Leave Me

Not Alone

ALSO BY LOUIS FLINT CECI

THE CROY CYCLE

If I Remember Him
Comfort Me
Jacob's Ladder
Leave Me Not Alone

AS EDITOR

Not Just Another Pretty Face

Leave Me Not Alone

Book 4 of
The Croy Cycle

Louis Flint Ceci

with illustrations by
Jennifer Rain Crosby

les croyens press

Published by Les Croyens Press
An imprint of Beautiful Dreamer Press
309 Cross St.
Nevada City, CA 95959
U.S.A.
lescroyenspress@BeautifulDreamerPress.com
www.BeautifulDreamerPress.com

This is a work of fiction. Names, characters, businesses, places, and incidents are the products of the author's imagination or are used fictitiously. Any resemblance to actual events, locales, or persons, living or dead, is entirely coincidental.

Some scenes on Virgil Craddock's farm were originally published as "Trestle" in *Jonathan*.
The verses to "The Midnight Train" were originally published as "Cargo" in *The Colorado-North Review*.
Lines from "In Temptation (Jesu, Lover of My Soul)" by Charles Wesley, from *Hymns and Sacred Poems*, published by John Wesley and Charles Wesley (London: W. Strahan, 1740).
Poem LXXXVI ("To the staunch Dust we safe commit thee") by Emily Dickinson, from *The Single Hound; Poems of a Lifetime* (Boston: Little, Brown, 1914).

10 9 8 7 6 5 4
Publication date: September, 2022
Printed in the United States of America

ISBN: 978-1-7347389-7-1
Library of Congress Control Number: 2021917298

Cover Design by Inkspiral.
Back cover illustration by Jennifer Rain Crosby.
Author portrait by Jennifer Rain Crosby from a photograph by Dot.

Contents

To Dorothy Frances Ceci, and to the memory of all those whom we love but see no longer

Leave Me

Not Alone

Fare forward, you who think that you are voyaging;
You are not those who saw the harbor
Receding, or those who will disembark.

. . . . .

Not fare well,
But fare forward, voyagers.

—T.S. Eliot, *The Dry Salvages*

life would be dead in the water
without unreasonable lust

—horehound stillpoint

Virgil's Problem

The problem is Arlene. She's just no luck in picking husbands. The first one died, the second one ran off. Who's she gonna get to run the farm when I'm gone? Virgil Craddock pulled a bud of alfalfa as he walked through the field, crushing it with his thumb and inhaling. Sweet. Almost sweet enough to mow. He could make it that far, the first hay. But the end of summer? Who'd help then? Frank? He had to laugh.

That was his grandson now, walking down the drive from the highway in a suit. *What the hell? It ain't Sunday.* He picked up his pace to cut him off at the porch.

Pain shot from his liver to his left shoulder. He came to a halt with a gasp. Frank looked his way. *Can't let him see.* "Where the hell you been?"

"The school, granddad. The basketball lunch. I told you."

"Lunch? It's nearly supper and them stalls still need muckin'."

"I'll get changed and meet Jim in the barn."

Virgil scoffed. "You'd better be quick about it. He's nearly packed."

Frank frowned. "Packed?"

Virgil couldn't move his left foot. "Well, don't just stand there, gapin'. Get changed."

Frank narrowed his eyes and headed into the house, shaking his head.

Think you're so clever? Well, think again. Jim's fixin' to leave this very day. Jim Newton was a good enough farm hand, and he was right smart on a horse. But they'd butted heads too often on how to run the farm. He wasn't sorry to see him go.

His leg unstuck itself, and he headed for the porch and

his chair. He hooked his arms in the bib of his overalls and stared at the fields. The deep smell of the crop calmed him. *Like money. It better be or the bank gets everything.*

He had to think things through. His daughter, her two kids, the farm. Something had to be done. And he knew, even without seeing a doctor, that he didn't have much time.

Frank bounded up the stairs to his room in the dormer.

"Is that you, Frank?" his mother called from below. "Come give me a hand in the kitchen. Angela's still sick and can't help."

She's no help even when she can. "Can't Mom. Jim needs me in the barn."

"No he don't." Frank turned to see his half-sister leaning against the doorframe.

"I thought you was sick. Chicken pox or hog cholera or somethin'." He shucked his sports coat and tugged off his tie.

Angela stuck out her tongue.

"Oh yeah, I see now. You're all better."

"You're in for a nasty surprise."

"You're in for a nastier one if you keep standin' there spyin' on me." He turned and pulled off his shirt. "Go help Mom."

"You can't boss me around."

"I'm sorry your highness, but your servants have the day off. You ain't princess today."

"I will be someday."

"Yeah sure, and I'll be a rock star on *American Bandstand.*"

"Not the way you sing."

"Who said anything about singin'?"

"Not the way you play guitar, neither."

He turned to face her and started dropping his trousers.

"Mom!" Angela yelled and ran down the stairs.

He followed as soon as he stepped into his overalls and boots, fastening the strap over his left shoulder as he headed for the back door.

"I'm sure you're exaggerating," his mother said as he strolled through the kitchen. Angela was pouting over a cutting board loaded with carrots.

"Your majesty," he said, bowing.

She glared and chopped a carrot in half.

He left the other strap unfastened, his shoulder bare as he rounded the corner of the barn. He stopped.

Jim was loading the last of his tack into the back of his pickup.

"Where you goin'?"

Jim didn't answer or look at him. Frank checked the back of the Ranger. All of Jim's stuff from his shed and bunk was crammed inside.

"You ain't leavin', are you?"

Jim stood rock still. "Got an offer in Colorado. Better pay than here."

"You can't leave. Not now." He grabbed his shoulder. "Why? What happened?"

Jim turned, his eyes like ice. "You know why."

Frank's heart pounded. He didn't want to hear what he was hearing. "What about the hay? We're mowin' in a few days."

"You'll manage. I've taught you everything I know."

"Not everything."

Jim's face twisted. "I've worked every farm, ranch, and homestead from here to Los Animas. I got a gal in every county and a man in more than a few. But no boys. I ain't never gone down that road, and I ain't about to start."

"You were pretty far down that road when I caught up with you."

Jim grabbed him by the front and pulled him around the corner of the barn, out of sight of the house. He pushed him against the rough wood with one hand and grabbed his crotch with the other. He kissed him hard on the mouth and squeezed. Frank whimpered from the pain in his balls but opened his teeth for Jim's tongue. Instead, Jim pulled away, breathing hard.

"Is that what you want?"

"If that's all I get."

Jim drew back. "I gotta draw a line somewheres. I'm drawin' it with you."

"I ain't a boy."

"The hell you ain't."

"Line or no line, you got me. For more than a month now, you got me. So *now* you're gonna run?"

Jim turned and spat and started back to his truck.

Frank followed. "You can't leave it like this." Jim got in the cab and started the engine. "Granddad's gettin' crazier by day, Mom's hopeless, and Angela . . . What am I supposed to do?"

Jim gave him a long look. "It's not up to me. I'm busy savin' myself." He put the truck in gear and pulled down the drive.

Frank chased after, eating dust. "No!" The pickup reached the highway and turned. "Fucker!" he screamed. He sank to the gravel in tears.

Virgil Craddock watched from the porch and shook his head. *Who'd marry a woman with a kid like that?*

And there it was. The problem wasn't Arlene. The problem was the boy. He'd have to do something about that.

The Cost of a 15¢
Root Beer Float

I'm thinking of starting a band," Beau Hamilton said, smiling from the front door of his house.

Jake Jacobs leaned against the porch railing, tossing a basketball from hand to hand. "What kind of band?"

"Maybe a folk-rock band. Or maybe something more like The Doors."

"You're nuts. That'd never fly around here."

The smile dropped from Beau's eyes. He crossed to the porch swing and sat, looking down.

Jake felt like a dick. He sat next to him and tried to make up for it. "Who'd be in it?"

"Nobody, I guess."

"No really, who?"

Beau sat up. "Well, me on lead guitar and Belle Craddock on drums."

"A girl drummer? That's cool. Like The Vevlvet Underground."

"Who now?"

"This group Vince introduced me to."

Beau's eyes lit up. "Oh, yeah. Vince."

Jake crossed the porch. *Why did I mention him? Forget all that.* "Who else?"

Beau took a breath. "Well, we'll need a rhythm guitar and bass, too. I'm thinking Al Mattingly on bass, if he's up to it. Do you think?"

"Haven't seen him much since he got out of the hospital. But his new leg shouldn't affect his playing none."

"Then Frank Pellegrini on rhythm."

"Frank? I didn't know he played." Beau looked at him. "Well, it never came up at basketball practice."

"Huh. I guess not."

Jake spun the ball on his fingertip. "Al's pretty into his church. Credits all that praying for stopping the cancer. I'm not sure where they stand on rock bands."

"So, we might still need a bass." Beau smiled at him.

"Oh, no. Don't look at me. I can't even play kazoo."

"Bass isn't that hard."

"Tell that to Paul McCartney. Besides, you wouldn't want me up there. I'm terrible in front of crowds."

"Says the guy who took us to state. I suppose no one was watching you then, though."

"That's different." He dribbled the ball on the porch, making it ring. "And we lost in the finals, anyway."

"You could be our roadie."

"Yeah?" He slammed the ball hard against the planks. "I like the sound of that."

The front door opened and Mr. Hamilton leaned out, frowning. "Beau? Everything all right?"

"Yeah sure, Dad. This is Jake. From school."

"Afternoon, Mr. Hamilton." Jake smiled.

Beau's dad nodded but didn't smile back. "Just thought

I'd check."

"We were talking about the band," Beau said.

"Oh?" Mr. Hamilton relaxed and came all the way out. "What do you play?"

"Left bench." Jake laughed, but neither of them got it so he said, "Naw. I can't play. I've got no talent."

"Have you tried?"

"Thanks, Dad." Beau launched himself from the swing. "Jake and I were just heading over to Herman's."

"Oh. Sure. But don't be late for your—" Mr. Hamilton glanced at Jake "—for your appointment."

"Don't worry. C'mon Jake." Beau headed around the back of the house.

"Sorry about that," Beau said as they started down the alley. "He's still a little jumpy since . . . you know."

Jake glanced at Beau's wiry hair and large glasses. The bruising was all gone, and you could barely see a line where the stitches had been. "Yeah, I know."

They walked in silence to the end of the block, crossed the street, and continued down the next alley. Beau looked up ruefully. "Hope you don't mind."

Jake shrugged. "I like alleys. People aren't putting on a show. They're just being themselves. You get to see all their secrets."

Beau smiled. "You mean their laundry and garbage cans."

"Exactly!"

"I always go this way when I go to the library. Or to St. Joe's."

Jake shook his head. "Your folks still making you do that?"

"Yeah. That's what all that 'appointment' stuff was back there."

"That sucks."

"It surely does."

They got to Herman's before they realized they didn't

have any money. Jake's pockets were empty, and Beau had only a nickel and a dime. "We could get a fifteen cent root beer float and split it," Jake suggested.

"Do you think the prices are the same?" Beau asked. "I haven't been since the new folks bought it."

"Sure they're the same. It's still Herman's, isn't it?"

The guy at the counter was neither one of Herman's endless supply of nephews nor a recent high school graduate. Clean-cut and enthusiastic, he wore a crisp white paper hat and greeted them with a smile and a cheery, "What can I get for you gentlemen?"

His flat vowels immediately identified him as not from around here. Somewhere up north, St. Louis or Southern Illinois, maybe. Jake didn't let it put him off. "We'd like a fifteen cent root beer float and two straws."

The smile didn't budge but the eyebrows went up. "I'm sorry, but we don't have fifteen cent floats. A float is twenty cents."

"That's all right," Beau said, pocketing his coins.

It irked him, both the guy's attitude and Beau's giving up. He was sure he'd had fifteen cent floats at Herman's before. He looked at the price board. "Okay then, how about a dime cone and a nickel root beer?"

"Sure thing!" The guy turned and started pulling the soft serve from the machine.

"And no ice, please."

"Sure thing."

"Hand me the money," he whispered to Beau.

"What are you up to?"

The guy placed the cone on the counter and poured the root beer. "You like a nice head on it, do you?" he smirked, handing it over.

"Yep." Jake laid the coins on the counter and handed Beau the cone. He took a big gulp of root beer, took back the cone, and scraped the top of it into the cup. "There you go," he said, handing it back to Beau. "And there's even some left for me." He took an elaborate bite from the cone and smiled at the guy behind the counter, who was frozen in the act of ringing up the sale. "Thanks!" he said and breezed out the door with Beau behind him.

They headed for the picnic tables under the trees.

"I don't think he'll ever let us in there again," Beau said, slurping fizz from the edge of his cup.

"Did you see his face?" Jake laughed. "It was like I'd thrown a brick through the window."

"It was kinda mean."

"If they're gonna keep the Herman's name, they gotta keep the Herman's customers."

They sat under a catalpa. Last year's seed pods clicked and twisted in the breeze. Beau set his cup on the table and stared at it.

"What?"

"Nothing."

Jake crunched through the bottom of his cone, watching.

"It's just, there's enough meanness in this town, y'know?" Beau said.

Jake cleared his throat. "Yeah, I know."

Beau looked him in the eye. "You're not mean, are you?"

"No." He felt his face flush as the lie caught up with him. "Well, maybe. Maybe I was, once."

Beau kept looking at him.

Jake cleared his throat again. "I know who beat you up."

"I know you do."

"I wanted to do something about it, but I chickened out."

"Because of the game. Because of state."

Jake looked down and nodded. "We lost anyway."

"You weren't with them. I know that, too."

Jake shook his head. "But I hung out with them. It was

Marcus and Tom, wasn't it?"

"Tom, not Marcus. I mean, Marcus started it. They stopped me on the street and said they wanted some pot."

"What do you mean, you don't got none?" Marcus said.

"We saw you talking to that guy. You were right friendly." Tom closed in. "So don't hold out on us."

Marcus started going through his pockets, pulling him this way and that. Tom snatched the paperback from his hand. "What's this? Poems?"

Beau tried to knock Marcus's hands away and grab the book at the same time. "Give that back! That's Mr. DeWitt's!"

"That fairy?" Tom laughed and tossed it to the ground.

Marcus gave up. "Shit, there's nothing here."

"Ain't you got nothin' for us, Beau-boy?"

"Let's go, Tom. This is a waste of time."

"Not if Beau pays for it." He reached into Beau's back pocket and pulled out his wallet.

"That's mine!" Beau yelled. "I got that for Christmas!"

"Ew!" Tom held it up and grimaced like it was a piece of maggoty meat. "Look at this fruity thing! It's got cute little rainbows and all."

"Give me that!"

"I'll give you something." Tom tugged the back of Beau's belt and reached inside and yanked. Expecting resistance, his hand came flying out with a shred of pink lace in his fist.

The world stopped.

"What the hell?" Tom whispered.

Marcus turned away. "Let's go, man, there's nothing here."

"What are you, some kind of freak?" Tom knocked Beau to the sidewalk and straddled him. "Freak! Homo!" He

started hitting him in the face. Beau tried to roll over, but the blows just scraped his face against the concrete. Tom was yelling and Marcus was trying to pull him off.

"Jesus Christ, Tom, quit it! Someone'll see."

Tom stood. "I better never see you again. Not on the street." He kicked him. "Not at school." He kicked him again. "Nowhere! You hear?"

He swung his leg for another kick but Marcus pulled on his letter jacket and his foot swung wide, tipping him off balance.

"Leave him be," Marcus said. "He ain't worth it."

Beau heard car doors slam and a car pull away before he blacked out.

Jake sat motionless. "Jesus, Beau."

Beau sat across from him, hands in his lap, watching his face. The catalpa pods rattled overhead. Jake took deep breaths to slow his heart before he spoke again. "He kept it. The wallet. He showed it to me."

Beau nodded. "A trophy for beating up a fag."

"Don't say that. You're not a fag."

"Yes I am."

"Well, not that word, then. Gay."

"Or queer?"

Jake shrugged. "Everybody's a little queer."

"Even you?"

He half smiled. "Maybe more than a little." Beau did not smile back. Jake leaned in. "You're safe with me."

"You won't hit me or kick me. But you could still hurt me."

"I won't. I promise."

"Really?"

Jake nodded.

Beau unbuttoned his shirt to the waist, showing a navy blue undershirt beneath. He held out his hand and Jake took it. Beau guided the hand to his chest, just right of center, and left it there.

It took a second for Jake to realize what he was feeling. "Is that . . . ?"

Beau nodded.

Jake leaned back and looked him in the eye. "Yeah. I promise."

They relaxed. Jake finished off his cone, a soggy mess by now, and Beau buttoned his shirt.

"So, that's why your folks send you to a shrink? The underwear thing?"

Beau shrug-nodded.

"And all the time, you're wearing that underneath?"

Beau looked up and smiled.

Jake laughed. "Man, that is a perfect Fuck You."

Beau picked up his cup. "It surely is."

Jake watched as he finished off the fifteen cent float. It had been too meager a thing to share, so Jake didn't ask for any. "Gotta go," Beau said, heading for his session at St. Joseph's Hospital.

Jake waved as he walked away. He marveled at how cool and even tempered Beau was about it all. If he had to talk to a psychiatrist, he'd freak out. *I don't want anybody in my head. It's crowded enough in there already.*

A bit of wafer cone was stuck to the back of his throat. He walked home by way of Tibbits Rexall, hoping to wash it down with a coke. Plus he could catch up on things with Joanie.

"How'd the sports banquet go?" she asked as he entered.

"Luncheon, not banquet. I got a trophy."

"Oh, lawdy. Croy's got a new hero. So, where is it?"

"Well, I wouldn't want to provoke envy."

She grinned. "That small, huh?"

He spread his finger and thumb. "About that much. I left

it at school." He placed his basketball on the soda counter. "So, what's a guy gotta do to get a drink around here?"

Joanie came around to the fountain and picked up an order pad. "Will this be on separate checks, sir?"

"Oh, shoot."

"What?"

"I forgot. I don't have any money. We blew it all at Herman's."

"With customers like you, we should be out of business in no time."

Jake looked around. The Rexall didn't look to be short of customers. The phone rang and Joanie called out, "I'll get that, Daddy."

"No, that's all right," her father's voice came from the pharmacy stacks. "I got it."

Jake rolled his ball back and forth on the countertop. Joanie loved gossip, and he had a really juicy bit of it. But he had promised.

"We who?" she asked.

"What?"

"'We blew it all at Herman's.' We who?"

"Oh." *Is she reading my mind?* "Um, Beau Hamilton. He's thinking of starting a band."

"What kind?"

"Rock'n'roll, I think."

"So, no need for a clarinet then."

He smiled. "I think you're safe. So far, it's just him and Belle Craddock."

"Belle? I didn't know they were friends. I mean, we're all in band together, but—" She raised her eyebrows.

Jake frowned. "But what?"

"Well, she's a bit of a hellion, and he's a bit of a . . ."

She let the sentence hang.

"A what?"

Joanie blushed. "Well, he's not like you. I mean, he *is*, but he's *not*. He's—you know—a little soft."

Joanie knew a lot. She knew about his crush on Randy back when the three of them first met. Last year, he'd told her about Vince. Even when that didn't work out, though, she'd never said anything against him, never called Vince "soft." *This is what Beau means, this everyday meanness. This is what I promised wouldn't happen again.* "Beau is plenty tough. Tough in ways I could never be. He's a match for Belle or anyone."

He watched this sink in. Her skeptical look turned to a smile. "That should be quite the band."

"Joanie," Mr. Tibbits said, emerging from the stacks, "can you close up? I've got to run this out to the Woolvine farm."

"Sure, Daddy."

"Afternoon, Jake. How was the banquet?"

"It wasn't— It was fine, Mr. Tibbits."

"Joanie, pull a coke for our champ. What will it be, Jake?"

"A Co-cola, please. But I don't have any money."

"On the house."

"Thank you, sir, but I'd really like to pay for it." A thought tickled his brain. "Tom's not running deliveries for you anymore, is he?"

"No, our young scholar is getting a jump on his studies at Northwestern. Early admission."

Jake pointed to the package in Mr. Tibbits's hand. "I could run that over. Or anything else."

Mr. Tibbits cocked his head. "On a regular basis?"

"Sure. Full-time or part-time. I got all summer. You could pay me—"

"The same you paid Randy and Tom," Joanie interjected.

Mr. Tibbits looked from his daughter to him. "It's a fair notion." He put on his coat. "We'll talk tomorrow, but without your agent present."

"Bye, Daddy."

"Bye, Princess. Tell Mom I'll be late for supper."

They watched him leave, then turned to each other and went, "Wheee!"

"I could fix the fender on the Dream Machine!" Jake said.

"Don't let him talk you down a dime from what he paid Tom Hansen. 'Young scholar' my foot. Young gangster is more like."

"I'm not supposed to drive outside of town, though. That was the agreement I made with Randy's mom when I got my license."

"Who's going to tell?"

Jake shook his head. "Virginia doesn't need to be told. She just *knows*."

Mother Knows Best

J oanie locked the store and offered Jake a ride to his place.

"With the top down?"

"No point otherwise."

They drove down South Main, Jake bubbling over with plans for his future income. It made her smile.

"There's these new high tops I've been eyeing at van-Doozer's. These clodhoppers don't fit and are shot anyway. And I need new dishtowels."

"That's amazingly dull."

"You haven't seen them. You can read a newspaper through them." He tapped his fingers on the side of the convertible. "The Dream Machine will need a tune-up, too. I don't want to be halfway to Dibble City when something falls apart. Or off."

"I'm surprised Randy's old heap still runs at all." They turned onto Choctaw, passing Assembly Park with its heroic statue. Jake waved.

"Afternoon, Aloysius!"

She groaned. "You don't have to rub it in."

"Aloysius Fenton Longstreet, co-owner and general manager of the Longstreet and Barnes Circus. *Not* General James Longstreet, commander of the Army of Northern Virginia."

"Yeah, yeah, so you were right and I was wrong."

"Actually, all I said is he wasn't a general. Beau dug up all that stuff about the circus. Did you know they buried an elephant outside of town?"

"Oh, gross." They crossed the tracks to Jake's side of town. "Did he say where, exactly?"

"Just over to Pesogi, or what's left of it."

"I wonder if I could find out. Is there anyone who would still know?"

Jake shrugged. "Coach Tucker's uncle still lives out there. Or Mrs. Oldfield. She's part elephant, you know. She never forgets a thing."

She turned into the alley, her mind racing through a hundred questions. She pulled to a stop behind the granny house at the bottom of the Oldfields' backyard and looked across the alley to Randy's house. "Do you miss him?"

He gave her a funny look. "The elephant?"

"Randy."

"Naw. Do you?"

"Of course not."

"Uh-huh. That's why you asked."

"Well I thought you might at least have seen him after he came back from Lubbock." She frowned. "He came back changed, don't you think?"

"I think all the senior boys who went did."

"I guess you can't see that kind of devastation and not be. We had one too, you know, years ago. They didn't call them F5s back then. They called it the TriCounty Twister. That's what wiped out Pesogi. It nearly wiped out Croy, too. Grampa John used to talk about it. There's all kinds of legends around it."

Jake grinned.

"What?"

"You're thinking about your next article for *The Clarion*, aren't you?"

"Don't be silly. It's months till school starts."

"But you're doing that thing with your hair."

She pulled her hand away. "I am not. Anyway, I didn't

get to see him. I wanted to say what a brave thing it was to go help those people. But then he left again."

Jake got out and cradled his basketball under his arm. "I haven't heard from him, but I haven't written, either."

"But you could? You'd know where to write?"

"He's in South Dakota, building houses with this guy he met in Lubbock."

She drummed her fingers on the steering wheel. "He didn't mention a Jack Huckleberry, did he?"

Jake looked uncomfortable.

"Never mind. See you tomorrow at the salt mine."

Boys and their secrets, she thought on her way home. *If Randy is in cahoots with his outlaw father again, I'd rather not know.*

Jake rounded the corner of the house and saw a man on a ladder installing a porch light over his door. "Afternoon, Reverend Jameson!" he called out.

Ethan Jameson looked down. "There's the champ." He climbed down the ladder. "Mrs. Oldfield was going to have you do this, but I was handy and volunteered."

"Thanks. How's Adam?"

Reverend Jameson smiled. "Adam is at the library, of course, working on his languages. He heard a rumor Latin and French are going to be dropped when school starts, and he doesn't want to lose a year."

"And Zach? He get that football scholarship?"

Mr. Jameson's smile turned bland. "Zach's working at Longacre Brothers, which is fine enough for now." He brushed his hands off and his cheerful demeanor returned. "I'll tell him you were asking after him. Is that the famous ball? The one that got us to the finals?"

Jake blushed. "Naw. This is just my ball. I was out shooting hoops around town."

"We thought you might be." He pulled the ladder down. "They're waiting for you, up in Mrs. Oldfield's kitchen."

Jake looked up at the house, a feeling of dread creeping over him. "Who is?"

"Mrs. Oldfield, Mrs. Edom, and your mother."

"Oh no."

Mr. Jameson hefted the ladder. "You look concerned, son."

"Anytime they get together, I get sent back to the fifth grade."

Reverend Jameson shook his head. "Best get it over with, then."

Jake ducked inside the granny house, tossed the ball in a corner, and changed into a fresher smelling shirt. Then he headed up to the large home that used to be the Oldfield farmhouse before the town grew in around it. *This is not good. This is very not good.* An awful thought came to him. *She wouldn't bring Vince with her, would she?*

He knocked on the back door and entered right away.

"There he is," Susan Jacobs said, rising from the kitchen table and extending her arms. Virginia Edom, Randy's mother and Jake's surrogate mom when Susan was away, sat on one side, and Clara Oldfield, his land-lady, sat on the other. Virginia twitched him a smile, but her fingers tapped on the table in front of her. Mrs. Old-field looked—*Oh God. She looks happy. This is very* very *not good.*

"Hi, Mom." He hugged her. "This is a neat surprise. I'd have been home if I knew you were coming. When'd you get in? Did Vince drive you? Again?"

Susan Jacobs pulled out a chair and he sat.

"You were right, Ginny. He has a million questions." His mother smiled at him. "No, Vincent's internship ended with the school year." Jake relaxed. "But they hired him on as a full-time production assistant." He tensed. "He's far too busy now to be my driver."

Jake smiled, frowned, forgot what to do with his hands. "So, he didn't drive you down."

"Reverend Jameson was kind enough to pick your mother up in Tulsa," Clara Oldfield said with a smile.

What's she so happy about? Jake was afraid to find out, but he had to. "So, what's up?"

"Don't be so nervous, Jake honey. It's good news."

"It's fantastic news," Virginia said. He saw her reach for a cigarette then think better of it.

"You remember those specials I shot in New Orleans?" Susan said.

"Sure. They were about Evangeline DuPere's family and all. Your character's backstory. Everybody watched them."

Virginia nodded. "You couldn't get a thing done in town when they were on."

"I thought they were charming," Mrs. Oldfield said.

Jake gaped. *I didn't even know she had a TV.*

"Well," his mother continued, "they were a big hit. And now they want me to do a feature film."

His eyes widened. "Mom! Wow, that's fantastic! In Hollywood?"

"No." Susan smiled. "In Paris."

Jake was speechless.

"France," Mrs. Oldfield clarified.

"Oh."

"Vince is over there now, doing advance work and scouting locations."

Jake locked eyes with Virginia. "Oh. Good."

"The question is, do you want to join me?"

His head snapped back to his mother. "Join you? In Paris?"

"For the summer. You'll be back in time for football practice and school."

"I . . . gee . . . I . . ."

"It's a golden opportunity, kiddo," Virginia said.

I'm just about to start a job. I'm just about to start a band. I'm just about to go crazy. He didn't realize his hands had risen and he clutched his head.

His mother looked to Virginia for help.

"It's a bit much, I know," Virginia said.

"You don't have to decide right now," Mrs. Oldfield said.

"And," Susan said, squeezing his hand, "you don't have to feel you *have* to come. I know you have a life of your own here. Your friends. Your teammates."

"Your church," Mrs. Oldfield said.

"What? Oh, yeah." He took a deep breath. He tried to visualize himself in Paris. With his mother. With Vince. *The guy who called Croy a shithole and tried to get me to run away with him last year.* Without Joanie. Without Randy. *Well, Randy's gone anyway.* Without Beau. *Yeah, but that's just starting.* Without . . .

Without everything that made him who he was. It would be like starting all over again, like when he first came to Croy two years ago. When nobody knew him, nobody cared. When he was Malachi Jacobs, the lost kid, not Jake Jacobs, the basketball star. *Do they even have basketball in France?* Things were just beginning to get solid, and now they were turning to Jell-O.

He exhaled. "It's wonderful, Mom. You're going to be great."

Susan's earnest smile relaxed, and she looked at Virginia. "Just like you said."

"Would anyone care for pie?" Mrs. Oldfield said, rising.

"So, you're staying?" Virginia asked.

Jake nodded.

"Good."

"But there's new rules," Susan said. "Ginny told me

what went on here last year. What *really* went on. It wasn't just driving Randy's car up and down the alley without a permit, was it?"

Jake hung his head. "No, ma'am. I had . . . I had a friend over."

"Other than Randy," Virginia put in.

"Yeah, other than Randy, and I didn't ask permission."

"And?" Virginia prompted.

"And I didn't tell anyone until I got caught. I'm sorry I didn't tell you, Mom."

"I had Jake take him back right away," Virginia told Susan. "But pretty soon I won't be on the lookout so much."

"That's where I come in," Mrs. Oldfield said, placing a slice of blueberry pie in front of each of them. "When Mrs. Edom's not around, I will be."

"That light Ethan installed goes on when you get home," Virginia added, "and stays on all night."

"That's how they'll know you're home safe," Susan said.

"Mom, I'm nearly seventeen. I know how to keep myself safe."

"Your adversary, the Devil, prowls around like a roaring lion, seeking whom he would devour," Mrs. Oldfield said. "Would you like some milk?"

"And you said *No*?" Joanie exclaimed when he told her about it. He was loading a paper bag with the afternoon deliveries.

"I'm just beginning to settle here. I don't want her tearing up my life again."

"Your mom can't help she's a TV star. Heck, most kids would kill to have a parent that glamorous."

"Would you? Could you picture your mom playing a seven hundred year old witch who looks like an angel and screams like the Devil?"

"Well, no. Not *my* mom."

"Besides, it wouldn't be just Mom and me. Vince would be there, too."

"Oh. But still, you're nuts to say no."

"Virginia thinks it was the right choice."

"Hah! She's never even been to Paris, Texas."

"I think she knows Vince spent the night with me last year."

Joanie blinked. "What? When?"

"New Year's Eve. At least, that's what we planned. But she got wind of it and came down on us like a ton of bricks before we got anywhere. I told her Beau came over, but I think she knew it was Vince."

"So, what happened?"

"Nothing."

"But you wanted it to?"

"Yeah."

Joanie shook her head. "Virginia would have killed him."

"Doesn't matter. We broke up. He was the wrong guy anyway. Just a fantasy." He squared his shoulders. "Nope. This is better. This is real. And this is my first real job. I better go."

He turned on the radio as soon as he started the car. A too-cheerful DJ announced Hal Orison's "Why Should I Believe You Now?" The familiar slide guitar intro began, followed by Orison's lonesome baritone. *Is that the kind of stuff Beau's band would play? I hope not.*

He decided to get some gas before starting his route, so he stopped by Longacre Brothers. "Russell & Raymond Longacre, Excellent Service For Excellent Prices" read the sign below the familiar green triangle. As soon as Jake's tires rang the bell, Zach Jameson came out, wiping his hands.

"Well, there he is," Zach said. He wore the same sweat

band around his afro he'd worn all last year, but he didn't look nearly as intimidating. Maybe it was the coveralls, which fit loosely over his solid build. "Still driving this old heap?"

"It gets me where I'm going, but not without gas. Mr. Tibbits has me going halfway 'round the county on deliveries."

Zach pulled the hose from the pump. "How much?"

He checked his wallet to make sure. His mother had given him a fiver "for expenses" when she agreed to let him take the job. He was feeling large. "Fill 'er up!"

Zach set the hose. "Check the oil?"

He wasn't feeling that large. "Maybe next time."

Zach turned away, watching the gauge on the pump.

Jake glanced at the open service bay. Marcus Longacre stood inside next to a Chevy on the lift, a filthy rag hooked in his belt. He smiled broadly at Jake and tilted his head in greeting. Jake's blood ran cold. *I used to hang out with that guy. We used to make fun of Beau together. Then he and Tom went and beat him up.*

He didn't want to acknowledge the link. He turned to Zach, but he was watching the pump. *Zach and I are more alike. We played a season of football and basketball together.* He turned down the radio on Orison's mournful lament. "This is my summer job."

Zach scowled. "Say what?"

"Deliveries. This yours?"

Zach gave a short laugh. "If it lasts that long. The new station out on the bypass is undercutting us. Or, undercutting *them*." He nodded at the open bay. "I ain't a Longacre."

"I kinda noticed." The pump kept dinging up gallons. "I talked to your dad the other day."

"Yep. He mentioned it." The pump stopped, and he squeezed out a few drops to round up the bill.

"I asked him if you got that football scholarship."

Zach smiled. "Won't be needing it."

"How come?"

"My draft number. Forty-eight. I'll be seeing all the sights Uncle Sam wants me to see."

"Oh shit, man. I'm sorry."

"I ain't. One way or t'other, I'll be gone. Don't matter to me how." He put up the hose and screwed on the gas cap. "I'll bet you'll miss me, though."

"Now, why would I do that?"

Zach leaned in the window. "Who else is gonna flatten your skinny white ass at football?"

Jake laughed. "Nobody can like you can."

"Damned straight." Zach slapped the roof of the car.

"Zach!" Russell Longacre called from the station. "If you're done with the customer, come give Marcus a hand with this here transmission."

"Yessir, Mr. Longacre," Zach called back. As he took Jake's money, he added, "I can't wait to get the hell out of here."

Marcus fumed beneath the chassis of the Chevy. He could feel Zach approaching him. *I don't need help. Not from some ignorant ape, anyways.*

"Russell says you need help."

"Uncle Rusty can go fuck himself."

"Sure." Zach stood a while like a block of wood. "I'll go work on Mrs. Armbruster's, then."

"Don't bother telling me."

Zach started off, then said, "You don't have to be like that, you know. Just because some toothpick of a kid don't say hey."

Marcus grunted. "Why would he? He's a guy with a future, ain't he? Unlike either of us."

Zach nodded and walked away.

Complete

Beau Hamilton fingered the envelope in his pocket as he walked down the alley. He was pretty sure he knew what was in it. It was a letter from his psychiatrist saying Beau was a disappointing patient and an insult to the medical profession. It was fitting he be required to deliver this news himself. Dr. Wallace would call his parents this evening to discuss it.

He approached South Main, intending to cross to the alley that ran between vanDoozer's and the Rialto, but he stopped at the sidewalk. A crowd had gathered in front of the theater. Some carried signs. Al Mattingly stood on a box, holding a bible and talking about sin and repentance. *He looks pretty good, considering. Not wobbly at all.*

Beau didn't like passing such a large group, but they all had their eyes on Al, so he crossed. He was about to start down the alley when he noticed Bobbie Littledeer in a sandwich board, standing off from the rest. The front of her board said, "Sodom Was Destroyed! Who's Next?" He couldn't read the back because she was standing against the building.

He hoped to pass unnoticed, but Bobbie saw him and her face turned red. He stopped. "Hey, Bobbie."

"Go away."

He looked up. The theater marquee announced the rerelease of *Midnight Cowboy*. "Best Picture!" exclaimed the posters out front. "Best Director! Best Screenplay!"

"Is this about the movie?"

"Of course it's about the movie. Go away."

"I hear it's really good."

"No, it isn't. It's really *bad.*"

"They cleaned it up, though. It's not X-rated anymore. See?" He pointed to the R rating.

"You can put lipstick on a pig, but it's still a pig."

That's not right. They took things out, not added things on. Bobbie kept her eyes on him, not looking at Al or the other folks at all, like she was expecting something.

"Have you seen it?" he asked.

"No."

"Then how do you know it's bad?"

"If you had to see smut to know it's smut, you'd be damned before you could blink." She looked at the marquee. "I know it's not about cowboys, though."

"You're just drawing attention to it with all this yelling. You'll probably pull more people in."

"That's not the point. You have to set a watchman."

He smiled. "That's you, then. Standing here. Watching." He meant it as a joke, but he saw tears start in her eyes. "Hey, I'm sorry. Look, it's not my thing, but if it's yours—"

"It's not!" She sniffed and took out a hanky. She gestured to the sandwich board. "I hate this. I feel like I'm on display." She wiped her nose. "He likes it, though."

"Reverend Mathers?"

"No. Him." She nodded at Al.

Everyone's eyes were on Al. He was winding away, feeding off the *Amens* and *That's rights* from the crowd. But he wasn't looking her way. *If she's going through all this trouble, you'd think he'd at least notice.* "Maybe you should be walking up and down. That's what people with sandwich boards do."

"No."

"Why?"

She glared at him.

"What's the back say? Nobody can see it with you standing there."

Bobbie pressed her lips together. She glanced at Al, quickly turned to show the back of the board.

The back said, "Get Thee Behind Me Satan!"

A snort escaped Beau before he could stop it.

"It's not funny."

He cleared his throat. "You could, you know, just lean it against the wall. Then you could join the rest of your friends, if you want."

"No. It's not what *I* want. It's not what makes *me* happy. It's what's *needed*. That's why I'm here. Because I'm needed." She took a deep breath and straightened up.

"Okay." He started to go. "But you're okay, right?"

"I'm fine." She dropped her head and said in a low voice, "Thank you for asking."

Beau shook his head as he walked down the alley. *I guess asking Al to join the band is out. But why would Bobbie do that? Just for him? For her church? Nobody should have to do that. It's humiliating.*

He stopped suddenly.

Then why am I sneaking down alleys?

A sinking feeling came over him as he approached his backyard. He could see the twins, Raphael and Sophia, playing in opposite corners. He called out. "Rafe? Keep Soph out here a while, will you? I need to talk to Mom and Dad." He didn't bother to see if his brother agreed and went right in. "Mom? Dad? Got a minute?"

His heart pounded but he knew what he had to do. They gathered in the living room, his parents on the sofa, him pacing in front of the coffee table.

"What is it?" his mother asked. "Has something happened again?"

"No." He stopped. "Yes. And no." He took out the envelope. "This is a letter from Dr. Wallace. He wants me to give it to you. But I think I know what it says. Or what it might say. It's one of two things. He might say he thinks I can't be cured."

"You've read it?" his dad said, taking the envelope.

"No."

"Then it's too soon to be pessimistic."

"No, Dad. That's not the pessimistic version. It might be much worse." He took a deep breath. "He might say I can."

He sat in the chair across from them. "This afternoon, we talked about sex. Between men. How it works."

His dad turned to his mom. "Rachel, maybe you'd better—"

"No." She kept her eyes on Beau. "I need to hear this. What did Dr. Wallace say?"

"He said sex between men was no better than a good bowel movement."

His dad colored. "Well, that's certainly . . . graphic."

"Actually, he said it's no better than a good shit. Sorry, Mom, but that's what he said."

She turned to his dad. "This is the doctor we're paying to talk to our son?"

"I'm sure he was just trying to be concise."

Beau shook his head. "No, Dad. He was trying to be disgusting. He wanted to gross me out. How does grossing me out help?"

"Well, he's wrong," his mom said.

His dad looked surprised. "Rachel?"

"Well he is, Scott. Sex *can* be disgusting. And it can also be messy and frustrating and hilarious and, well, fun."

"I don't think that's Dr. Wallace's point."

"Mom, Dad, that's not *my* point. Sex is not what I am. I mean, sex would be nice. I mean, it would be fantastic. At least I think it would. But that's not the point. This—what I am, what I feel, what I want to be—it's not about sex.

It's about being *me*. The whole me, the real me." He looked at them. "Nothing taken away, or hidden, or disguised."

"This thing you do—" his dad began.

"Cross dress."

"Yes, okay. How is that not a disguise?"

Beau closed his eyes. *How do I explain? What are the right words?* He shook his head. *There are no right words. Just tell them.* "When I was maybe six, I had a dream. There was this boy, lost, lying on the ground, all wrapped up in a jacket and gloves and a hat, like it was winter. Yet he was cold. He was miserable, alone, and scared. And then I came along and I lay down on top of him. I was wrapped in something like a sheet, billowing, soft, flowing. And the minute we were together, we were warm and safe." He opened his eyes. "I gave my heart to that boy and he gave his to me. We were complete."

His dad cleared his throat. "Is this some boy you know? Someone at school?"

"I've never met him. I hope to someday."

His dad didn't look him in the eye, but took his hand and squeezed it. "Your mother and I will do anything to keep you safe and happy."

"I don't think you can do both."

"Let's go for happy then," his mom said. She looked at his dad. "We did, didn't we? It worked for us."

"For most of us."

This is something they've never talked about. "What worked?"

"Tell him, Scott."

His dad took a deep breath and nodded. "You know about Poppa and Memaw Rosen, right?"

"Sure."

"And Grammy Pritchard."

"Yeah. When I was sick, she came to help. Mom was having the twins, I think."

"But Grampa Pritchard never visited. You never met him."

Beau shrugged. "Well, he died, didn't he? A couple of months later? After the twins were born."

"But even when Raphael and Sophia were born, he didn't visit. Didn't come to see his grandkids. And our last name isn't Pritchard."

Beau shifted and looked away.

"The Rosens are Jewish."

"Sure, I knew that."

"And I'm Jewish," his mother said.

Beau shrugged. "Yeah. Okay."

"I'm not," his dad continued, "but that doesn't matter to some folks. To some folks, if your mother is Jewish, you're Jewish, too. My dad, your grandfather, was one of those folks. He forbid us to marry."

"My parents were against it, too," his mother said.

"But you convinced them, right?" Beau said. "I mean, obviously."

His mother took his dad's hand. "I still remember what you told them. 'I know you don't see God's blessing in our love, but that is neither God's fault nor ours.'"

His dad looked into her eyes. "I would never ask you to convert. It just wouldn't be you." He kissed her on the forehead.

"That was enough for Poppa," she said, smiling.

Beau blushed. He thought talking to his parents about his feelings would be painful. Hearing about theirs was worse.

His dad turned to him. "But it wasn't enough for my father. When I told him we were going to marry anyway, he disowned me. So I returned the favor and took Grammy Pritchard's maiden name. That's why we're Hamiltons, not Pritchards." He sighed. "My father never spoke to me after that. Said I was dead to him. Said all of us were dead. You, me, Rachel, the twins. All of us.”

“Dad—”

“It was hard, but giving up your mother would have been harder. She’s my other half, Beau. Without her, I’m just not a whole person. I’m half a human being, and a pretty sorry half at that. So when you say you need this thing to feel whole, and you need to feel whole no matter what, I get you. I know what you feel. But I’m still scared, son. I don’t want you hurt.”

“I got friends. There’s Jake and Belle.”

“Jake’s a good kid. From good people.”

“We’re starting a band.”

“Oh, boy.” His mother sat back. “Frilly underclothes and lying on top of boys is one thing, but a band?” She picked up the letter. “And what about this?”

Beau tensed. “He’s going to call to make sure you got it.”

“Well, let’s see what it says.” His dad opened the letter and started reading. His face went pale, then red, then redder.

“Scott?” She touched his dad’s arm.

“You were right, Beau. He thinks he can cure you.” He shook the letter. “There’s a new technique, he says. Aversion therapy. First, he arouses the subject’s sexual response—”

“Arouses?” His mother stood. “Arouses how?”

“—and then he administers an emetic. In time, the subject learns to associate the stimulus with the response, and an aversion is formed.”

His mother’s voice got cold and sharp. “Arouses how?”

His dad gripped the letter. “Porn. He wants to show our boy porn. And then make him throw up.”

Beau’s throat tightened. “He needs your permission first though, right? He’s calling tonight.”

Rachel crossed her arms. “What are we going to tell him, Scott?”

His dad looked at her, at him. "We're going to tell him to go take a good shit."

The doorbell rang. At the same time, his brother burst through the back door. "Can we come in now, please? Soph says she's gotta pee."

"Sure, hon," Rachel said, bustling him into the kitchen. "Scott, could you get the door?" As soon as his dad left the room, his mother crooked her head at him, and he followed into the kitchen.

Sophie came in and Rafe went out. His mother leaned close and spoke. "But there is a boy, isn't there?"

Beau blushed. "No. Well, sorta. We've talked about . . . all this."

"And he's okay with . . . all this?"

"Yeah. But I haven't told him how I feel or anything. About him, that is." His words were suddenly clumsy and his face was hot.

"You're sure about this boy?"

Beau nodded.

She leaned closer and whispered, "Tell him."

"You don't have to ring the bell," Kyle complained. "You can just walk in."

Joanie looked down at her little brother. "That's rude. I've never been to their house before."

"I have."

"Well, I haven't." She was about to give him more points on etiquette when Mr. Hamilton opened the door. "Good afternoon, Mr. Hamilton. I'm—"

"Is Rafe home?" Kyle interrupted.

"He's out back."

Kyle squeezed past them and raced through the house to the back door. Joanie was horrified. "I'm so sorry, Mr. Hamilton. I don't know what's happened to his manners."

"It's quite all right," Mr. Hamilton said. "We're all used to Kyle around here. You're his sister, I take it?"

"Yes. Joan Tibbits—Joanie," she added, thinking she sounded too formal.

"Won't you come in?"

"Thank you." She entered the living room and felt suddenly that she shouldn't have, that she was intruding on something.

"Can I get you anything?" Mr. Hamilton said. "Ice tea?"

"No thank you, sir. I've come to see Beau, if he's in. We're in the same classes at school."

"Band too, right?"

"Yes." Beau's father seemed to know more about her than she knew about Beau.

"Beau?" He called. "Someone to see you." He walked toward the kitchen and added, "A girl from school."

Beau popped out of the kitchen. A woman, his mother she assumed, also came out, gave her a look and smiled. "Can we get you anything, hon?"

"Hi, Joanie." Beau turned to his mother. "It's Joanie. From band."

"Oh?"

"Marching band," Beau's father clarified.

"Oh. Can we get you something, some ice tea?"

"No thank you, ma'am."

"Scott?" Beau's mother said. "Have you got a minute?"

"Hmm?" his father said. He was grinning for some reason. His mother looked at him levelly. "Oh, yeah, right." And the two of them disappeared into the kitchen.

"I'm sorry for just dropping by," she said as Beau showed her to the sofa. "I can come back later if it's not a good time."

"No, now's a good time. Really good."

Now he's grinning, too. Weird family. "It's just that I was talking to Jake, and he mentioned some research you did."

"Jake was talking about me?"

"Yes. Well, about your research."

"Huh."

The back door slammed and she jumped. "It was last year. You found out something about General Longstreet—I mean, the Longstreet statue."

"Aloysius Fenton Longstreet," Beau said proudly. "Of the Longstreet and Barnes Circus."

Kyle and Rafe came hurrying through, each with a sandwich in hand. A big bite had been taken out of Kyle's, but that didn't stop him. "No he ain't. It's General James Longstreet. Everybody knows it."

"Kyle! Don't contradict and don't talk with your mouth full."

"Maybe everybody's wrong," Beau said calmly.

"C'mon, Kyle," Rafe said, nudging him to the door.

As they headed out, Kyle turned. "If it's the Longstreet and Barnes Circus, why is there only a Mr. Longstreet? Where's Mr. Barnes?" He took another bite out of his sandwich and left.

Joanie sighed. "I'm really sorry. He's been so sweet lately, especially around Julia Mae. He takes his role as a big brother so seriously. But I'd forgotten at heart he's still a brat."

Beau shrugged. "He's a little brother. Little brothers are supposed to be brats." He shifted his shoulders and adjusted something under his shirt. "He's got a point, though. There are Fentons in town, but no Barneses."

"And no statue of Mr. Barnes?"

"Nope." He smiled. "It's a mystery."

She smiled back. "Good. I was hoping it was."

"Where we headed?" Rafe asked, chomping through his egg salad sandwich.

"Courthouse." Kyle's voice was muffled by his mouthful, but Rafe could make it out. "There's this door on the second floor landing, leads to this attic kinda place."

"Won't we get caught?"

Kyle shook his head. "Nobody checks. Anyway, if you walk along the rafters a ways, you get to this spot that's right above the sheriff's office. You can hear the dispatcher and all the calls and stuff."

"Cool!" He licked his fingers, finishing up. "Sorry about my brother and all."

"Aw, you can't help it if your brother's a weirdo." Kyle threw his crust into the weeds. "My sister's a bitch, but it don't affect me none."

First Letter of Jake
to the Edomites

Big Man,

I'm moving in on your territory and I don't mean Joanie. I'm taking over your delivery route for the Rexall. What glimpses I get of Joanie will be fleeting as I fly out the door and down county roads, gay as you please.

The paper plant is running again and your mom is all eager to start back on swing shift. Apparently this leaves me free of an evening to run riot through the fleshpots of Croy. (Where are they, by the way? Surely you know.) The odious Mrs. O now has carte blanche to drop in on me whenever to make sure I'm not doing whatever. Imagine my thrilledness.

My mother is in Paris. France, not Texas. She's making a film. I could have gone with her, but things in Croy are so, you know, <u>exciting</u>. To wit:

Beau is starting a band. We don't know what <u>kind</u> of band yet. All we have so far is Beau's guitar and a drummer, Belle Craddock. I offered to play kazoo, but they turned me down. Mostly I just lug stuff from Belle's place to Beau's garage and back. We get more done out at Belle's. Her only neighbors are the brick works across the highway and they don't complain much. Her uncle is the plant supervisor there and would clobber them if they did.

Fourth of July and my birthday are coming up. Do you realize we were born 9 months apart? We're practically twins.

Speaking of twins, one of Coach Ardmore's little girls has a heart defect. They're on the prayer list at St. Elizabeth's. It's kinda sad.

They may have to put the whole Croy Athletic Program on the prayer list, too. There's talk of a teachers' strike. (Can teachers go on strike? It ain't natural.) Anyhoo, Ardmore is looking for higher pay to cover his bills. I hear Tulsa Memorial is drooling at the prospect. That will leave Tucker and Webb in charge of sports and that would be <u>really</u> sad. Tucker's okay, but I can't stand Webb.

That's all the news that'll fit in print.

Yours in some regards,

—Jake

P.S. Joanie doesn't say "Hi."

Taking Stock

Jake was doing inventory in the back of the Rexall when Zach appeared at the side door. He blocked the light, making Jake look up. Zach was in a suit and tie, which was odd. It was midweek. "Hey, Zach."

"Hey." Zach shifted and thrust his hands in his pockets.

"What's with the suit?"

Zach raised his chin, looked aside and smiled.

He's nervous. What could make Zach Jameson nervous? "Come on in. Wanna coke?"

"Naw."

"It comes with the job."

Zach cleared his throat and stepped inside. "No thanks." He brushed the front of his sports coat and laughed. "I'm trying to make a good impression."

Jake laughed. "The only impression you make leaves a bruise." He expected Zach to laugh, but he didn't. "Jeez man, what's the matter?"

"I need a job. They're closing down the Conoco. It's just Marcus and his uncle now, but they won't last."

"Crap."

"I tried Herman's, but . . ."

"No dice?"

Zach shook his head.

"You wouldn't want to work for him anyway. He's a nimrod."

"Hell, I've worked for the Longacres. Can't be worse than that. Money's money. But that son of a bitch wouldn't even let me inside. Interviewed me out back. By the toilet."

"Shit. Soda jerk just graduated from nimrod to asshole. I'm not going there again."

Zach smiled and looked down. "Thanks." He took a breath. "So, I hear Mr. Tibbits sometimes hires help. Randy and Tom, last year."

"Yeah, but—" *But that's* my *job.* "—things have been slow. Not much deliveries."

Zach scowled. "Don't be thick. Can you see me heading down country roads, making farm deliveries? Alone?"

"Oh. Right. I didn't think."

"'Cuz you don't have to." He softened. "But maybe something around the store. Stock room stuff."

Jake looked around. "There is a lot of stuff. And I don't have time for it and the deliveries."

"Thought you said deliveries was slow."

Jake cleared his throat. "I mean, I need more time for the band now, so I won't have time to do that and this *and* deliveries—you go all over the county, you know, sometimes for hours. I could put in a word with Mr. Tibbits."

Zach nodded and rubbed his chin. "Good. Good. Thanks." He looked up. "Is he in?"

"You mean, now?"

"Yeah."

Jake thought quick. It wasn't a lie about the band. *I'll have to say something to Mr. Tibbits sooner or later.* "Sure, why not. Come with me."

Zach hesitated. "How do I look?"

"Good. Non-bruising."

Mr. Tibbits took the news about Jake pretty well. "A band, huh? Well, can't keep a musician from his music. It doesn't end well." He looked at Zach. "You have your own car?"

"Actually, Mr. Tibbits," Jake said, "I was thinking of keeping the route, and Zach here taking over for me stocking shelves and such."

"Oh you were, were you?" He looked over at Joanie, who was ringing up a sale. "You kids will be running the place all by yourselves if I don't watch out." He looked at Zach, like he was sizing him up. "All right," he said, extending his hand.

Zach grinned and shook it.

Jake felt proud. "At the same pay as me, right?"

Mr. Tibbits's smile disappeared. He opened his mouth, but Zach spoke first. "Not right away, sir. I've still got to learn the job. From Jake."

"That's right," Mr. Tibbits said. "Jake, you can start by showing him how to do inventory. That is what you were doing back there, wasn't it?"

"Yes sir. Right away." He started for the back room.

"Now hold on."

The two of them turned to see Mr. Tibbits standing with his arms crossed. "We can't have two of our championship basketball team join the firm without a bit of ceremony. Joanie? Set 'em up. Cokes all around."

Joanie was all smiles as she set up the drinks. "Well, this is exciting. Welcome to the salt mines."

"Thank you, ma'am."

"Oh, for heaven's sake. We're going to be working together. Joanie, please."

Zach smiled but didn't repeat her name. Instead he looked sideways at Jake. "A band, huh?"

"Yeah. So far, we've got a guitar and drums."

"Which are you?"

Joanie leaned on the counter. "Don't tell Daddy, but he's just their roadie."

"Hey, I'm important. Amps don't plug themselves in." He turned to Zach. "We're still looking for a bass and a second guitar. Or a keyboard."

"You play, don't you?" Joanie asked. "You should join."

"I play lead," Zach said.

Of course you do. "We really need a bass."

"I play that, too. Who's in this band?"

"Beau Hamilton and Belle Craddock."

"Hamilton? Ain't he the kid who brought down the talent show last year?" Zach rubbed his chin. "Could be interesting."

"They're rehearsing tonight at Beau's," Joanie said.

Jake frowned.

"What? Well, they are. You said so yourself."

"I ain't got the time," Zack said to the last of his coke.

"No, you should come," Jake said. "Really."

"Uh-oh," Joanie said, looking up. "Here comes Daddy. Break time's over."

Afterward, when Zach had gone and they were closing for the day, he asked her, "What's got into you today?"

"It's historic!"

"Oh, here we go."

"No, really. It wasn't so long ago he wouldn't even be allowed at the counter. Not that Daddy ever believed in that nonsense."

"I'm not talking about that. I'm talking about the band."

"What? You said you were looking for a bass. He plays bass. Problem solved."

The way throwing a lion into a flock a sheep solves your sheep problem. Aloud, Jake said, "It's really up to Beau. It's his band."

Beau's eyes widened as Zach pulled not one but three guitars from their cases: a Fender Stratocaster, a dobro, and a bass. *If he can play even one of those, this is going to be great!*

They tried a few Dylan tunes to warm up, Zach on bass and him on lead. Then some Creedence. Finally, Zach looked over at Belle. "That's quite a trap set. I'm thinking we ain't heard nearly the half of it yet."

Belle grinned and looked at Beau.

"Do it," he said.

She hammered out Ric Lee's "Three Blind Mice" from *Stonedhenge*.

Zach smiled for the first time. "That's pretty fly."

"Your turn," Belle said. "Show us what you got."

Zach picked up his Fender. "Hang on to your ears, kids." He launched into Jimi Hendrix's version of "The Star-Spangled Banner." The first verse started out melodic enough, with a loose and stylized rhythm. The second drew out more riffs and harsh discords. Then Zach swung into "the rockets' red glare" like he was felling a tree. The Stratocaster blasted out whistling screams and explosions Beau didn't know a guitar could make. He hopped up and down to the sounds, laughing. Jake grinned and covered his ears. Belle looked like she was howling, but he couldn't hear her.

They didn't notice Beau's mother standing in the door until Zach finished.

"Is everything all right out here?" she asked. "I thought maybe your guitar had broken. Or exploded."

"Wasn't that great, Mom? This is Zach. I think he's going to be our new lead guitar."

"Oh. That's very nice." She smiled and looked baffled. "You're Reverend Jameson's boy, aren't you?"

"I'm his son, yes ma'am."

"Well, you kids let me know if you need anything, like water or ice tea or . . . Band-Aids."

"Thanks, Mom."

As soon as she left, he turned to Zach. "That was *amazing*."

Zach grinned. "I don't get to play that at home."

"Did you mean that about lead?" Belle asked him.

"Sure! I can take over at bass." He winked at Jake. "It's not that hard."

"Still need rhythm," Zach said.

"How about Al?" Jake offered.

Beau shook his head. "Al's out. There's still Frank, if you can get him off the farm."

"What do we call this outfit, anyway?" Zach asked.

Belle snorted. "Well, definitely not Belles and Beaus. That's my uncle's square dance club."

"How about The Quirks?" Beau offered. "We're all a little quirky."

Zach frowned. "I'm not."

"Maybe we should get some gigs first," Jake said. "There's the VFW hall Saturday nights."

"Bunch of drunks," Belle said.

"We gotta be in front of people if we wanna improve. The Teen Center?"

"If we wanna improve, we need to practice," Zach said. "Let's do that."

They did some more folk-rock. Beau hit a high falsetto on "I'll Be Your Baby Tonight" that sounded like Barry Gibb. Belle's husky voice did well on the mellow bluesy numbers. They tried it on "Summertime" from Big Brother and the Holding Company, and it didn't sound half bad. Jake even joined in the chorus on some songs. Zach didn't sing.

When they were done, Jake and Zach helped Belle load her drums into her pickup. "Next week, my place," she said. "My uncle's used to the racket."

Beau nodded happily. "I have ideas for our outfits. I'll bring them."

"Outfits?" Zach shook his head. "We ain't even a band yet. Two guitars and a drummer."

"Jake'll get Frank to join. It'll come together. You'll see."

Jake was the last to leave. Beau was glad to have some time alone with him. "He's perfect."

"Hmm?"

"Zach. We're going to take off like a rocket!"

"Like a rocket's red glare!"

He wrapped his arms around Jake and squeezed. "Thank you, thank you, thank you!" Jake didn't squeeze back. Beau broke the embrace, embarrassed.

But Jake was smiling. "It's good to see you happy."

Beau let out a long breath. "It's good to finally *be* happy."

Jake hurried back from a delivery at the Woolvines late in the afternoon on July fourth. The sun was already headed for the trees. He wanted to get home in time to shower, make supper, and meet Joanie at Little Bushy Park for what she called his pre-birthday fireworks. From the hints she dropped he knew she wanted to tell him about some discovery she'd made. *If she brings up that statue again I'll just plug my ears and hum "The Star-Spangled Banner," Hendrix style.*

He had just passed under the railroad bridge when his car gave a loud *clunk!* and clattered to a stop. He tried the usual remedies, but none worked. He tried cursing and kicking, but they didn't work either. He looked at the sun then down the road. He was three miles north of town. It would be twilight before he could get to Longacre Brothers, arrange a tow, and get the Dream Machine back to town. And he'd be a sweaty mess. "Shit, I'll miss the fireworks."

He looked up the road. The Santa Fe tracks passed over the highway and headed east. Frank's farm was out that way, maybe half a mile. Maybe Frank would give him a tow with the tractor, or at least let him use the phone to call Longacres. Plus he could finally get around to asking him about joining the band.

He climbed the embankment and headed down the tracks. He wondered if he'd arrive around suppertime or if they'd already have eaten. It would be nice if they hadn't.

Virgil's Solution

Virgil Craddock sat on the wide front porch of his farmhouse, his hands tucked into his overalls, his right hand fingering three shotgun shells. Two other shells were already loaded into the shotgun that leaned against his chair. He breathed in the evening air as deeply as he dared, gritting his teeth.

The pain in his belly was worse. The pills Doc Lewis had given him were nothing but sugar. He'd figured as much, being treated like some helpless baby that had to be tricked into keeping quiet. The cancer was eating through him, and there wasn't anything anyone could do about it. He knew how these things went. He had seen it with his own daddy, lying in the big bed, stinking of his own filth.

So he knew what had to be done, and he was determined to do it. After supper was when.

But the shells were a puzzlement. Two in the shotgun, three in his hand. He rolled them around in his palm. Him, Arlene, Arlene's ruined boy, Frank, and the beautiful little Angela. He hated to do it to Angela, but there would be no one to take care of her with him and her momma gone. So who was the fifth shell for? It had been so clear yesterday. It was someone he had to take care of first, someone who would stop him, but who?

He drew an angry breath and the pain shot from his belly clean up to his shoulder and down into his left thumb, paralyzing his arm. "Arlene!" he bellowed through clenched teeth. "When the hell's supper?"

"In a minute, Daddy," she called from the kitchen.

Frank maneuvered around his mother, trying to salvage the meal. She was stirring ground beef with onions and potatoes in an iron skillet, ignoring the pot of carrots she had put on earlier. Frank had pulled them from the garden this afternoon, golden and full of promise, but they would soon be a tasteless pulp. The kitchen was tight, and when he reached for the pot he bumped Arlene's arm.

"Frank, get out the way!" his mother scolded. "Your granddad is cross enough without you setting supper back an hour."

"I'll just take the carrots—"

She slapped his hand.

"They'll be all mush!"

"He likes them all mush."

Frank looked at his stepsister, Angela, already seated at the table, twirling a lock of hair over her right ear. She was pretending to be somewhere else, waiting for servants to serve up supper on burnished plates. He shook his head. Angela gazed blandly in his direction, stuck out her tongue, and went back to her fairyland.

"It's now or never," his granddad announced from the kitchen doorway. "I'm sitting down and there'd better be something in front of me right quick." He pulled into his chair and glared.

"Getting it now, Daddy," Arlene said.

"Howdy, Granddad." Angela leaned in and whispered, "Don't touch the carrots. Frank put poison in them. I seen him."

"I heard that," Frank muttered, taking his seat across from her.

Arlene brought the skillet to the table. "Heard what?"

"I'm just taking care of Granddad." Angela turned to him and patted his hand. "You're my favorite, you know. I like taking care of you."

A huge grin broke over his face. "You're my favorite, too, little angel. And I'll take care of you, too. I'll see to it."

All through dinner his half-sister and his grandfather played their little game. He always looked her way before he started in on the beans or the hash or the cornbread, and she always gave him her little signal to tell him if it was safe to eat. When she shook her head as he lifted a forkful of carrots, Frank had had enough. "Quit it," he said.

"Quit what?" Angela said, the picture of innocence.

"You know what."

"Mom?" Tears quickened in her eyes.

"Frank, stop pestering your sister."

"I'm not pestering her. Don't you see how she's carrying on?"

"I don't see a thing and neither should you. Eat your beans."

"You just don't like me, that's all," Angela sniffed. "You *never* liked me. You wish I was dead."

"Oh for God's sake!"

"Frank Pellegrini! You watch your mouth!"

Angela started whimpering.

"What the hell's all this?" his granddad said.

"Frank's gone and upset his sister."

"I have not. I haven't said a thing."

"Frank, apologize."

"The hell!"

Virgil Craddock slammed his fist on the table. "There will be no yelling at supper. Do you hear me? No yelling!"

There was a second of silence, then Angela burst into tears.

"Now look what you've done!" his mother said.

"I don't believe this." Frank got up.

"Where the hell do you think you're going?" his granddad asked.

"Frank, sit down, please," his mother said.

"You're all a bunch of loonies, and this is nothing but a loony bin."

"Frank!" His mother reached for him, rising from her chair.

"You stay away from him!" Virgil Craddock roared. They all froze in place. The old man glared across the table. "You stay away from that Newton fella."

Frank looked quickly at his mother. Her eyes were wide.

"You heard me," the old man said. "You keep away from him. He'll be the ruin of you, if he ain't ruined you already."

The color drained from Frank's face. "What?"

"Daddy?" His mother's voice had an edge of panic.

The old man leaned forward. "I seen you," he hissed. "I seen the two of you, playing buck-buck out behind the shed."

Frank's face turned blood red. "You're a crazy, miserable old man!" he yelled. He looked at his mother, who stared with pain-filled eyes. "Are you just going to sit there?" But she didn't move or say a word. He flung back his chair. "I don't have to put up with this bullshit!" He slammed out through the kitchen door.

He crossed the barnyard, his jaw clamped against anger and tears. He glanced at the shed where Jim Newton had bunked as a hired hand. But Jim was gone, his gear and rodeo tack crammed into his truck. He had driven off, leaving Frank to eat dust like a fool.

The anger burned inside him. *They all go away. They all leave. Jim, Dad, that dumb-ass Pellegrini. Gone or dead or just plain run off. They leave, and I'm left to clean up their shit.* The one man he wished would go away forever never did.

He tore off his shirt as he strode through the thick summer evening. He thought of flinging it across the field, then of throwing off all his clothes and taking a running jump into the White Horse River. Maybe he could burrow into its fetid bottom, or swim all the way downstream—under the Santa Fe trestle, down past their neighbors' fields, all the way to the Canadian River, and rise from its banks a creature of mud and instinct. Or maybe just drown.

The tracks drew a sharp line against the straw-colored sky. They cut across the north end of the farm, then stepped in two spans across the bottomland before jumping the White Horse itself. Frank climbed the embankment and scrambled into the space beneath the rails. He used his wadded-up shirt to clear dirt and mouse droppings from the cardboard sheet that lay atop a wooden pallet he and Jim had dragged out here months ago. He sat with his back against the concrete wall and looked out from the underside of the bridge. The smell of tar seeped from the sun-soaked ties overhead.

A stone skittered across the ties, then dropped between them and fell fifteen feet to the ground. Frank held his breath. Someone was walking the rails. He held perfectly still, wondering if the figure would climb down and discover him, wondering if he wanted him to, wondering what would happen when he did.

The footsteps turned into scrabbling sounds as someone climbed down the slope and came around the corner.

"Howdy, Jake," Frank said nonchalantly.

"Jesus!" Jake exclaimed and began toppling backward.

Frank grabbed him by the hand. Jake flailed wildly, then slid roughly to his butt, catching his fall with the other hand.

"Holy crap, Frank!" he said, breathing hard. "You scared the shit out of me."

Frank pulled him to his feet. "All I said was howdy."

"Howdy my ass," Jake said, straightening up. They stood beneath the trestle now, their heads bent low to clear the ties above them. "Do you always lurk under bridges?"

"Sometimes." He sank to his haunches. "What about you? Do you always go for a stroll along the tracks?"

"My car gave up the ghost out on the hardtop. I thought I'd hike in here and ask for a tow." He slid down beside him and started picking pebbles from his hand. Frank could smell the sweat and dirt on him.

"Sure. Tow it to town?"

"Yeah. Longacres. If they're still open."

"You'd be halfway there by now if you walked."

"Yeah, but I wanted to ask you something. Something else."

A dark smear of blood covered the fleshy part of his palm. "Here, let me see that." Frank reached out.

Jake pulled away. "It's nothing."

"No, come on. It's my fault for spooking you."

Jake looked at him a moment, then offered his hand. Frank took it. Jake twitched. "Man, that's gotta sting." He reached behind him and got his shirt. He folded a corner and spat on it.

"What are you doing?" A laugh worked its way through Jake's words.

"You patched me up plenty. Remember the Holiday Tournament? You wrapped my ankle to keep it from buckling."

"Coach Tucker taught me that."

Frank brought the hand close to his face. Jake twitched again. Frank frowned. "Hold still." When he was sure Jake wouldn't flinch, he wiped away the dried blood and gently dabbed the raw flesh. The bleeding stopped. They relaxed.

"Thanks," Jake said.

Frank kept hold of his hand. "Why'd you jerk away like that?"

A grin crept up Jake's face. "I thought you were going to lick it."

"You mean, like this?" Frank brought Jake's palm to his face and drew his tongue slowly across it, looking him in the eye.

Jake's grin grew broader. "Yeah. Kinda like that."

"What else were you going to ask?"

There was a muffled explosion in the distance. They both twitched.

"What was that?" Jake asked. "Fireworks?"

Frank shook his head. "Just my granddad, shooting coyotes. Crazy bastard."

They had dropped hands. Now they both looked at the one Frank had licked. "Look . . ." Jake started.

A high-pitched keening floated across the field. Frank stood, his head cocked.

"What is it?"

Frank looked at him. "That's my mom." Then he whirled around. "That's my mom!" He bolted from the trestle and flew down the slope.

The two of them raced through the field toward the house, the screams getting louder as they got closer. They ran into Frank's little sister stumbling toward them, one continuous high-pitched scream pouring from her twisted mouth. Frank scooped her up, then saw his mother on the porch yelling incoherently and tearing at her hair. He shoved his little sister at Jake and dashed up the steps and began to pull his mother by her arms and dress, trying to get her off the porch and into the house.

Angela clung to Jake and shook violently, her fat arms nearly choking him and her chin digging into his shoulder. In the race through the field, all Jake had seen was Frank's naked back, shoulder blades flashing in the late sun. Now that Frank had cleared his line of sight, he could see the porch plainly. His stomach lurched to his throat and he turned away. Angela's screams started winding up again, so he turned back to face the porch, knowing now he couldn't look away.

The front of Virgil Craddock's skull was completely blown off, the back of it plainly visible like the inside of a shattered melon. Above and behind, a brilliant red V spread up the wall and fanned out across the underside of the porch roof. Bits of bone and white matter dripped from it. There were already flies.

Wake

J oanie could have just killed Jake for standing her up. She asked Zach at the store the next day if he had seen him.

"Not after he left."

"He was supposed to meet me at the park."

He shrugged. "Guess he got busy."

She knew there was no point trying to get more out of him. It bugged her, but two men sat at the soda fountain so she quit trying to figure out boys and turned to her customers. One was an overweight man with soft brown hair, the other a wiry cowhand with eyes like ice and hair like a crow's wing. That made remembering their orders easy: a chocolate phosphate and a coffee, black.

They were still at the counter talking when Jake came in. She practically pounced on him. "Where on earth have you been? You missed everything."

"Huh?" He sat at the fountain, his hands barely touching the countertop.

"And not just the fireworks. Guess who interviewed the last surviving member of the Longstreet and Barnes Circus?"

He stared blankly. She tried again. "He has all these stories, and bits of old statues and things, and parts of a flying jenny."

"Virgil Craddock's dead."

"What?"

"Frank's granddad. Blew his head off with a shotgun yesterday. I was there."

She noticed his hands were trembling. "Jake?"

"I couldn't sleep all night. I kept seeing it, over and over."

She came around the counter and sat next to him. "That's horrible. Are you all right?"

"I can't sleep. Do you think your dad could give me something to sleep?"

"Daddy!" she called. It came out more like a cry than she meant. Zach stepped from the storeroom frowning.

Her father came over right away. So did the men.

"Craddock's dead?" the cowhand asked. "What about the boy? What about the little girl?"

Jake looked at the stranger.

"What's wrong, Joanie?" her father said.

Jake's head whipped around to him.

"Mally?" the other stranger said.

Jake twitched in his direction, and then his face just dissolved. He clutched the man and buried his head in his shoulder and cried.

The man held him and rocked him. Her father gave Jake something to drink. The cowboy looked like he wanted to punch somebody. The whole scene was utterly baffling.

"Thank you, Mr. . . ." she began.

"Anderson," the large man said.

"Oh." Jake pulled away and wiped his face. "I'm sorry. Mr. Tibbits, Joanie, this is Mr. Anderson. He was our neighbor in Oklahoma City."

"What about the boy?" the other man insisted. "What about Frank?"

"Frank's fine. They're all fine. It's just him. Just Mr. Craddock."

The man left quickly. Jake started trembling again.

"We need to get you home," Mr. Anderson said. He looked at Joanie. "Where is home, exactly?"

"I'll take him," she said. "Zach can cover for me, can't you Zach?" She didn't wait for his answer or her father's approval.

Jake fell asleep on the way to the granny house, curled up against Mr. Anderson in the back seat. She glanced at them in the rearview mirror. *Like a mother and child.* "So, you were Jake's neighbor in Oklahoma City?"

"Jake?"

"That's what Mally calls himself now."

"Oh. Yes, they lived next door with their aunt Margaret. I got Susan her first job on television, you know. As a weather girl. Look at her now."

She glanced in the rearview mirror. Anderson had a big smile on his face, but his eyes were shadowed. "What brings you to Croy?"

"I'm writing a book, *Crazy Woman Weather*. Legendary tornadoes of Oklahoma."

"Well, you've come to the right place. We've had some doozies."

"Oh yes, you're quite famous. The TriCounty Twister and the seventeen-year curse."

What curse? I never heard of that. But they had arrived at Jake's house, so she held her questions while they got him settled in bed. Joanie removed his shoes and stepped out as Mr. Anderson undressed him to his underwear. She was standing in the living room when there was a knock at the door and Mrs. Oldfield stepped in. "Is something wrong, Joanie?"

Mr. Anderson came from the bedroom. He stopped when he saw Mrs. Oldfield.

"No ma'am," Joanie said. "Jake's had a shock, that's all."

Mr. Anderson took a breath. "I'd better be going."

"Mr. Anderson was in the store when it happened. He helped bring Jake back."

"Mr. Anderson?" The crease between her brows deepened. "Oh."

"I just happened to be there, at the drugstore." The two of them eyed each other. "I really should be going."

"I can drive you back," Joanie offered.

"No, no. I'll walk." He nodded to Mrs. Oldfield. "Good day to you, ma'am."

The moment he left Mrs. Oldfield stepped closer. "Is Jake all right?"

"He was at the farm when Mr. Craddock shot himself."

"Oh, dear Lord." She looked at the closed door to the bedroom. "I just heard myself. The poor boy."

"My dad gave him something so he could rest."

"Good." They stood silent a moment. "I'll look after him."

I'm being dismissed. Fine. "I've got to get back to the store." She glanced at the bedroom. "He'll be all right now."

"Of course he will."

Joanie got in her car and gave the granny house a long look. *There's something she's not telling me. Something between this Anderson guy and her.* She looked around. *And where's Jake's car?*

Jake's room was uncomfortably warm when he woke up. He wriggled out of his underwear and got his toes tangled in his socks trying to tug them off. That woke him enough to realize he had to piss something fierce. As soon as he opened the bedroom door, a voice called from the living room, "Just so you know, I'm out here, in case you were wondering." It was Joanie's voice.

"Just so you know, I'm putting my clothes on as soon as I— I'm putting my clothes on."

He went out when he was ready. Joanie sat in the recliner with a book, a glass of ice tea on the floor. "I'm glad it's you and not Mrs. O," he said.

"Oh, she's been here. She dropped off her magic potion."

"Three parts sugar, one part tea?"

"I think she may have skimped on the tea."

He poured himself a glass. "I suppose Virginia's been, too."

"The busybody network is in full gear."

He sat with a sigh. "Not my mom, too?"

"Um, no. She's still in Paris."

"Oh, right. Say, what did your father give me anyway?"

"Actually, Daddy said it was just water."

"Sure." He took a gulp of tea. "Sorry I stepped on your big scoop."

"I'm just glad I was there. I mean, not *glad* glad, but, you know, glad."

He nodded.

"You seemed glad Mr. Anderson was there."

"Yeah." He saw that look in her eye. *I'm not going to have to tell her the whole story, am I?* "Mr. Anderson was our neighbor. We were friends."

"Was he the guy with the telescope? The one who showed you the universe?"

"The Milky Way, yeah."

She got a dreamy look on her face. "'Out there, somewhere, there's got to be a home for each of us.'"

"Do what?"

"That's what you said about the Milky Way."

He shrugged. "I don't remember. Sounds like something I would say though, back then."

"I miss back then. I miss Mally."

"I don't."

She stopped being dreamy. "So what's the deal with him and Mrs. Oldfield?"

He sighed. "The busybody network, O. City branch.

Somehow, Aunt Margaret got the idea Mr. Anderson was a bad influence on me. That's when she and Mrs. Oldfield concocted their scheme to send me down here. I never thought I'd see him again. He seemed just as surprised to see me."

She squinted. "What kind of bad influence?"

He was awake now and tired of explaining. "He'd never do anything to hurt me."

"Good, 'cuz I'd scratch his eyes out. With an ugly stick."

"You and Aunt Margaret and Mrs. Oldfield." He stood. "I don't need protecting, Joanie. Not from Mr. Anderson. He's one of the good guys."

The phone rang.

"That's probably Virginia, checking up on me."

But the voice on the other end was Frank's. It was flat and hoarse, like he'd said the same thing a million times today. "Funeral is on Saturday if you want to come."

"Do you want me to?"

"If you want."

He didn't. "I'll come."

"It's closed casket, so you won't have to . . ."

"I'll come. Are you all right?"

There was a long silence. "And there's a wake. At the farm."

"Sure. I'll be there." He hung up and turned to Joanie. "I don't want to go."

"To the funeral?"

"To the farm. I don't want to go back there."

"You don't have to if you don't want to."

He nodded. "Could you drive me? My car's kinda out of commission."

The service at the Southern Methodist church was short. Reverend Crawford's eulogy praised Virgil Craddock's virtues, including taking his daughter in when her first husband passed and sticking with her during her difficulties. That the difficulties were mostly with her second husband, Lorenzo Pellegrini, and that Lorenzo's difficulties were mostly with Virgil, was not mentioned, nor was the means by which Virgil ended his own particular difficulties.

"God knows us from before we were knit together in our mother's womb," Reverend Crawford said. "He knows what our gifts are, and what our flaws are. He alone knows the difference, and He alone can love us whole. And all He asks of us is that we sing His praise. See the darkness, believe the light, and sing."

The only kids Jake and Joanie saw at the service were BT Crawford, Zach Jameson, and Belle Craddock. The guys had been on the championship basketball team with Frank. Belle was some sort of cousin. She helped Mrs. Pellegrini down the church steps as the casket was loaded into the hearse. Frank stood nearby, holding his little sister by the hand. The child had been silent throughout the service.

BT shook Frank's hand solemnly. "My father and I will see you at the cemetery."

"Sure. Thanks."

Zach thumped him on the back and left.

Joanie spoke softly. "I'm so sorry."

"Sure. Thanks."

Jake stepped up and Angela ducked behind her brother. Jake bowed his head. "Man," was all he could say.

A brace of women helped Frank's mother into a car. He looked at Angela. "We should go." She shook her head. "You comin'?" he asked Jake.

He said it with such hollowness Jake had to say yes. As the entourage pulled away, he apologized to Joanie. "This is turning into an all-day thing."

"Don't be stupid. Let's go."

After the interment, Joanie drove them to the farmhouse. They parked as close as they could. There were more cars in the drive than there had been people at the funeral. As he and Joanie approached the house, he froze.

"What?" she asked.

He stared at the porch.

"Oh."

"It's been painted."

"Do you want to . . . ?"

He shook his head. "No. Let's go in."

It was hot and humid in the parlor. All the men were in dark suits, the women dressed as if for Easter. The noise of all those people eating and talking, some even laughing, made Jake's ears hot. Angela sat in a chair with a plate heaped with food in her lap. She ate with her hands, her eyes darting from one face to another.

He spotted Frank in a corner, looking strangled in his suit and tie and holding a glass of water. People would come up to him and touch him on the elbow and mutter something. He never responded. Jake went over and stood beside him but didn't speak.

Across the room, Reverend Crawford spoke to Frank's mother. Over the din, Jake heard him say something like, "Love covers a multitude of sins."

Suddenly, Mrs. Pellegrini's voice rose above the crowd. "Such a beautiful service, Pastor! All of Daddy's favorites." She sang out,

> *Other refuge have I none,*
> *Hangs my helpless soul on thee;*
> *Leave, ah! leave me not alone,*
> *Still support and comfort me.*

She broke off abruptly, choking. Reverend Crawford pulled her into an embrace and gestured some ladies over to help.

Frank snarled, "She's drunk."

Jake looked at him. "Do you want to get out of here?"

"Fuck yeah." Without another word Frank headed out through the kitchen. Jake followed.

Trestle

They walked quickly through the fields, heading for the railroad bridge. Frank tore off his tie and flung it aside, then shed his suit coat and threw it to the ground. "Bunch of phonies!" he yelled, wrenching his shirttails from his pants.

Jake was breaking a sweat keeping up with him. He took off his sports coat and unbuttoned his shirt, stuffing his tie into his pants. "I'm sure they mean well."

Frank turned on him. "Mean well? Hell." He turned and continued striding toward the trestle. "Did you see that fat slob, Woolvine? That son of a bitch shook my hand, actually *shook my hand*, looking me in the eye. Said he'd make good on the deal to buy the alfalfa. Fuck! He knows that deal was a handshake and Granddad didn't keep records. He'll cheat us. He'll drop the price and say it's what they agreed on. And Reverend Crawford? What's he mean, 'Love covers a multitude of sins'? He has no idea what was in the old bastard's heart."

They reached the embankment and scrambled up, ducking under the span. Frank flopped onto the cardboard-covered pallet. "He should rot in hell. That's where he belongs."

Jake slid down beside him. "I was there when my granddad died. It was drawn out and miserable. It tore me up to watch."

Frank spat over the edge. "You don't know shit about it."

"I'm just saying, maybe your granddad did the best thing, ending it quick."

Frank glared at him. "Fuck you." He stood and turned his back.

There was a rumbling like thunder in the distance. Jake hadn't noticed any thunderheads on their way out here. If it came up a storm, they'd be drenched. Jake reached out and touched Frank on the leg. "Hey."

"You want to know what he was thinking?" Frank trembled. "You want to know what that son of a bitch had in his heart when he pulled the trigger?" He pulled something out of his pocket and turned. "This! This is what he was thinking!"

Jake looked. Frank held three shotgun shells in his hand. The bright red cartridges were smeared with a darker red. "I don't get it."

Frank crouched down, his face close to Jake's. "It's simple. Dead simple." He placed one cartridge on the pallet between them. "Mom." He placed another. "Angela." He placed the third. "Me."

Jake shook his head. "That's crazy."

"I fished them out of his pocket before the cops came. Who goes to blow their brains out and takes extra ammo? It's not like he's gonna miss."

"But why would he want to kill you and your mom and sister?"

Frank snorted and sat back on his heels. "You've seen my mom. She's hopeless. Angela? I don't know. Fucking crazy bastard."

Jake swallowed. "And you? Why would he want to kill you?"

Frank looked at him. "You know."

The thunder sounded closer now, continuous, just across the river. Jake couldn't take his eyes off Frank.

"I wonder what it was like," Frank said, picking up a cartridge. He turned it over in his hand. "I mean, can you feel it? Is it hot? Or heavy?" He curled his fingers around the shell, leaving one end sticking out. "Or sharp, maybe?" He brought his hand to his mouth and wrapped his lips around the red paper.

"Stop it," Jake said.

Frank moved his hand slowly back and forth, the cartridge slipping in and out of his mouth.

"I said stop it, Frank. There's a train coming."

"I can taste him."

"He's dead. Who cares what the fuck he thought? He's dead and gone. Let's get out of here."

Frank shook his head, looking at the cartridge. "No, he's not. He's right here."

The bridge began to throb as the train's engines started crossing the White Horse.

"Let's get out of here, Frank. Let's go back to the house."

"Can't." Frank's mouth twisted. "Don't you see? He's still there. He'll always be there. I picked bits of bone and brains out of that wall, but I couldn't get it all. He'll always be there. I can't go back." Suddenly he slammed his fist into the wall behind him. The primer scraped against the concrete. "That's how you set them off, isn't it?" He slammed it again. "Come on, god damn it! Do it!"

"Frank! Stop!"

The roar of the engines was almost on top of them. Frank was slamming his fist against the wall and then into his mouth. "Do it! Do it!" His hand and lips turned bloody. Jake was yelling, but he couldn't hear his own words and he couldn't make Frank stop, so he lunged at him hard and threw him to the pallet. He lay on top of him as the diesels pounded overhead. Frank convulsed beneath him over and over as the boxcars beat their rhythm above. The sound entered their bodies and soon they were heaving against each other in time. They tore at each other's belts and jerked open their pants.

The train took forever to pass. When it did, they lay exhausted beneath the trestle. "Fuck," Frank said.

Jake looked down at the mess between their open shirts. "Too late," he said. He spotted a rag between the pallet slats and pulled it out. It was Frank's shirt from before. "Here," he said. "We better clean up."

Frank stopped him. "I'm not crazy. He's still there."

Jake nodded. "Maybe so. But so are you. And so am I. That's two against one."

Frank winced, bringing his hand to his ruined mouth. "Ow. Remind me not to do that again."

Jake traced a circle on his stomach. Their spunk was turning clear and beginning to run. "I'll be around."

On their way back, they looked for Frank's suit coat and tie. They found the coat. It didn't look too bad once they dusted it off.

"You don't have to stay," Frank said. "You're with Joanie, right?"

"She drove. My car's still at Longacres." Jake rustled through a tangle of alfalfa. "No sign of a tie."

Frank tucked in his shirt. "You never did ask me that question."

"We're starting a band. You play guitar I hear."

"Sorta. Who's in it?"

Jake took a deep breath. "Belle."

"Rebel Belle? On drums, right?"

"Right. And Zach."

Frank nodded.

"And Beau."

"Beau Hamilton? Blowin'-in-the-Wind Beau Hamilton?" He shook his head. "But Zach, huh?"

"He's lead guitar."

"Figures."

"Beau's bass. We need a rhythm."

Frank looked at the house, his expression hard to read. "What do you play?"

"I just hang around." He pushed a clump of dry hay with his foot. "It's a reason to hang out. *We* could hang out. If you aren't too busy out here."

Frank shook his head. "There won't be any out here once the buzzards pick it over." He started toward the house.

"What about the tie?"

"Some crow's made off with it, most like."

"Wait." Jake pulled his tie out and looped it around Frank's neck. He gave it a tug and Frank stepped closer. "Hey."

"Hey." Frank pressed against him. He was hard again.

"Don't you have a funeral to enjoy?"

Frank laughed and started walking, knotting the tie as he went. He looked at Jake's unbuttoned shirt. "What about you?"

"I'm good. No one will notice I haven't got a tie."

Joanie was talking to Belle Craddock when they walked in. She immediately broke away and came up to them. "Where have you two been?" She looked at Jake. "Where's your tie?"

"I left it in the car."

Frank looked around. "Where's my mom?"

"Some church ladies took her to her room. She was a little wobbly." She scanned Frank's face.

He tried to cover the dried blood, but that just showed his scraped hand. "I'll be right back," he said and headed for the bathroom.

Joanie whispered to Jake. "Have you been fighting?"

"We were up at the trestle. Frank slipped and fell."

"Uh-huh."

"He's thinking of joining the band."

Joanie opened her mouth, but before she could speak, Angela let out a shriek and rushed to the hall. She threw her arms around a tall dark-haired man. The front door stood open behind him. All talking in the room stopped. The man patted Angela's hair as she cried and gripped him tightly.

Frank bolted from the bathroom and came to an abrupt halt. "Oh hell," he muttered.

"Who is it?" Jake asked.

"It's Lorenzo. It's my stepfather."

A Letter to the Jacobites

Jake of All Trades,

Mr. Huckleberry had to be somewhere else, so I headed out, too. I'm in Wyoming now so it took a while for your letter to catch up with me. Did you know there's a pretty girl behind every tree in Wyoming? The problem is, no trees.

Tell Joanie I don't say "hi" back. And while you're not telling her things, don't tell her she was right about my money running out. Things are expensive here.

So Virginia is back at the plant? I thought she'd rather punch her supervisor than punch a clock. Maybe now she'll get to do both.

Sorry to hear about Coach's little girl. As for Tulsa, they can drool me a river. It ain't gonna happen.

A two-person band, huh? There's a name for that, Buford, and it ain't "snazzy." Try asking Al. Besides cars and booze and basketball, pickin' and grinnin' was one of his skills back in the day, before he got all holy roller.

I'd watch myself around Belle. They don't call her Belle of the Balls for nothing.

And watch out for those cart Blanches. Also lazy Susans. And pots of flesh. For other kinds of pot, ask Marcus. And don't call me Shirley.

What else is new? Anyone die this summer?
I'm available if Chief Owen wants an out-of-
town Edom to hang things on.

Not missing you a-tall,

—Randy

Band

Jake read most of Randy's letter aloud to Virginia the afternoon it arrived. It was good to hear her throaty laugh, just like when he first started sharing things with her, back when she was just Randy's mom and he wasn't officially in her charge. She chuckled at the Wyoming joke, muttered "Damned straight" about punching Mr. Smalley, and said "Don't be so sure" when it came to Coach Ardmore not jumping ship for more pay. She *tsk*-ed at the dig at Belle Craddock. "That girl's had it tough since her folks left. It's hard making it on your own. I should know." But she laughed out loud at the dig at Chief Owen. "Just like his father!" Then her laughter turned into a coughing jag and she had to lean on the kitchen table.

"Are you all right?" Jake asked.

Virginia straightened up. "It's nothing. Just a touch of something from last winter. Doc Lewis says he's looking into it."

"Into what?"

"Now don't get your undies in a bunch. I couldn't catch my breath on the line the other night is all. I wouldn't have gone to the doc, but that toad-sucker Smalley made me."

Jake put down the letter.

"It's not serious, kiddo." She refilled her coffee. "Just a spot from the pneumonia."

What pneumonia? She never mentioned that. "It sounds pretty serious. Maybe I should write Randy and—"

"Don't you dare. He's finally getting out from under

the shadow of his father. And me. Don't you ruin this for him."

"But if Randy can help—"

"Help how?" She sat. "Doc Lewis said he thinks it's probably nothing. He'll probably just give me a shot of vitamins or something and I'll be back on the line in no time." Her hand twitched to the pocket where she kept her cigarettes but came up empty.

"I'll come by and check on you."

She frowned over her cup. "Tell you what. You come by if you want, but you have to promise not to pull Randy into it."

He frowned right back.

"Promise me," she insisted. "Be on my side on this one, kiddo."

He crossed his arms. "Okay. But tell me what's going on, will you? Don't leave me in the dark."

She smiled and patted his hand and poured him a cup of coffee.

He wasn't fooled. She was worried, but it seemed important that she handle it herself without dragging Randy into her business. *Or dragging her into Randy's, I suppose.* He hadn't read her the entire letter. Naturally he skipped the bit about Marcus and pot, but he also cut the coded reference to Randy's dad. If Virginia wanted to believe Randy was on his own, free from his parents' tangled relationship and his father's troubles with the law, then who was he to spoil it for her? He sighed. *Parents are so fragile. Sometimes it takes a whole bunch of kids to keep their world together.*

He left the Edoms' and drove out to Frank's farm. Mrs. Pellegrini met him at the door and directed him to the barn, but Frank wasn't there, so he went to the tack shed.

He found Frank putting bridles and bits up on hooks. "Howdy, cowboy," he called.

Frank turned, the light slanting across his body. "Not no more. We sold the horses." He smiled dryly. "The buzzards have landed."

"How can you run a farm without horses?"

"We do have tractors, y'know, it bein' the twentieth century and all."

"Sure, but you still have stalls in the barn and that stuff there."

"This is just junk Lorenzo couldn't sell. It's mostly Jim's, our hired hand. But he's gone, and now the horses are gone, too. Everything's gone. Except these." He stroked a pair of leather chaps. "Jim left in kinda a hurry." He gave them a slap. "They're all that's left. That and the smell of horse piss. That'll be here till the barn burns down." He rested his hands on his hips. "What brings you out here? Car break down again?"

"You never did say about the band."

"Never did make up my mind."

"We're meeting at Belle's Sunday afternoon. You could maybe sit in, see if you fit."

Frank regarded him. "You come all the way out here just to say that?"

"Sure. What else?"

"I thought maybe you might be havin' the same problem I'm havin'."

"What's that?"

He cocked his head. "I've got a tickle in the back of my throat."

Jake's own throat tightened. "Are you coming down with something?"

"Yeah. Here, I'll show ya." He grabbed Jake by the belt and tugged.

Mr. Pellegrini came around the corner of the shed, trailing a plume of cigarette smoke. "Aren't you done yet?"

Frank straightened up. "Yes sir."

"Well?"

"Jake was just asking me about joining a band."

"What band?"

Jake cleared his throat. "Me and Belle Craddock and Beau Hamilton." For some reason, he thought it best not to mention Zach.

"Yeah, right." Mr. Pellegrini tossed his cigarette to the floor. "A band of freaks and weirdos." He walked off.

Frank ground out the butt, clenching his jaw. "Fuck him."

"Is that a yes?"

"To what?"

"To joining the band. Of freaks and weirdos."

"You heard him. 'Yeah, right.'" A smile curled his lips. "That's a yes in my book."

"Good." Jake turned to leave but looked back. "And that other thing? That tickle in your throat?" Frank raised his eyebrows. "That's a yes in my book, too."

Jake hummed as he walked to his car. *It's all coming together.* He passed Mr. Pellegrini on the porch. He sat in the same spot where Jake last saw Virgil Craddock. He nodded. "Mr. Pellegrini."

The man didn't look up. "This is a working farm. No visiting hours."

"Sorry, sir. I should have called ahead."

"It better not cut into his chores."

"Sir?

"This band nonsense. And don't expect me to pay for outfits or gas or anything."

"No sir. We make our own outfits. And I'll take Frank to gigs."

"Paying gigs?"

"Yes sir."

"Where?"

Jake shrugged.

"So long as he gets his fair cut. And it doesn't interfere with his responsibilities."

"We thought we'd do Sunday afternoons until school starts."

"And then?"

"Just an hour after school."

"Every day?" Mr. Pellegrini shook his head. "Can't be every day. Too much to do here."

"Sure."

Mr. Pellegrini squinted at him.

"I mean, yes sir."

Mr. Pellegrini stared. He pulled a knife from his back pocket and held it a second. The blade sprang open. He looked down and started digging under a nail. "You got somewhere to be, don't you? Deliveries and such?"

"Yes sir." He walked up the drive. He turned at his car and yelled to the porch, "Good afternoon, sir!" He added a big cheerful wave to show he meant it.

His stepfather cornered Frank in the barn just before supper. "Any money, you hand it over to me, understand?"

"What?"

"Don't get smart with me. The band."

Frank shook his head. "I don't think I'll be bringin' in any money. I ain't that good."

"This isn't about you. Whatever you make, you hand it over. Do you get me?" He stepped closer. "This is about supporting your mother and sister."

"I thought that's what you're supposed to do."

Lorenzo clipped him across the ear.

"Are we clear?"

The whole side of his head burned, but he kept his face blank. "Yes sir."

Summer Sessions

Frank fit perfectly as rhythm guitar and had a full baritone that gave their harmonies a solid base. "Hot damn!" Belle exclaimed. "Look out Hal Orison. There's a new kid in town."

"It's a real circus," Zach said.

"We finally sound like a band," Beau said. "Now all we need is outfits and a few gigs to make it real."

Under the trestle, Jake and Frank were making it real their own way. Frank hated kissing at first. "That's girly stuff." But Jake had picked up a few tips from Vince and soon had him convinced. Before long, their mouths were as busy as their hands.

Frank had a few tricks of his own. He would swirl his mouth around Jake's hardened cock and have him squirming as he edged closer and closer. One afternoon, Frank stopped before getting a mouthful and moved down to his nuts. All Jake could think was, *A mouth full of teeth and I've never felt more safe, more open to anything.* He leaned back, closed his eyes and sighed.

Blue jeans hobbled their ankles. Frank tugged Jake's off completely. A breeze from the river cooled Jake's balls, and he wanted nothing more than to have them stuffed into Frank's warm haven again.

Instead, Frank slipped his hands under Jake's thighs and lifted, folding Jake's ass up in the air. Jake's eyes popped open. Before he could get out a word, Frank pressed his face against his butt, then a warm wetness glided slowly over his hole. A wordless cry flew from his mouth and he trembled. He grabbed the backs of his thighs and pried them apart. Frank's tongue worked its way in and out. Jake's eyes went wide, but he wasn't seeing anything. Everything was centered on that one radiant point and the heat that filled his body.

Frank pulled away with a gasp and slid his body up Jake's torso. He pressed his mouth against his. Jake could smell his sweat on Frank's face.

Frank pulled back. "That's what you taste like."

"Jesus Christ," Jake panted. "Where'd you learn that?"

Frank smiled. "Jim. That and a few things besides."

"Jesus." He put an arm behind his head to cushion it against the pallet. "Blow jobs and jerking off were as far as Vince and I got."

"That guy from last year? The old guy?"

Jake frowned. "Not old. He's in college. Or was."

Frank stroked his chest. "Jim's old. Thirty at least." He sighed. "I keep thinking he'll be back. He left his chaps. A guy doesn't leave his chaps unless he's coming back."

"I don't care where Vince is."

Frank looked at him. "Yeah you do."

"Okay, yeah, I do. Or did." He wrapped his hand around Frank's cock. He was still amazed at how much meat protruded from his fist. He sat up and wrapped his other hand around it. The sheathed tip still poked out. He slid the foreskin slowly up and down. "We have a lot of things in common."

Frank smiled. "That ain't one of them."

"Not that, fuck face. I mean people. Jim, Vince. Older guys. And your father and my father."

"You mean Queer Andy?"

Jake stopped his slow jerk-off. "Who calls him that?"

Frank shrugged. "Everybody."

Jake leaned back.

"Hey, don't stop. That felt good. Nice and slow."

Jake looked at Frank's bobbing member. A clear bead shone at the tip, tempting him. "I meant they're both dead. They both died in car accidents."

"Mine died in a truck. Crushed in a pileup in California, hauling tomatoes. On his way to makin' ketchup, turned to ketchup himself."

"Jesus, you're gruesome."

"You get used to gruesome on a farm."

Jake took a breath. "My dad's death wasn't an accident. They said it was, but it wasn't. He was no different than you grandfather, except he used a train to do it."

"Fuck. I could never do that. Just wait for it to come? Hell no. I'd take granddad's way out. Quick."

"You'd never do that, would you?"

Frank stretched out beside him. "If I did, I wouldn't yak about it first. I'd just do it."

Jake reached out and tweaked Frank's nipple. He twitched. "Good. You're still alive." Frank grinned. "I love that. I wish mine were like yours."

Frank pinched his tit, but Jake shook his head. "Nope. You might as well be pinching my elbow."

"It's okay. You got other features."

"Like what?"

Frank slid his hand between Jake's legs and crooked a finger up his ass.

"Ah!"

"Like it?"

"Put a little spit on it, will ya?"

Frank put on more than enough. He went down on Jake while his finger worked his butt. Jake gripped Frank's hair and started bucking his hips. He held out as long as he could. When he climaxed, Frank gagged but held on. Jake stayed hard while Frank suckled his cock, pulling contractions out of his belly even after his seed was spent.

Eventually he softened and Frank let him slip through his lips. He slid his finger out of his ass and he uncurled across Jake's chest and kissed him. A line of cum dribbled from his nose. He kissed him again and Jake realized he was tasting himself. He got hard again, but that didn't seem fair. "What about you?"

Frank smiled and sat back. "Watch this. It's pretty cool."

He started playing with his nipples. When they got hard, he started digging into them with his thumbnails. Jake winced but couldn't take his eyes off the show. Frank's cock stirred and hardened with each pulse. Soon it thumped against his belly. Frank closed his eyes and leaned his head back, the muscles on his neck standing out. His mouth hung open and his breath came short. Precum pooled on his stomach, a glistening thread tied to his cock. Still his hands never left his nipples. His face and chest flushed. His cock stopped throbbing, inflated even more and went rigid and stayed that way. And then—

"Yeah," Jake admitted, wiping off his shoulder, "that is pretty cool."

Beau asked Belle to go with him to sign the band's contract at the VFW.

"Why me?"

"You and Zach are the only ones old enough to sign a contract, and he's at work."

"But the vets hall, B? Those old geezers wouldn't know 'In-A-Gadda-Da-Vida' from 'Turkey in the Straw.'"

"But they'll pay us. The Teen Center never does. If they like our first gig, they'll have us back the next Saturday. Besides, the hall is nearly the size of the gym. Jake can work out the mikes and amplifiers before we do the Halloween Dance."

"*If* we do the Halloween Dance."

"We'll get it. Jake's working on it. And we gotta sound great."

"Because sounding bad would be tragic since everyone at school has such high regard for us." She shook her head. "I don't know how you talk me into these things, B."

"C'mon, B2. It's our first real gig."

But Mr. Smalley, the VFW rep, laid some last minute conditions on the signing.

"No Kinks," Smalley said, sitting behind a desk and wearing a black officer's cap. "No Rolling Stones, no Lovin' Spoonful. None of that druggy stuff."

Belle cast Beau a look.

"Is that in the contract?" Beau asked.

Smalley didn't answer. "Nothing anti-war. No 'Waist Deep in the Big Muddy' or crap like that."

"Sure."

"And no Hendrix."

Belle smiled. "How about some Patsy Cline?"

Smalley leaned back. "If you think you can fill the shoes of the great Patsy Cline, you go for it, missy."

Belle clamped her lips and signed the contract before there was blood.

Outside, she erupted. "Missy!"

"Belle, it's done. We got the hall."

"The great Patsy Cline! What does he think 'Walking after Midnight' is about, anyway?" She turned to him. "What are you going to tell Zach?"

Beau shrugged. "We don't really have much Hendrix in our sets."

They told the rest of the band that evening. Zach didn't react much. "Figures," is all he said.

"How can the VFW object to 'The Star-Spangled Banner'?" Jake said.

"That's in three," Frank said. "It wouldn't fit anyway."

"Sure it would. You just have to swing it a little." He was noodling around on a spare guitar and demonstrated.

"Guys," Zach said. "It doesn't matter. Let's just work on what we got. The goal is getting the dance at school."

Their first Saturday night went well. They even worked Tammy Wynette's "Stand By Your Man" into a set and got applause. But when Beau went to collect their money, there was a hitch.

"What do you mean, a hitch?" Zach asked.

"Mr. Smalley says the contract is for two Saturdays, so he isn't going to pay us until we finish the second one."

Zach slammed his fist into the wall. He looked down at his skinned knuckles. "I was counting on that money." He didn't say another word as they packed up. When they split up to go home, he didn't answer any of their good-byes.

"He'll show up next week, won't he?" Beau asked.

Belle shook her head. "Would you?"

"Virginia always said Smalley was a toad-sucker," Jake said. "Now I know why."

But it wasn't Zach who was missing when their second gig came around. It was Frank.

Frank showered and put on a fresh shirt and pants and started down the stairs with his guitar case.

"Where do you think you're going?" Lorenzo drawled.

"The VFW hall. Our gig."

"I don't think so."

"I told you about this. We got a second gig tonight."

"Did they pay you for the first one?"

"No, but—"

"They don't pay, you don't play. You can't let them walk all over you, son."

Frank bristled. "I told you. We have to play the second gig to get paid for both."

"I know what you told me." Lorenzo sat in a large chair, his eternal cigarette turning the air in the living room blue. Angela lay sprawled on the floor reading a comic book. His mother sat nearby darning. Neither looked at him. It was like he and Lorenzo were talking in an empty room.

"I can't hash this out with you now. I'll be late."

Lorenzo smiled and held up his hand. Frank's car keys dangled from it. "Unless you can show me some cash from last Saturday, you're staying put." He stood, pocketing the keys. "You wouldn't be holding out on us, would you?"

"This is nuts. Mom, reason with him."

She looked up but didn't say anything.

Lorenzo squared his shoulders. "As long as you're under my roof, you'll do as I say."

"It's not your roof. It's Mom's. She's a Craddock, you're not."

Lorenzo stepped closer. "And you're a Pellegrini. Like it or not, I'm your father."

"Stepfather. My father was Jack Fenton. And as soon as I turn eighteen, I'm changing my name back to Fenton. And you can't stop me."

Lorenzo backhanded him. He dropped the guitar case and it popped open. One of the strings snapped.

"You son of a bitch!" Frank lunged at him.

"No!" his mother yelled. It startled Frank and he hesitated. Lorenzo pulled back for a second blow, but his mother got between them and it struck her instead. She fell to the floor.

"Now look what you made me do!" Lorenzo went down beside Arlene.

Angela launched herself at Frank. "Stop it! Stop it!" She

hit him with both fists. "Everything is supposed to be perfect! Everything is supposed to be fine now that Daddy's back. You ruin everything!"

Frank tried to pry himself away from her.

Lorenzo sprang up. "You touch her again, I'll kill you!"

His mother screamed, but it wasn't fear. It was a feral shriek that stopped them all. She had gotten up and held Frank's guitar by the neck in both hands. "Everybody stop! Stop now! Or I swear to God I'll smash this to pieces and everything in this room."

Frank panted but couldn't get air into his lungs. Three sets of eyes stared at him, pushing him away, making him the stranger.

He ran up to his room and slammed the door. He sat on the bed hugging his knees and rocking. Tears poured out of his eyes but he wasn't crying. He was thinking. And the more he thought, the slower he rocked. He finally stopped altogether. So did the tears.

They had to start the first set without Frank. "Here," Beau said, pushing a guitar into Jake's hands. "You know the chords."

"No I don't!" He looked wildly at Beau, at Belle.

"Then play real quiet," Zach said.

He made it through the first four songs but made a major gaffe on the fifth. It threw him into a panic and he stopped playing altogether. Playing his bass like nothing was happening, Beau walked up and murmured in his ear, "D minor, E flat, B flat." Jake swallowed and picked up on the next chorus. He finished out the set.

Frank showed as their break was ending. He was out of breath and sweating. "Where the hell you been at?" Zach growled.

"Where's your guitar?" Belle asked.

"The farm," he said. "Broken. No car."

"Jeez, Frank," Jake said. "Did you run all the way here?"

He collapsed on Belle's stool, nodding.

"Well, you're a sight." Jake handed the guitar to him. "Please take this before I kill again." He saw Beau shaking his head. He walked over to him and spoke low. "Things can get a little nuts at Frank's house."

"He should have called. One of us could have picked him up." He looked at Frank. He was calming down and chatting with Belle, who handed him a glass of water. "He may be sexy as hell but he sure is dumb."

They got paid the full amount at the end of the night. Frank wanted them to dock his cut because he was late, but they were in good spirits and insisted on an even split.

Driving back to Frank's place, he told Jake what had happened. He was horrified. "He hit her?"

"He meant it for me, but yeah, he knocked her flat." He squirmed in his seat. "Look, don't come down the drive. Drop me off under the bridge and I'll walk in the rest of the way."

"I'm coming with you. At least as far as the trestle."

A waning gibbous moon rose above the White Horse as they walked along the rails holding hands, saying nothing. When they reached the trestle, they climbed down to the top of the embankment and stood in the dark, looking at the barn and farmhouse. There were no lights on.

Frank turned his head. "Hear that?"

Jake listened. A distant thrumming carried through the air.

"That's the midnight train. Wait till it passes before you leave."

Jake put an arm around him. "Will you be all right?"

"Yeah." He dug in his pocket and pulled out his share of the take. "Here. You keep this."

"I can't take that. It's yours."

"It won't be if I bring it home."

The thrumming grew louder. Jake could see the light moving through the trees, coming closer. Frank started down the slope. "Wait," Jake called in a loud whisper. "What about next time?"

Frank came back. "See that window in the dormer? That's my bedroom. If I leave the top half down, that means I can't make it. If the bottom half's up, though, I'll meet you here." The train started crossing the river. "Gotta go."

"Frank."

He came back again. Jake held his face in both hands and kissed him. Frank suddenly gripped him and hugged him tight, then turned and slid down the slope and disappeared through the field. Jake lost sight of him in the shadow of the barn. He sat on the dark embankment as the train thundered past until he saw Frank crouch along the roof to his window and slip inside. He stood and started back along the rails. Ahead of him, the train announced its passage through town, its voice getting farther and farther away.

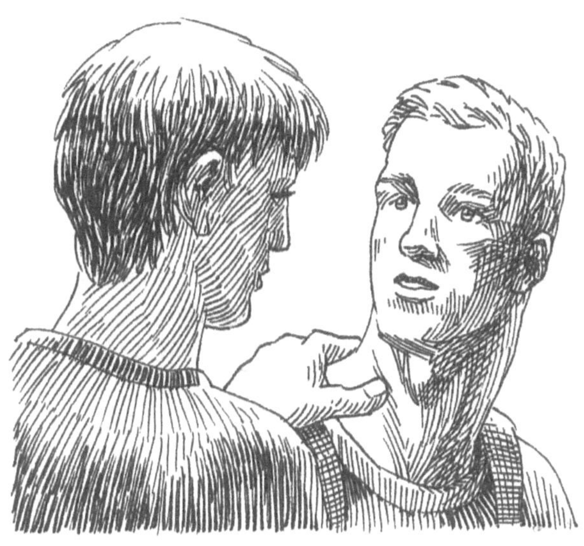

Second Letter of Jake
to the Edomites

Ramblin' Randy,

The afeared changes in CCHS coaching staff
have come to pass. Ardmore took the head
b'ball position at O.S.U., and Tucker moved up
to head coach here, and Webb moved--oh who
the hell cares? One week of football practice
and I called it quits. Frank Pellegrini's out too
after he and Webb nearly came to blows.
DeWitt is Freshman coach. Ain't that a laugh?
How would you like the Junior English and
speech teacher for a football coach? They won
their first game, though.

Tucker was a dick about me quitting the team.
He cornered me and said, "You need an
anchor." I told him, "I have an anchor. I'm in a
band." He just turned and walked away, like I
had disappeared.

As for who's died, well- - -

Remember last year when you told me
Frank's granddad was a crazy old coot? Turns
out you were right. He crazied himself with a
shotgun on their front porch last month. I was
there talking band stuff with Frank, but we
were way over on the other side of the farm.
We heard the shot and came running. I wish
we hadn't. You never seen such a mess.

Frank's stepdad is back, supposedly to run the
farm. He keeps a tight rein on Frank. It cuts

into our ^*band* sessions. He is a Grade-A #1 Asshole. Doesn't anyone have normal parents?

We lost Zach, but he wasn't the same after Hendrix died anyway. He would arrive late and not talk to anyone and leave before we finished. Then one day Adam shows up (that's his brother--maybe you never met him? He's in my class) and tells us Zach's been drafted. So Frank is our lead guitar now.

I bought a guitar myself and am learning how to strum in a mostly rhythmic fashion. I leave the more complicated stuff to Beau and Frank. But we got paid for a couple of gigs at the VFW, so we are now officially A Band.

Joanie is now officially An Author, having published an article in <u>The Croy Evening Call</u> with an actual byline. It was about locals who used to be part of the Longstreet and Barnes Circus. Lots of praise in the Letters to the Editor from folks who remember it. Now she's obsessed. She keeps bugging me to go on sleuthing trips with her to the Historical Society Museum, enthusiasm for which I got none. Remind me again why I like this girl?

Wishing you more trees to find girls behind (not more girls' behinds to find trees),

—J

A Curse

J oanie knew she'd find Jake at his locker. She cornered him as lunch hour swirled around them. "What do you know about a seventeen year curse?"

He shrugged. "Locusts?"

"No, doofus. Tornadoes. Mr. Anderson mentioned it for his book. I think it has something to do with the TriCounty Twister."

"I haven't seen him since—you know, that day."

"He comes into the Rexall from time to time. And I've seen him at Randall's Diner."

"Well there you go. Ask him."

"Oh, I couldn't. He'd think I'm trying to scoop him."

"Jeez, Joanie. One article in *The Call* and you'd think you were working for *The New York Times*."

"Mighty oaks from little acorns grow."

"Well, that fits. An acorn is a kind of nut."

"You're no help."

"I'm kinda busy with the band."

"More 'practicing' with Frank Pellegrini?"

He pretended to look for something in his locker.

"Oh, don't be coy. At the wake, you two went out and came back and he was wearing your tie."

"What can I say? You got us. Me and Frank and Beau and Belle. We're all in a satanic cult involving drums and amplifiers and swapping ties. Beau's is a bow, of course. Whoever ends up with it gets to be king. We make the Manson Family look like the Osmond Brothers."

She harrumphed and leaned again the next locker. "Nice

try. I happen to know Belle, and she'd never let anyone else be king."

"What about that guy you interviewed? Coach Tucker's uncle. Maybe he'd know. Or Mrs. Oldfield. Or Miss Lancaster. Or What's-her-name at the historical society."

"Anybody but you, in other words."

"Sorry. My turn to quiz now. Who's on the organizing committee for the Halloween Dance?"

"Adam Jameson and Mary Kay Halliday. Why?"

"It's for the band. We want to bid on being the entertainment."

"Well you'd better get cracking. They've picked a theme already."

"It's Halloween. Why do they need a theme?"

"It's not the Halloween Dance anymore. It's the Harvest Dance. Mary Kay objected to Halloween because it's a pagan orgy or some such."

"A pagan orgy would be right popular. But they're still looking for a band, right?"

"Right."

"Thanks." He started to walk off. "Wait. There *was* something about a curse."

"Are we still talking pagan orgies?"

"No, tornadoes. Someone made a sculpture about the TriCounty Twister. For the Memorial Library."

She frowned. "There's no sculpture in the library."

"Not in it. *On* it. On the outside."

"There's nothing there, either."

He shrugged. "All I know is I saw it in a back issue of *The Croy Evening Call*. It wasn't what I was looking for, so I didn't pay much attention. But pictures of it were all over the front page."

"Pictures? That's great! I don't suppose you remember the date?"

"October 13, 1952."

"So you *were* paying attention."

"Not really. But the pictures the next day were all about my dad. That's what I was looking for. The accident."

"Oh. Right. Sorry."

He shook his head. "It's all ancient stuff. It doesn't matter anymore."

The way he carried himself as he walked away said differently. *That's how he looked when he said losing state didn't matter either.* But now she had a solid lead for her article in *The Clarion.* The headline was already forming in her head, "Croy's Lost History." *Do I have time to track down those pictures before—?*

"Oh!"

October 13! That's Randy's birthday. She stopped and turned. Jake's head was visible above the other kids in the hall, but he was too far away to call out. She shook her head. *It's just a coincidence. The paper is due out next week. Concentrate.* If *The Call* had pictures of the sculpture, she could pull them from the morgue and run them in the school paper. That would catch people's eye. If *The Call* let her, that is. If there really were pictures. If there was anything at all to what Jake said. *Too many ifs. Narrow it down.*

She hurried to the Memorial Library after school. Miss Lancaster confirmed that a sculpture had been commissioned.

"What happened to it?" Her excitement echoed in the rotunda.

"It was removed," Miss Lancaster answered lightly.

That raised more questions, but she mustn't get sidetracked. "Have you ever heard about a seventeen year curse?"

"There are several. Do you mean locally?"

"Yes ma'am. At least I think so."

Miss Lancaster drew a slip of paper from her desk and started writing. "Here are three references that can help. I recommend the one on Seminole, Choctaw, and Chickasaw legends. You will also find the subject card catalog helpful. Have you used the card catalogs before?" She looked up. "Oh, of course you have. One doesn't get to be senior editor of *The Clarion* without knowing how to look things up."

Joanie thanked her for the references and wandered over to the catalogs, but her mind wasn't on what she came for. *Miss Lancaster is not the sarcastic type, so that wasn't sarcasm. She's being—cagey?*

She's not the only one. Mr. Tucker's uncle had the same attitude when I interviewed him about the circus.

That interview had been strange from the get-go. Coach Tucker had given her directions to the scattering of houses that were all that was left of Pesogi. "He can be a little vague sometimes, so ask him short, direct questions. Keep him on track. But be respectful. He's old, but he's still sharp."

"Thank you, sir. What's his name?"

Coach Tucker rubbed his chin. "That's not as simple a question as you might think."

"What do you call him?"

"'Sir' usually works."

She had found the house with the carved horse on the front porch just like Coach Tucker said. Flakes of white paint lay beneath it like dandruff. A crate with uneven sides wrapped in a tarp filled the other side of the porch. She was gazing up at it when her interview subject appeared.

"Have you come for it?"

"I beg your pardon, sir. Come for what?"

"Is it time?"

"Yes, sir. I'm Joanie Tibbits. We spoke on the phone. I've come for my interview. For *The Call.*"

He looked at the large tarp and shook his head. "Not time, then. Better hurry, though." He smiled and sat on the sloping porch and waited for her questions.

She spent the rest of the afternoon getting details that became the core of her article. He talked about the horse he carved for the merry-go-round, which he called a flying jenny. "But she never flew."

"Was there a statue of Mr. Barnes to match the one of Mr. Longstreet?"

"No. No Mr. Barnes. Longstreet just made up the name. Thought it made the outfit sound classy. Didn't help in the end, though."

The collapse of the circus cut the troupe of performers and roustabouts off without a dime. "They were all out East and no ticket home."

Some eventually straggled back to their two- and three-room homes in Pesogi, the only solid things left in their lives, only to have the twister take that and their lives with it.

But he never referred to the crate on the porch again, she recalled. *He never even looked at it.*

Lost in her musings, she rounded the corner of the subject catalog and nearly ran smack into Bobbie Littledeer.

Bobbie was peering at an open drawer of the catalog, making a list of references. She slid her glasses up her nose, closed the drawer, and tucked the list in a pocket of her skirt in one smooth movement.

"Bobbie!"

"Hello." Bobbie looked at the floor to one side.

"How are things at New Life Academy?"

"Everything is fine." She looked up and smiled. "We have more students every day. The Lord's work is growing stronger by the hour."

"I'm sure it is. I miss you, though."

"Well . . ." Bobbie looked away again.

"So, it's nice running into you. I'm researching an article for the school paper. I'm senior editor now. Are you here doing something for school, too?"

"We don't have a library."

"What? What's a school without a library?"

"I mean, we have one, but it's spare. This place has more . . . things. What's your article about?"

She's never asked about The Clarion *before. What's up?* But she was happy to talk about it. "The TriCounty Twister. Did you know there used to be a sculpture about it? It was made for the library, but now it's missing. I'm going to find out what happened."

Bobbie's expression went through a series of changes. Surprise, consternation, embarrassment. "I've got to go," she said.

"Aren't you going to look up your books?"

Bobbie's face tightened, as if Joanie had said something insulting. Then Bobbie looked past her and she saw a flicker of something else.

"Come along now, child." Mrs. Littledeer's voice carried across the rotunda. Miss Lancaster lifted her head at the circulation desk, ready to hush them if this continued.

"Yes ma'am." Bobbie ducked her head and joined her mother.

"Have you got your shopping list?" Mrs. Littledeer said.

Bobbie looked back at Joanie, her face red. "Yes ma'am."

Joanie shook her head as they left. She looked up the books Miss Lancaster suggested and brought them to the reading table. Adam Jameson was seated there, wearing a brown and tan dashiki. He was engrossed in a book that appeared to be in Latin.

"Sorry about that," she said, sitting across from him.

"Hmm?" He looked up through round glasses.

"I guess the Littledeers aren't used to library protocol."

Adam smiled. "Sorry, I didn't notice. I was lost in Virgil's *Aeneid*. Things are looking dicey for Nisus and Euryalus." He pointed to her books. "Looks like you're about to dive into something more recent."

"I'm doing research on the TriCounty Twister. I have a hunch it's connected to some kind of curse."

He nodded. "The seventeen year curse."

"You know it?"

"Of course. It started with the lynching of a young mixed blood Seminole woman during the Green Corn Rebellion. She was only seventeen. She cursed the land before they hanged her. She said the Great Spirit would rain agonizing death from the skies every seventeen years until her blood was avenged. It's nonsense, of course, but when the TriCounty Twister struck, everyone remembered. Everyone who survived, that is. Crazy Woman Weather, they called it."

"That's the name of Mr. Anderson's book!"

"Who?"

"This guy from Oklahoma City. But never mind. So," she did quick math in her head, "there was the TriCounty twister in 1935, then the tornado that tore up the east side of town in 1952."

"That destroyed the first Mt. Zion, my church. So you see, we have a connection."

"And the storm in 1969."

"That wasn't a tornado." He adjusted his glasses. "It did damage Garvey High, though, just before the schools consolidated. But those were all acts of God, not the workings of a heathen curse. Besides, the Green Corn Rebellion was in 1917, so the TriCounty Twister was eighteen years later, not seventeen. It's just legends. Just stories people tell themselves to think they know what's going on."

"Oh." Her enthusiasm slumped like a wet bag. "Shoot. I guess I'll just focus on the sculpture, then."

"What sculpture?"

"Of the TriCounty Twister. They made one for the library, but nobody knows where it went."

"I do."

"What?"

"It was hanging in the main stairwell at Garvey High. It took up half the wall."

"Are you kidding? Is it still there?"

"Well, no. They tore Garvey High down last year."

"Oh darn. It's lost for good then."

"No it isn't. We have it."

"Who?"

"We do. My family. We're kind of proud of the role our family played in the disaster of '35. The tornado panel has my grandfather on it."

She ran out of time before she could look up Jake's newspaper story from 1952, but she had plenty of exciting material to make her deadline without it. She bubbled over with it, practically writing the article out loud at the dinner table before her astonished parents. "And the Jamesons had it all along!"

"That's wonderful news, dear," her mother said, spooning creamed peas into Julia Mae.

"I got news, too," Kyle said.

Mr. Tibbits leaned back in his chair. "Your grandfather was on that sculpture, you know."

"Grandpa John? On the tornado sculpture?"

"No, not that one."

"But I guess nobody's interested," Kyle said.

"Kyle honey, we'll get to your news in a minute." Her mother turned to her father. "He was on the center panel, wasn't he? The large one?"

"Center panel?" Her heart quickened. "You mean, there's more than one?"

"There were three. Or was it four?" Ruth Tibbits shook her head. "It's a shame, really."

"Why?"

"Lerner Alquist, the man who paid for it, didn't like it and had it torn down."

Her father sat forward. "No, that's not it. Alquist went bankrupt before they could install it, and the bank took it. They cut it up for bricks."

"Oh."

"Told ya," Kyle said. They looked at him. "Told ya there warn't no Mr. Barnes, and there ain't no library statue neither."

"Kyle, *wasn't* not *warn't*, and *isn't* not *ain't*."

"The Barnes statue isn't missing. It never existed," Joanie declared.

"Told ya."

"But the library statue *does* exist. Or did. Jake's seen pictures of it. If one panel survived, maybe all of them did."

"I suppose we'll never know." Julia started fussing and her mother turned her attention to her.

"There must be people around town," her father said. "A lot of townsfolk posed for Sunny."

"Who's that?"

"Sunny Sohi. The sculptor. A pretty flashy fellow. Talented, but flashy."

"Well, he would know, wouldn't he? Where is he now?"

"Don't know. He left town, I think. There was a—" he frowned. "It was a very busy time."

Kyle proceeded with his news, which had to do with *Bucky Firestorm and All His Friends*, a comic book he and Rafe were putting together about cops and robbers with sheriffs and posses and a heroic dispatch caller and some kind of time travel. "And he's listening real hard when this ball of lightning hits and *zhizzzp!* He ends up . . ." She let it drift past her.

She couldn't interview everyone in town. Not by herself. But the students of Croy Consolidated High School could. Her article would be a call to arms.

And there was one person she would interview herself. *Lerner Alquist. That's Randy's grandfather. I'll ask his mom. I'll ask Virginia.*

The Quirks

J anis Joplin Found Dead" the headline declared in large black type. Beau had never seen Belle cry before. They were getting ready to play the Teen Center when she found out. "We can call it off."

"No! God damn it, no. If she's so stupid to go kill herself, let her." Belle wiped her nose. "First Hendrix, now this. I am going to live past twenty-seven if it kills me."

"Maybe she didn't kill herself," Jake said. "Maybe it was an accident."

"Or the C.I.A.," Frank said. They looked at him. "What? Everybody knows they killed Kennedy."

Beau blinked. "Which one?"

"Screw it," Belle said. "Let's get ready."

It was their first gig in the outfits Beau created. Their shirts had ruffles down the front and at the cuffs, each with a different piping: Beau's was teal, Belle's bright purple, Frank's black, and Jake's red. The pants were bell bottom blue jeans he had bleached then dyed purple. "It wasn't supposed to come out so dark," he apologized.

Frank waved his arm. The cuff fluttered. "How am I supposed to play with these things?"

"Like you always do," Beau said. "Vigorously. And this is for the drum, but not tonight, there's not enough time." He held up a stencil that read, "The Quirks."

"I thought we were going to vote on a name," Jake said.

"Belles and Beaus is taken."

"So is Nads."

"Beats The Fatherless Five," Frank said, tuning his guitar.

Beau looked at Jake, who shrugged and said, "Okay, Quirks."

"*The* Quirks."

Al Mattingly was in charge of the Teen Center that night. He helped Jake set up the amps and showed him a bank of colored footlights he could toggle with a toe switch. Frank showed him his twelve-string and they noodled around on a couple of Leo Kottke songs. Beau started the opening to "Classical Gas" on his acoustic Gibson, but Al turned away. "The kids are arriving. I gotta watch the door." He smiled and walked off.

They got to play more R'n'B and psychedelic rock than they did at the vets hall. When "Summertime" came up in the set, Beau looked to Belle, wondering if she was up to it. She nodded, but held up her sticks and leaned into her mike.

"This is for someone who was always rising up singing. Spread your wings, beautiful one, and take to the sky."

She performed flawlessly. Beau was in tears at the end. Even the kids knew something special was going on. They didn't dance to it, though it was one of the few numbers where they could dance slow and close. They stood and watched, and when it was done, there was nodding and shuffling but no applause.

Beau felt electricity in the air. There was a fire in Belle's eyes as she looked at Frank. They exchanged a wicked smile. "Ready?" she said. He nodded.

She leaned into the mike again. "This is dedicated to certain people in this town. Certain powers. Pontificators. Administrators."

There was a rebel yell from the floor.

Beau didn't know what they were up to. Jake walked up and whispered in his ear, "Stand back. This is just them."

Belle started the *Stonedhenge* "Three Blind Mice" drum

solo. The kids got the joke immediately and yelled, "You tell 'em, Belle!" But when she started through the second time, she vamped on the opening phrase. All of a sudden, Frank dropped in with "The Star-Spangled Banner," Hendrix style, in 4/4. The kids went wild. When Belle and Frank finished, there was cheering.

"Great balls of fire," Beau gasped.

Frank grinned shyly. "Zach showed me how. It was Jake gave us the idea."

"Imagine doing *that* in the Talent Show."

"Imagine Superintendent Boyd going up in flames." Jake added.

Beau nodded. "It would almost be worth it."

"It would *definitely* be worth it," Belle said. "But it's not exactly the sort of thing the dance committee is looking for."

"That was, uh, pretty amazing," Al said, walking up to them. "I mean, wow, Frank! I couldn't play something like that." He smiled and slapped him on the back, but Beau thought there was a double meaning to his words. "Now let's give the kids something to dance to, right?"

"Sure thing," Beau said.

Al gave him a funny look, like he didn't expect him to speak.

"Sure, Al," Jake said.

Al nodded, satisfied, and they started their next set.

But the feeling lingered with Beau. *He doesn't really think I'm here. It's just Frank and Jake and maybe Belle to him. I don't even exist.*

And there was something else. Frank and Belle had obviously been working on "The Stoned-Spangled Banner" for some time. Even Jake knew about it. But he hadn't.

It doesn't matter. We're a band now. We're ready to show people what we got.

All the students who signed up for the Talent Show met with Mr. DeWitt in the auditorium the day before the show. The Quirks sat together with the other kids and groups, including their rivals for the Harvest Dance, The Father's Five. The meeting was to go over the order of performance and run through any set changes between acts, but the minute Mr. Boyd showed up, Beau knew there was trouble. Boyd had practically thrown Beau off the stage for his performance of "Blowin' in the Wind" last year, and gave him a week in detention for "suggestive lyrics."

Boyd was having none of that this year. "Any scripts, poems, or lyrics have to be approved by Mr. DeWitt first," Boyd said.

"Approved by *him*, he means," Belle griped.

"And the judging will be different. Mr. DeWitt?"

DeWitt used his Freshman Coach voice so they all could hear. "We're going to be more democratic this year. Instead of the faculty voting on the acts, it will be students."

"All of them?" someone asked.

"Not all. Just the four class officers from each class."

"Great," Jake muttered. "Remind me who they are again?"

"And no costumes." Boyd smiled. "Just your normal everyday clothes. That makes everyone equal. We want this to be a showcase for your talent, not your fancy dress."

"Hell," Frank muttered. "Al ratted us out."

"That goes for all the contestants," Mr. DeWitt added. "Dramatic readings as well."

"Oh yeah, that makes it fair." Jake leaned forward so Boyd and DeWitt couldn't hear him. "And while we're at it, anyone taller than six foot gets their feet cut off."

"That's not funny," Beau said

Jake dismissed him with a wave.

It stung. *They're giving up. I can fix this. I have to fix this.* "Guys." They all looked at him. "Meet me at the band shed right after this."

An hour later, they stood against the warm bricks. "I'm so mad I could spit nails," Belle said.

"I used to think Mr. DeWitt was pretty cool," Jake said. "Guess he's not, really."

"It doesn't matter," Beau said. "Look, all those kids, they already know what our outfits look like."

"Only the kids at the Teen Center."

"It doesn't matter. The Quirks will still have a look. But each of us will be different. That'll be our look. It'll be cool."

Frank shook his head. "No it won't. It'll suck. It'll suck big wet weenies."

"Tsk," Belle said. "Language. What would Mr. Boyd say?"

"He can suck my big wet—"

"Guys, guys—"

"How is that even a look?" Jake asked. "It's just us."

"You don't get it," Beau said. "We'll dress *like* us, but not *as* us. We'll quirk it up."

"What d'ya mean?"

"Frank, what's your everyday dress on the farm?"

"Overalls."

"Exactly. Do that, but more so. Jake, you've got this clean-cut image—"

"Do what?"

"So go the other way. Think James Dean in *Rebel without a Cause*. Belle—"

"Way ahead of ya, B. Frank, gimme your shirt."

"What? Now?"

"No, big wet one, your Quirks shirt. It's the only one whose piping no one can call a costume. But on me," she smiled, "can you imagine me in a frilly front and a skirt?"

"I truly cannot," Beau said. "It's genius."

"It won't fit," Frank said. "You've got more . . . stuff up there."

"Don't worry. I got ways."

"What about you, Beau?" Jake asked. "What will you wear?"

"Don't worry. It'll be everyday. But I need to talk to Adam Jameson first."

Backstage before the show, they showed each other their outfits. Beau wore one of Adam's dashikis with a pattern of purple and gold diamonds. His Quirks bell bottoms poked out beneath. The dashiki glistened.

"Is that silk?" Jake asked.

Beau sighed. "No, rayon. But it feels slinky."

Jake whispered, "Tell me you're wearing what I think you're wearing underneath." Beau smiled. "Way to go! Classic Hamilton FU."

Frank joined them wearing a flannel shirt, blue jeans, and chaps. "Howdy."

"Excellent!" Beau breathed.

"Mr. Dean, you're looking downright rebellious."

"Check this out." Jake turned sideways. A small box was rolled under the left sleeve of his T-shirt. "I was going to use one of Virginia's empties, but the Marlboro logo showed through. This is just a prescription box Joanie got me."

"Boys, I feel like a new woman," Belle said.

"You look like a new man."

"Where are your—" Frank made shapes with his hands.

"Ace bandages, wide. Thanks again to Joanie."

Beau looked at each of them, feeling like he could float on air. "Guys, we are amazing."

Mr. DeWitt passed by with the lineup sheet. He gave them a long look but smiled and said, "Good luck."

Mary Kay Halliday and Adam Jameson alternated as

emcees. Adam not only loaned Beau his brightest dashiki, but wore a more subdued one himself to squash any question about everyday student wear.

When The Quirks were announced and the curtain parted, they got a few catcalls. "Beau-in in the Wind," someone yelled. "The Lion Sleeps Tonight," someone else called out.

Belle stared them down with a fierce grin. She started a slow rhythm on the drums, Beau added bass, Jake strummed softly.

Belle spoke low into the mike. "Some men just ain't happy unless they're telling some other men how to be a man. It takes a whole lot of instruction, apparently. But you guys think you got it rough? You don't know the half of it."

Frank hit the familiar opening chords and Belle sang, "Sometimes it's hard to be a woman—"

The students cheered.

The band had more for them. On the second verse, Frank entered an octave below where Belle left off, giving them the full Hal Orison treatment. Girls swooned. Beau came in high and sweet with "Make sure you love him," and Belle topped it off, smiling and shaking her head with "After all, he's just a man." All four of them piled on for the chorus, and the whole student body joined in.

The whistling and stomping went on for minutes after they finished.

The four Quirks celebrated their talent show win with cokes and fries at Herman's. Joanie joined them later to say the dance committee had met and picked them for the Harvest Dance. "The Father's Five didn't have a chance," she reported.

Beau clapped his hands. "Yes!" His eyes shone behind his glasses as he grinned at Jake.

the
QuirkS

"Well, hot damn," Belle said. "Come on, B. I gotta get the drums back. I'll give you a ride home."

"Oh." He looked at Jake and Frank. "You coming?"

"Naw." Frank leaned back, trailing a fry through a puddle of ketchup.

"I'm staying, too," Jake said. "Think I'll have a burger."

"Well, the Rexall's open if you need anything later," Joanie said, rising. "We're running a special on Pepto-Bismol. And call me later, will you? I want to ask you something."

After they left, Jake and Frank sat on opposite sides of the booth, grinning at each other.

"Burger, huh?" Frank said.

Jake smiled. "Naw."

They drove to the farm. Energy ricocheted between Jake's groin and his heart. He was ready to burst into stars. "Did you see Beau's face? He was like to fly off into the blue yonder."

"Yeah, I wondered what he was on."

"He was on Beau. He doesn't need anything else."

"I reckon not. Fairies got wings."

"Hey, come on. He's one of us."

"One of us? He's nothin' like us."

Jake didn't want to spoil things, but he had to know. "So he's what? Like Queer Andy?"

"Hey, I don't mean nothin' by it. It's just what people say."

"We wouldn't have the band without him."

"Yeah. Sure. I mean, he's awright, I guess. It's just— It's kinda much, sometimes."

The late afternoon sun slanted through the trees as they passed the cemetery. The October air was chilling rapidly.

"He's different, that's all," Jake said.

"Yeah." Frank laughed, a short bark. "Quirky." He took a deep breath and seemed to let something go. "I guess we all are." The Santa Fe overpass was coming up. "It's gonna be chilly out there."

Jake knew he meant the trestle.

"Let's stop by the shed and pick up a blanket."

Jake turned the car around. "Your folks'll know you're home."

"They don't wait supper on me anymore. You can park up on the hard road."

In the shed, Jake sat on the bunk, running his hand over the coarse blanket. The bed was fully made, but the sheets smelled stale and sour. Frank hung the chaps on the wall.

"Those were Jim's, right?"

"Yep. This shirt too." Frank started unbuttoning.

"He leave that behind too?"

"Naw. I stole it from him when he was still here." He took it off and sniffed it. "It used to smell like him, but I used it so much it got stiff enough to walk." He sat beside him and held it out. "Smells like me now."

Jake inhaled. "It does." He lifted his T-shirt over his head. "I used my gym shirt."

"You still got it?"

"Burned it last year. Part of a campaign to put all this behind me."

"Get thee behind me, Satan!" Frank laughed and leaned back. "If only he would."

"You're thinking of him, aren't you?"

"Yeah." He looked him in the eye. "You wanna fuck me?"

The outline of Frank's cock was growing distinct against his overalls. Jake laid his palm across it and rubbed. "Actually, I was kinda wondering what that would feel like inside me."

Frank grinned. "We can take turns."

The farmhouse was dark and quiet when Frank slipped inside and up to his room. He got out of his clothes and under the sheets without making a sound. A breeze brought the scent of autumn silage and river mud through the window. *It'll be cold come morning. I should close it.* But his body was relaxing, the knots inside dissolving like they always did after a good plowing. He closed his eyes and started to drift.

Click.

He stopped breathing and listened. A strange tang lingered in the room, then was gone. It was nothing. He relaxed again.

Click.

Frank reached over and turned on the light.

Lorenzo Pellegrini sat on a chair in the corner. "Did you think I wouldn't find out?"

Frank didn't move.

Lorenzo folded the switchblade and slid it into his back pocket. "You hear a lot of things down at the vets hall. The price of hay. Who to trust. The latest pop songs. " He stood. "But I guess some people don't like to share. Some people don't want to be part of a family. They don't know their responsibilities." He unbuckled his belt. "It's time some people learned."

Sharper Than a Serpent's Tooth

Joanie wove her way through the halls, looking to catch Jake before they got to Mrs. Taylor's English class. The school was humming. The last home game was tonight. It hadn't been much of a season except for the freshmen team, but that didn't stop the spirit club from putting up banners and posters everywhere. There would be a pep rally seventh period.

She found Jake hanging out by the Boys' Gym stairs, where the varsity jocks gathered. He wasn't talking to anyone but looking up and down the hall. She crooked her arm in his and dragged him away.

"You didn't call last night. Again."

"I went to bed early."

"Got the trots?"

"What?" Jake looked over his shoulder.

"Herman's special. Ptomaine on rye." He shook his head, not getting it. "Never mind. Look, I can't get ahold of Randy's mom. She doesn't come to the door and she won't answer the phone."

"She's back on swing shift again. You have to get her before two, when she goes to the plant."

"Rats. I'll have to catch her before school."

They entered Mrs. Taylor's room and took their seats, opening their copies of *King Lear*. He leaned across the aisle. "No, not before school. She sleeps in late. Try around ten. Or maybe come over on Saturday. Have you seen Frank?"

"Maybe Mrs. Taylor can write me a pass for third hour."

"Joanie, have you seen Frank?"

"Of course not. We're on different tracks."

Jake pulled back. "Frank's smart."

"I didn't say he wasn't. Just on different tracks. He's in FFA and auto shop and stuff like that. And we're—" the class bell rang "—here."

Mrs. Taylor stood. "*How sharper than a serpent's tooth it is to have a thankless child*. What does that sound like to you? Where have you heard language like that before?"

The King James Bible, Joanie thought, but she didn't raise her hand. She was busy writing herself a note to call on Mrs. Edom on Saturday.

She got a seventh period pass from Mrs. Taylor after class and skipped the rally. *If I can't talk to Virginia until Saturday, I can at least get some research done.* The date of the article she was after was easy to remember: Randy's birthday, October 13, 1952.

She was chagrined to find Mr. Anderson in the Memorial Library stacks pulling out the bound volume of *The Croy Evening Call* for the very year of she wanted.

"Good afternoon, Joanie," he said smiling. "Your article has certainly created a buzz around town."

She blushed. *The Call* had picked up her school article, giving her a second byline, and backed it with an editorial, "Saving Croy for History." They linked tracking down the missing library statue to restoring the old Santa Fe depot and preserving other landmarks around town. "We need to act before our unique frontier town is washed away in the flood of modern life, fast food franchises and the banal wasteland of television. We must commit to being who we are and celebrate who we were, or we will become yet another town whose only notice is an exit sign on the highway."

She smiled and thanked Mr. Anderson and hovered

nearby while he laid open the aging newsprint on the reading table.

There was a commotion at the circulation desk, and she turned to see Reverend Mathers, Mrs. Littledeer, Bobbie Littledeer, and a man she thought was Mr. Swofford from the feed store. She drifted to the reference books and kept her ears open.

"I was there," Mr. Swofford said. "I seen them. Unfit for public display."

Miss Lancaster kept her voice low but firm. "I was there too, Mr. Swofford. The mood I recall was one of jubilation."

Reverend Mathers smiled. "Nevertheless, Mr. Alquist had them removed and destroyed. Or so we were led to believe."

Miss Lancaster said nothing.

"Does the library still have them?"

"They are still in the catalog, yes."

"There's more than that in your catalog," Mrs. Littledeer hissed.

Mathers calmed her. "We'd like to see them."

"The panels are in our catalog because they are library materials. But they have been checked out."

"By whom?"

Miss Lancaster folded her hands. "Patron records are private, Mr. Mathers."

Mrs. Littledeer sucked her teeth.

"Where are they now?" Mathers asked smoothly. "What is their status?"

She smiled. "Overdue."

Mathers stood motionless, then nodded. "Thank you, Miss Lancaster. I think we have everything we need. May God bless you this day." He turned and left. The two adults went with him, talking in excited whispers.

But not Bobbie Littledeer. She had seen Joanie and joined her.

"I'm so sorry," she said. "I should never have let Pastor Mathers see your article. I never thought they would take it this far."

"Who was that?"

"That's the Committee of Like-Minded Saints. Mr. Swofford, my mother, and some of the other elders at Mt. Hermon."

"But why are they interested in the panels?"

Bobbie shook her head. "It's my fault. They're looking for corruption."

"In a *library*?"

Bobbie pulled her farther into the stacks. "That day you caught me making lists? That was my mother's idea. She wanted to know if the library had certain books. On certain subjects."

"What subjects?"

"I— I can't even say the word. But it's in the Bible, if you want to look for it."

That hardly narrows it down. "Well, that's not your fault, if your mother told you to do it."

"I don't understand her anymore. Why would she even have me look up those words? They aren't words I know or want to know, and those aren't books I want to know even exist." Though she whispered, her voice carried through the rotunda.

Joanie put her arm around her. "Do you want to go somewhere and talk?"

"No. They'll miss me in a minute." She looked around. "It's like they revel in them. The words. Even Al says them. And there are more and more people in church every week. People I don't know. Pastor Mathers prays over them and heals them. But I've never seen them in church before, and they never come back."

"Let's go outside. Or tell you what, let's go to the Rexall. We can talk there."

Bobbie drew herself up. "No. It's fine. I'm fine now." She gripped Joanie's arm. "Please don't hate me for this."

"Bobbie, I could never hate you. I could never hate anyone."

Bobbie shook her head. "That's how it should be. That's what they say. But that's not what they do."

She walked Bobbie out the door. As they passed the circulation desk, Mr. Anderson was summoning Miss Lancaster over to the reading table. "It's unbelievable!" he said. They both looked upset.

Jake looked for Frank in the halls that morning. He had seen him during first period P.E., but Frank handed coach a note and sat out the class in the bleachers. When it was time to hit the showers, he was gone.

Jake wanted to tell him so much, but most of all he wanted to touch him.

Their night in the tack shed had been glorious and clumsy. Jake had gone first, lying back on the scratchy blanket while Frank worked his magic with his tongue. Then he moved up and leaned over him. Frank was a free milker and that got him part of the way in, but Jake had to ask him to pull out.

"Have you got something?"

"Wait a sec." Frank rummaged through a shelf and came back with a tin. He slathered it on and greased Jake's butt. This time, he slid easily past the first ring of muscle, then hit some kind of magic spot that made Jake gasp, "Holy shit!"

But Frank was only halfway in. He continued pushing slowly until he was all the way. Jake couldn't feel anything past that first wonderful pang, but every time Frank slid in and out, it sang again. His back chafed against the coarse wool, but he ignored it. Beautiful and jabbing heat radiated from his core. He felt each thrust in the soles of his feet, and each breath filled his lungs and opened him more.

Frank came pretty quickly.

"Sorry about that," he panted. "It's just, you're so, wow."

"You're pretty wow yourself."

Being on top of Frank was even better. Frank lay on his stomach, and Jake started by straddling him, bracing himself with his arms while rocking his hips forward. Frank bucked beneath, which pushed Jake deeper. He slid his arms under Frank's and lay fully across him, gripping his shoulders. It was like riding a horse, but you were part of the horse too, part of something muscular and unstoppable. Their sweat sealed them together, then let go with a sudden farting noise that threw them into giggles. After that, their rhythm got serious and steady. Frank's breathing told Jake he was going to come again, and that sent him over the top. He emptied himself, groaning and biting Frank's neck and shoulders. They lay wrapped in each other, breathing in the dark until they fell asleep with Jake still hard inside him.

The shed was cold when they awoke, and they dressed quickly. Rounding the corner of the barn, Frank peered at the house. All was dark and quiet. "They've gone to bed." He kissed Jake. "Go. You're shivering."

His James Dean T-shirt really wasn't up to the damp autumn night, so he ran all the way to the highway. On the way home he felt an urgency in his bowels, but he made it to the toilet on time. He looked down before he flushed, amazed and appalled at the mess of him and Frank.

In the morning, none of the gross details stuck with him. All he could remember was the feel of Frank's skin on his, Franks's body in his, and he wanted it again.

But Joanie dragged him to Mrs. Taylor's class before he

had a chance to check the halls. Over lunch, Beau came bubbling up to him with details of a new Creedence Clearwater song they had to play for the Harvest Dance. Jake kept hinting that he wanted to be elsewhere, but Beau was oblivious. *He really is a bit much sometimes.* "Let's talk it over with Frank, huh? Do you see him?"

But neither of them did. When seventh period came around and the kids started streaming to the pep rally, Jake ducked into the locker room to check again. It was empty. Cheering started in the Boys' Gym, and he went out through the back and scanned the parking lot.

There he was, leaning against Jake's car. Jake waved and ran over. "I've been looking all over for you."

"Crap. Same here. We've probably been chasing each other's tails."

Jake laughed, but Frank wasn't being playful. "What is it?"

"Have you still got it? The money I gave you after the vets hall."

"Sure. Well, not on me. I put it in the bank."

"Shit!" Frank kicked the car. "Why'd you do a fool thing like that?"

Jake flinched. "I thought it'd be safer there."

"Fucking bank's closed by now."

"I'll get it in the morning." Frank shook his head, angry. "What's wrong?" He reached out and squeezed his shoulder.

Frank cried out and pulled away.

"Jesus, Frank. What is it?"

"Lorenzo was waiting for me in my room. He found out we got paid. Now he wants the money. Right now. He's really pissed."

"You could say it was my idea to bank it. Let me come out there. I could explain it to him."

"No, I don't want to take the chance. I don't know what he'd do."

"What could he do?"

"This." Frank turned and dropped his shirt. His back was covered with broad red welts.

"Son of a bitch!"

"He's going to keep it up. Every night till he gets his money."

Jake dug in his wallet but only came up with a fiver and two ones. "Shit! I shouldn't have filled the tank. Wait, I can ask Beau or Belle. We'll scrape it together tonight."

"No. I want to keep this between him and me. I don't want you mixed up in it."

"I *am* mixed up in it."

"But I'm used to it. You're not. You don't know what he's like."

"I can't let him hurt you again. I love you."

Frank shook his head. "Don't say that. Don't make this messy."

Jake tried to hug him but Frank recoiled. "Sorry. Shit. What can I do?"

"You'll get it tomorrow?"

"Sure. As soon as the bank opens, I'll bring it right out."

"No. Just leave it in the mailbox out on the highway. Don't come near the house." He started to walk away.

"I can't bear it, Frank. I've got to see you again. I've got to touch you again."

"We can't. Not for a while." He looked at his boots. "We've still got the band.

"Fuck the band."

Frank nodded. He looked up. "There's something we can do. You hear the train when it crosses the river, right?"

"Yeah. It's a booming sound."

"That's when I'll start. You start, too."

Jake knew what he meant. "The last crossing is just a block from my place."

"That's when we'll finish."

"Yeah."

Frank nodded.

"I can't bear it, Frank."

"Me neither." He started walking away again then turned. "If anything happens to me— Well, you know."

Jake watched him walk to his car and leave. *To hell with this. I'm getting the money out there tonight.*

He caught up with the others coming out of the pep rally. Neither Beau nor Belle had more than a few bucks. Beau gave his readily, but Belle was suspicious.

"What's this for?"

"I'll pay you back tomorrow afternoon. I just need it tonight is all."

She frowned but forked over what she had.

He was still twenty dollars short. He thought of asking Virginia, but she wouldn't be home yet. Then he thought of Joanie. *She left school early. Is she at the Rexall?*

At the store, Mr. Tibbits told him she was at the library.

"Oh." He licked his lips. "Mr. Tibbits, can I ask you a favor?"

John Tibbits smiled. "Anything, Jake."

"Can you advance me twenty dollars on my pay?"

The smile became a frown. "Borrowing on credit is a bad habit, son."

"It's just for the weekend. I need to get something tonight, and I can't get to the bank till morning."

His eyebrows went up. "Something special?"

"Yes sir."

"For someone special?"

"Yes sir." It wasn't a lie if he and Mr. Tibbits were thinking of different someones.

"I'll write you out an I.O.U." He moved to the till.

The bell over the door rang. Mr. Anderson came in, red and perspiring though the afternoon was cool. He smiled when he saw Jake, but went immediately to Mr. Tibbits. "Excuse me," he said.

"Afternoon, Mr. Anderson. Something I can get you?"

"Well, sort of. Miss Lancaster tells me you're on the library board."

"I am indeed."

Mr. Anderson smiled again at Jake. Something about his face looked odd.

"Here you go, Jake." Mr. Tibbits handed over the twenty and the I.O.U. "Just sign and date this."

"You'll have it back tomorrow," Jake said.

"No rush."

Jake turned to Mr. Anderson. "Mr. Anderson?"

"Hmm?"

"I'd like to talk to you later. I have something to ask you."

"Of course. Though I may be going out of town soon."

"Oh."

"I'm staying at Mrs. Chisholm's. You can call me there."

"Thanks. And thanks, Mr. Tibbits."

"Don't make a habit of it, Jake."

"I won't, sir."

At his place, he double-wrapped the money in lined yellow paper and sealed it in an envelope after checking that the bills wouldn't show through. He addressed it to Frank Pellegrini and debated putting his name on the return address. Remembering Frank's warning, he put just a street number. He even put a stamp on it and drew a cancel mark to make it look legit. Then he drove out to the farm. The mailbox had *Craddock* painted out in white and *Pellegrini* over it in red. He put the envelope in and got in his car and waited. Fidgety, he turned on the radio.

Why should I believe you now
When you lied to me so many times before?
Tell me why should I—

"Jesus." He snapped it off in disgust. *So what if Hal Orison is from Elk City? Don't they have anything new to play?* He bit the cuticle on his thumb and stared at the mailbox.

But how would Frank know it was there? He hadn't thought that far ahead. *Should I call?* He felt stupid. *Why would anyone come out now? They got their mail hours ago.* He waited half an hour anyway, suffering through two airings of "Sugar Sugar" on two different radio stations, but no one came out to check the box.

He drove home, turned around and drove back, then thought checking the mailbox would look suspicious to anyone driving by and went home again. KOMA out of O. City mocked him with "Spirit in the Sky" and "One Toke Over the Line" on the way out, and "House of the Rising Sun" on the way back. All he could hear while "Rising Sun" played was Frank's yearning voice:

It's been the ruin of many a poor boy
And God I know I'm one.

He couldn't eat that night, not knowing if Frank was getting another beating. Waiting for the train made the night stretch forever. He thought he heard it twice only to see from the glowing kitchen clock dial it was too early. He took off his clothes and flopped down on the bed and stared at the ceiling.

At last he heard the booming from the river. He slowed his breathing and ran his hand across his chest and down.

How will Frank manage to hold out? He can come just by pinching his tits.

He imagined the two of them together, arms wrapped

around torsos, legs wrapped around legs, riding waves of skin as they rose and fell like the sea pulled by the moon. He had to stop stroking, afraid he would shoot too soon and ruin it.

Finally, the engines rattled the walls and vibrated the bed and the last whistle blew. He released himself into the night, crying out as it flew past.

He usually fell asleep right after coming, but tonight he couldn't. The throbbing engines faded away to the south. The last of the watchful dogs stopped their barking. Wind pushed against the windows and trees, and yet sleep wouldn't come. There were unfinished dreams in the air.

He turned on a light and started writing.

The Midnight Train

I need to sleep near a railroad line
Where in midnight dreams I can feel
The deep throat drum and the diesel whine
Pushing a cargo deep, deep in the night.

There is no pull on the midnight line
Where the only movement is down and under,
Under the riverbank, under the rails,
The rhythm the river hums over and over.

> *I am the night*
> *I am the rails*
> *I am the cargo of hair, skin, and nails.*
> *I am the river and*
> *I am the deep.*
> *I am the reason you weep.*
> *I am the reason you sleep.*

I wait for the engine, near and deep,
With its cargo pushing on mine.
I wait for the image to rise in sleep
And dance on the rails of the river of night.

> *I am the night*
> *I am the rails*
> *I am the reason that love never fails.*
> *I am the river and*
> *I am the deep.*
> *I am the soul of your pain.*
> *I am the midnight train.*

Confluence

For Saturday morning breakfast, Joanie's parents served scrambled eggs, collards, bacon, biscuits, and a side of nagging.

"Application deadlines are coming up," Mr. Tibbits said.

"I know. I won't miss them."

"The sooner we know, the better we can plan."

"Yes, Daddy."

"Can Julia Mae have her room?" Kyle asked.

"I thought you enjoyed having your baby sister so close," Mrs. Tibbits said.

"Yeah, but not *so* close."

"Maybe Julia will keep your room, and you'll get mine."

"Ew! Who wants some old girl's room?"

"Have you decided where to apply?" Mrs. Tibbits asked.

Joanie ticked off the list. "University of Texas at Austin. University of Colorado at Boulder. The University of Missouri, Columbia. And," she watched for her father's reaction, "Northwestern."

"Whew! That's one we'll definitely have to plan for."

"Is it because Tom Hansen's going there?" her mother asked.

"No! Not in the least."

"I suspect the Medill School of Journalism is the main draw," her father said.

"They're all so far away. It'll be hard to come home on weekends."

"I'm not going to O.U., Momma. I'm sorry, but I'm not."

"Well, it was worth a shot. Oh!" Her mother got up from the table. "I almost forgot." She brought a letter from the dining room. "This came for you yesterday."

It was from Oklahoma State University. She raised her eyebrows.

"Don't give me that look, young lady," her mother said. "I had nothing to do with it."

She opened the letter and started reading.

"Are you gonna finish your bacon?" Kyle asked.

"Oh, my goodness!"

"What, Princess?"

"It's from some researchers in library science at Oklahoma State University. They're building a database of Carnegie Libraries in the state, both past and those still in use. They saw my article in *The Evening Call*, and they want to know if they can incorporate my notes. They're interested in 'historical pictures of the library, its furnishings, ornaments, and especially any details of the sculpture mentioned in your article.'"

"Well, that's wonderful."

"Somebody read it! Somebody read my article."

"Well of course, dear. Everyone in town read it."

Her father frowned. "May I see that?"

She handed it over. "I can't wait to tell Jake. He thought this was all a wild goose chase."

"What are you going to say? To the scientists."

"Library science, Momma."

Her father cleared his throat. "Don't say anything just yet. I want to speak to Miss Lancaster first."

That's strange. Why would he need to do that? "Of course, Daddy. May I be excused? I want to call Jake."

Kyle dove for her bacon the second she got up. Jake's line was busy, though. *I can tell him when I go to interview Mrs. Edom. It's not too early to do that now, is it?*

She decided it wasn't. Then she decided to ask Jake in person and drove to his place. He looked surprised when he opened the door. "Oh good," he said. "I need to talk to you."

She waved the letter like a pennant. "I'm going to be interviewed by researchers at Oklahoma State University!"

"Swell."

They sat at the tiny kitchen table. His leg jittered up and down like a piston.

"Swell?" she said. "It's more than swell. It's— what's with your leg?"

"I'm on my third cup of coffee. Plus I haven't slept all night."

"Good Lord, Jake. That much caffeine will fry your brain."

"Too late. Already fried. Coffee crispy. Want some?"

"No, I don't like it. And you shouldn't either."

"A cup a day keeps the doctor away."

"No it doesn't, and you're not making sense."

"I know!" He sprang up. "My head is full of *things*. I've been writing them down. A song. A pretty good song, I think."

"You can write music?"

"No. But I did. I'll show you." He grabbed sheets of paper with words and chords and arrows all over them. He pushed them across the table and leaned over.

"I can't read this, Jake. And I hate to say this but . . ."

"Hmm? What? What but?"

"You smell like a boy."

He pulled back. "Oh."

"In fact, like a whole lot of boys. All jammed together."

"Sorry."

"Why don't you take a shower while I fix you something to eat? Something to smooth out those crispy brains."

When he came back he seemed much calmer. Or at least slower.

"I've scrambled you an egg and poured a bowl of Cheerios. I'd eat the Cheerios first. I think that milk expires at noon today."

"Sorry." He gobbled it down. "You got good news?"

"Yes, very. My stories about Croy's lost history got noticed by some researchers at O.S.U. They want to interview me and maybe use my notes in their database. So it's real important I interview Randy's mom and get those pictures of the library sculpture."

"Yeah." He looked thoughtful. "I should talk to her, too. And Mr. Anderson."

"Oh please, Jake. Let me get the scoop on this."

"Huh? Oh. No, not about that. Something else."

"So it can wait?"

He shook his head. "I don't think so." He looked over her shoulder. "There she is, coming out of Mrs. Oldfield's."

She turned. Virginia Edom was coming down the lawn, heading for her house across the alley. "Can we go over right now? Is it too early?"

He shrugged. "She's up. You're here. And I've got about forty-five minutes before I crash and burn."

The interview with Mrs. Edom started well. Joanie had her questions all lined up and her notebook ready to take things down in Speedhand. The first thing she noted was that Virginia didn't call it the memorial sculpture or the library sculpture.

"It's Ada's Memorial," she said. "Daddy never called it that, but that's what he meant it to be. In fact, he meant the whole library to be called the Ada Alquist Memorial Library, but for some reason he changed his mind."

"Oh, that's a great detail." She wrote it down.

"You know, I thought Ada's Memorial was lost. There was quite a backlash when it was unveiled."

"How come?"

Virginia shrugged. "The soldiers' panel upset folks. The 45th liberated Dachau, you know, and folks didn't like seeing that. Too gruesome, I guess. Others said the tornado panel wasn't accurate. Mrs. Oldfield is on that one."

"Really?" Jake grinned.

"And Mayor Pautler hated his pose on the Main Panel. Said it was disrespectful. Knowing Sunny, he was probably right.

"But all I remember is how Momma looked at the top, seated on a throne with rays of light shooting out behind her. You know, that's the only image I have of her. When she died, Lerner destroyed all her pictures."

"Why did Lerner—Mr. Alquist—do that?" Joanie asked.

"The tornado. The way she died. He didn't want to remember her like that. It was almost like he didn't want to remember her at all, except as a building. Something solid he could get his hands on and take charge over. But he kept this one portrait in a silver frame in a locked drawer. That's the one Sunny used."

"Is that Sunny Sohi?"

"Yeah, the sculptor." She shook her head. "We were great friends when we were kids. But kids grow up. Sunny didn't." She looked longingly at an empty ashtray on the kitchen counter and seemed to drift off. "I don't remember my mother at all, except sometimes certain sounds, like a song, or a smell—they kinda echo. I guess that's her."

"So, were there three panels in all?" Joanie asked.

"Yep. That's all that would fit out front, on the whatchamacallit over the entrance."

"There's the soldiers' panel, the tornado panel—"

"And the main panel, the biggest. The Goddess of Prosperity." Virginia laughed hoarsely. "Folks didn't like that, either. Anti-Christian, they said. Idolatry. They wanted to dump it in the White Horse, where the Little Bushy runs in. 'Back to the mud that spawned it!' Idiots."

Jake looked puzzled. "So, for years you thought they dumped it in the river?"

"Until Joanie's article came out. But if the soldiers' panel is still around, maybe my mother's is, too."

"How could you stand not knowing?"

Virginia stood. "I thought I did know. I called Miss Lancaster that night when the uproar started, to warn her they were coming for it, but Harry and I had our hands full. I went into labor with Randy, for one."

"I knew it!" Joanie blushed. "Sorry."

"Yeah. Well, he was a few weeks early, and there were complications. I was pretty much out of it, laid up in St. Joe's. Harry took the brunt of it. By the time I came around, the panels were gone, Daddy was dead, and there were other things on our mind. The memorial wasn't high on the list." She poured herself a cup of coffee and drifted over to the window.

"The folks at O.S.U. are going to love this, Mrs. Edom."

"Who now?"

"These researchers in library science. They're putting together a database on Oklahoma's Carnegie libraries."

"Oh? But it's not a Carnegie library."

Joanie nearly dropped her pen. "What?"

Virginia looked out the window. "Jake, were you expecting someone? There's this man walking around the granny house."

Mr. Anderson joined them at the Edoms' kitchen table. Virginia poured him a cup of coffee and offered to pour Jake one, too. He really wanted one, but a glance from Joanie told him to decline.

"Mrs. Chisholm said you called and wanted to see me," Mr. Anderson said. "I'm leaving this afternoon for Norman."

Jake licked his lips. *There's no putting it off. Here goes nothing.* "Yes. I was going to ask each of you separately, but you're all here, so here goes." He took a deep breath. And couldn't speak.

Virginia looked at him. "Jake?"

"Mr. Pellegrini is beating Frank."

There was silence.

"What?" Joanie whispered.

"Frank showed me. He has welts, bruises on his back. His skin is torn up."

Virginia sat down.

"What on Earth?" Mr. Anderson said.

"Mr. Pellegrini says it's because Frank won't give him the money from our shows, but I don't think that's it."

"He can't do that," Joanie objected.

"Different families have different rules, Joanie," Virginia said.

"That doesn't make it right."

"It's not our place."

Jake swallowed. "I don't think the money is all. I think it's because of Frank and me."

Joanie raised her eyebrows. "Oh."

"What about Frank and you?" Virginia asked.

"We see a lot of each other."

Anderson sat back. "Oh."

Jake looked at Virginia. "A lot."

Her face turned red. "I *knew* I should have had that Vince character's balls on a plate!"

"This has nothing to do with him. Vince and I never did anything."

"That's the truth, Mrs. Edom," Joanie said.

Virginia squinted. "And how would you know?"

"They broke up way last year. Jake told me. We share everything. Well, almost everything."

Virginia's breath came short. It didn't look like she was buying it. "Frank and me," Jake said, "we just found each other, that's all."

Anderson interrupted. "I'm not sure we should be talking about this now."

"We shouldn't be talking about it at all," Virginia said. "You kids are too young to be fooling around."

"We're not just fooling around. That's why Mr. Pellegrini is so mad."

"How Frank's dad wants to raise his kid is up to him."

"He's not raising him. He's whipping him. For something we did, we *both* did."

Mr. Anderson folded his arms. "How long has this been going on?"

"I only found out yesterday. Frank didn't want to tell me. He said it was between him and his dad."

"It is," Virginia agreed.

"And if I tried to stop it, he didn't know what his stepdad might do."

"To him?" Anderson asked.

"To me."

Virginia started to rise but sank back in her chair. "The hell." Mr. Anderson extended a hand but she batted it away. "I'm fine." She searched her pockets frantically. Finding nothing, she stood and opened a drawer, then slammed it shut. "Are you sure you aren't exaggerating?"

"No ma'am. Frank was really scared, more for me than him."

"You should go to the police," Joanie said.

"Percy Owen?" Virginia scoffed. "Don't make me laugh."

"The sheriff, then."

Anderson shook his head. "And tell him what? A man is beating his son for being—I beg your pardon, but—for being queer? He'd probably give him a medal."

Virginia shook her head. "Half the town would. More than half."

"So, what do we do?" Joanie asked.

Jake covered his face. "I don't *know*! That's why I'm asking *you*!" Joanie touched his shoulder and he dropped his hands. "I'm afraid Frank might do something to himself."

The adults were silent.

"Like his grandfather did?" Joanie said quietly.

He nodded. "He's already told me he's thought about it, how he'd do it."

Virginia crossed her arms. "No. You tell Frank if he ever feels that way, call me. Or Mr. Tibbits."

"Thanks. I will."

"And if he needs a place to stay, a safe place, he comes here."

"That's great and all, but he doesn't know you." He looked up. "I want him to stay with me."

"Mrs. Oldfield will pitch a fit," Anderson said.

"I'll handle Clara Oldfield," Virginia said. "Whatever happens, make sure Frank knows he has a safe place to go."

"But they're miles from town," Joanie said. "We can't keep an eye on them. If anything goes bad, it will be too late."

Anderson let out a breath. "There may be something I can do. Let me talk to a friend."

"I'm sorry to lay this on you all," Jake said. "I just didn't know what to do, but I have to do something."

Anderson leaned across and hugged him. "You *are* doing something. You're being his friend. That's the best thing a person can do."

"I feel like I'm messing up."

"No," Virginia said. "If anyone's messing up, it's the adults."

"I'd like to stay and help," Anderson said, "but I've got to get going. I have to be in Norman this afternoon. They have archive copies of *The Call*, and I need pictures of the sculpture for my book."

"But we have archives here," Joanie said, "in the library."

Mr. Anderson looked at Jake, then at Joanie. "I thought your father would have told you. All the pictures are gone. They've been cut from the paper. The article, the photographs, all of it."

"That's crazy," Jake said. "I saw them a couple of years ago. Miss Lancaster helped me find them."

Anderson shook his head.

"But *The Call* has them, don't they?" Joanie asked.

"No, they're gone too. We checked this morning. They don't know how or when it happened, but all photos and articles about the memorial and its dedication are gone. Someone wants it erased and forgotten."

Jake's heart hammered in his throat. "How about articles for the day after the dedication? Are they still there?"

"I only looked for the dedication, but I suppose I could look further."

"No we'll do it, Joanie and me." He stood. *Those three coffees better last me.* "You're coming back, right?"

"Of course. We'll talk more then."

At the library, Miss Lancaster was reluctant to show them the damage. "The board will be meeting to discuss the issue. In the meantime, the volumes are under lock and key for their protection."

"You let me read them two years ago," Jake said. "I didn't damage them then. You know I won't damage them now."

"That's not the only issue." Miss Lancaster looked at her desk. "There are things that are too personal, too painful for young people to see. It's a form of bullying."

Jake set his jaw. "How old do I have to be to learn the truth?"

Miss Lancaster studied him for a moment. "Old enough to ask that question." She rose and took a set of keys to her office. She came back bearing the 1952 volume of *The Croy Evening Call.* "Turn the pages slowly," she said. "The mutilations have compromised the paper's integrity."

Jake turned to the October 13th issue. The front page and several others had gaping holes. Then he turned to the October 14th issue.

Joanie gasped.

Every picture of Andy Simms had been cut out. There were pictures of the mangled car and the crash site, but none of him. Nor were there any with his obituary. Nor in the article reporting the coroner's verdict. He leafed back to the beginning of the year. There was a neat hole in the middle of the column announcing Andy's appointment as music minister at Mt. Hermon Bible Church.

"They're all gone," he said.

"I'm terribly sorry, Malachi," Miss Lancaster said. "The vandals were thorough."

He closed the volume and handed it back. "Thank you, Miss Lancaster. Thank you for letting me see the truth."

Jake and Joanie sat on the steps outside the library. "Thanks for driving."

Joanie leaned against his shoulder. "It's what friends are for." She sighed. "It's awful."

"I should check on Frank, but I'm out of gas."

"We can take my car."

He laughed. "Not that gas. I mean *pffft!* I'm out of gas."

"Oh."

The sun was beginning to slant toward afternoon.

"It's not just Frank, is it?" she said. "There's other kids, too."

Jake nodded. "Beau got beat up last year. Belle's own family kicked her out. We get beat up or kicked out or treated like we're less than human because we don't fit. We're a mistake."

"You're not a mistake. You and Frank aren't a mistake."

"My father wasn't either. But he felt it, that scorn, that look of disgust. So he tried to make himself disappear." He stood. "But it's never enough. It's not enough to kill the future. They have to kill the past, too. They don't want us to exist, ever." He clenched his fists. "They can't win. They can't be the ones who get to tell the story, or bury it, or keep others from hearing it. They can't win *any* of it. I won't let them."

"*We* won't let them."

"I'm really tired."

"I'm tired and angry. Butchering the paper like that is barbaric."

"No, I'm really tired."

"Oh. I'll take you home."

Mrs. Oldfield was waiting for them at the granny house. She held a jelly jar in her hands. "Mrs. Edom spoke to me. I don't understand what's going on with people. I'm going to speak to Pastor Mathers about it."

"Um, thanks," Jake said.

"Children looking after children. It's not the way it's supposed to be. The adults, the parents, we're the ones who are supposed to be in charge. But how on earth are we to keep up?" She held out the jar. "Here. It's strawberry rhubarb preserves."

They watched her walk up the lawn to her house. "I think we may have just witnessed a miracle," Joanie said.

"Joanie, can you go out to Frank's? Just out to the highway, to their mailbox. I left something there for him. Can you check that he got it?"

"Sure."

"And then come back and tell me." He looked at the jelly jar. "I don't really like strawberry rhubarb."

She took it from him. "You get to bed before you fall over."

"Right." He turned as he got inside. "And come to our session tomorrow. I want you to hear my song."

Rehearsal

Belle's uncle was the plant supervisor at the Croyen Top Clay brick works southwest of town. Gilbert Frye had a house, three-car garage, and a few acres across the highway from the plant. When things fell apart between Belle and her parents, he gave her a place to stay. When the rest of the family packed off to Cameroon to found a mission, he backed her decision to stay in Croy. But she was not his ward. Belle was an emancipated minor, and although she had to check in with a judge from time to time, she was her own person. She paid her uncle rent for the space above the garage, and they pretty much let each other be. The property had no neighbors, so Belle practiced her drums whenever she pleased. And when the band assembled at her place, they were free to raise the rafters.

On their way out to Belle's, Beau kept reeling off different sequences of songs for the upcoming Harvest Dance and asking Jake's opinion. Jake seemed distracted and gave non-committal answers.

"I'd like to add The Kink's 'Lola' to the mix, but I don't think we'd get it past the dance committee," Beau said. "What do you think about Three Dog Night's 'Out in the Country'? Too corny?"

"I've got a song of my own I'd like to try."

"Really? Terrific! We don't have a signature yet. Is it an anthem, like 'Born to Be Wild'? Or more like a ballad?"

"It's a waltz, really, but kinda edgy."

"Edgy. I like that. Fits our image."

"I invited Joanie to the session. I hope you don't mind."

Their rehearsals had always been private. He wished Jake had checked with him first. "No, not at all. Hey! She could write an article about us for *The Clarion*."

Jake rolled his eyes. "Don't encourage her."

Joanie and Frank were already in the loft-like space above the garage with Belle. Beau plugged in his amp and turned to ask Jake to run a mike check, but he and Frank were off in a corner. There was a look of concern on Jake's face as he touched Frank's sleeve. "No, it's okay. I got it," Frank said. "Everything's fine."

Beau wished they'd get down to business. He wanted a mike check. He wanted to go over the play list. He wanted Jake and Frank not to stand so close together.

"Jake says you're going to try his new song," Joanie said.

"We've got to run through the stuff for the dance first." He focused on tuning his bass. "And we're going to try 'Out in the Country' today, see if it fits."

Joanie drifted away.

Their run-through was awful. The band wasn't listening to itself. Belle complained that Beau was behind on the beat. Frank fumbled his entrances. He and Belle both said they couldn't hear vocals on the monitors and Jake spent half an hour trying to get the balance right. Whenever they did manage to get all the way through a song, Joanie clapped and exclaimed, "That was wonderful!"

Beau wanted to strangle her. "Let's take a break." he said.

"Wait," Jake said. "There's something I'd like us to try. It's called 'The Midnight Train.'" He handed out sheets.

Belle turned the paper over. "How am I supposed to follow this? It's all chicken scratches."

"It's easy. You'll see."

Most of the melody was around B flat, perfect for Frank. But the chorus started more than an octave higher and went up from there. Belle shook her head. "Shit, Jake, this range is wider than 'House of the Rising Sun.'"

Beau started to hear the melody in his head. His fingers tingled. *This could be it.* "Other songs have that range."

"Such as?"

"Bridge over Troubled Water."

Frank shook his head. "I ain't no Art Garfunkel."

Jake said, "It's written for your range. Can you hit the top?"

"I can hit it, but I'll sound like my nuts are in a vice."

"I can hit it," Beau said.

Joanie raised her hand. "Why don't you split it up, like you did 'Stand By Your Man'?"

Frank nodded. "Sure. I'll take the verses, Beau the chorus."

They ran through it twice. It clicked.

"Slide guitar would sound great on this," Frank said, switching instruments.

"We should repeat the first chorus," Belle added.

"And let's add a two bar lead-in before each verse," Jake said.

They ran it again. As the last note faded, a charge hummed through the group.

"Wow," Joanie whispered.

"Damn," Belle said. "That's our song."

Beau swelled with joy. *This is why I created a band. To tap into this flow. To create dark and brilliant things in a mean, drab world.*

Jake frowned. "Beau, it's 'I am the *soul* of your pain,' not 'the *source* of your pain.'"

"*Source* makes more sense," Belle said.

"No, it doesn't," Frank said. "The train doesn't cause him pain. It marks the distance between them. It intensifies it, but it connects them, too. It consoles him." He looked at Jake as he spoke. Jake smiled and nodded.

Beau's wave of elation collapsed. *Oh. This is a song about them. This is their song.* He turned to his amp to hide his expression. *But it's a really good song.* "We should play this at the end. It will close out the dance." He put on a smile. "It'll kill 'em."

Two hours later, as they were breaking down the equipment, Belle called out, "Guys, we can't just keep playing sucky music out at the vets hall. We're getting too good."

"Amen to that," Frank said.

"Where do you suggest?" Jake asked.

"I got connections at The Corners."

"The Corners?" Beau looked up from his case. "That's kind of a rough crowd, isn't it?"

"They're pussycats. Trust me."

"It's a bar," Joanie said. "Can you play in a bar?"

"I'll work something out. There are ways. What d'ya say?"

They looked at each other.

"Sure, what the hell," Jake said.

Beau had his guitar and amp ready to load up, but Jake and Frank had stepped aside again and were talking.

Belle came up to him. "You all right?"

"Sure, sure." He smiled and nodded. A bit too much, he realized.

"It's still your band," she said.

"It's still *our* band."

"I mean," she nodded at Frank and Jake.

"They're all right. I'm happy for him. I mean, yeah, I had hopes, but . . ." He looked at Frank. "He's got everything. Confidence. A great voice. Shoulders. A big jock with a big dick."

"I wouldn't know."

"How can I compete with that?"

"You don't. If just being you isn't enough for Jake, then Jake isn't enough for you."

"I *would* be enough if he'd just see me. But he doesn't. I'm more of a pet project to him." He shook his head. "Boys can be so stupid."

"They surely can." Belle looked at Joanie, who had joined Jake and Frank. "Girls, too."

Joanie drifted up to the boys. *They're speaking in normal voices, so it's not eavesdropping*, she told herself.

"You're coming over, right?" Jake asked Frank.

"Sure, but I gotta talk to Belle first."

"That works. I gotta take Beau home."

Frank shook his head. "Why don't he get his own car?"

"It's his eyes. He keeps failing the vision test."

"But why is it always you?"

Jake smiled. "What goes around comes around."

He looked her way. She smiled her innocent smile. He frowned and looked past her.

"Are you ready, Beau?"

"Belle's giving me a ride, okay?" he called back.

"Sure."

"See you next time," Belle said. "Same Bat-time, same Bat-place."

"Hold up, Belle. I wanna ask you somethin'." Frank smiled at Jake. "Looks like you're free. See you soon."

Joanie dogged him as he carried his guitar and amp to the car. "I know, I know," he said as soon as he stowed them. "I'm an idiot."

"Sorry, Buford. Not a scoop."

"I knew it as soon as we ran the song, the minute I saw Beau's face. It's the same way I used to look at Randy."

"It was kinda obvious. As are you and Frank."

Jake sighed. "I never wanted this to happen. I promised him. I said I'd never hurt him. But I never expected him to fall for Frank."

Joanie opened her mouth.

"I know all's fair in love and war, but that's not how I wanted this to work. Beau's special. He's really the spirit behind us all. He's our Number One Quirk." He smiled ruefully.

"Jake, I don't think you've got the whole picture. Or even the right frame."

Beau came out, lugging his amp.

"Here, let me," Jake said.

"I got it. Joanie, can you give me a ride? Belle and Frank are deep in the weeds about something, and I want to get back."

"I can take you," Jake said.

"You shouldn't be my taxi all the time."

"It's no problem."

"No," Joanie said. "I'll take him back."

Jake smiled. "Great."

His relief was painfully obvious. She checked Beau's face, but he wasn't even looking. He sat silently beside her on their way back to town. Finally she said. "If you want to talk, I'll listen."

"No thanks. All talked out. Everything's smooth."

Joanie shook her head. *Boys can be so stupid.*

Frank rolled up the alley to the granny house and knocked on the door, eager to share the notion he'd discussed with Belle. There was no answer. He pounded. Jake's car was gone, and the whole neighborhood was eerily quiet. He tried once more. "Damn it." He got back in his truck and headed out to the farm. He had things to say to Lorenzo.

His family was in the living room in their usual spots. "Angela," he said, "can you go to your room, please? I want to talk to Mom and Dad alone."

She didn't even look up. "I got just as much right to be here as you do."

"Okay. But keep quiet."

She looked at Arlene. "Mom?"

Lorenzo answered. "You stay right there, honey. If you've got something to say, boy, say it."

"Sure." He squared his shoulders. "I want you to know I'm not waiting to turn eighteen. I'm going to file papers to change my name back to Fenton. There's forms, a procedure."

Lorenzo coolly tapped his cigarette on the ashtray. "Fine. You don't want my name, you don't want your family? You don't get our house."

Arlene gasped. "You're not sending him away, are you?"

"I'm not sending him anywhere. He's leaving."

"I don't want to leave. But I want control of my own money. Not what the farm earns, but what I earn on my own."

"On your own means on your own. You get no help from me. And that includes room and board."

Arlene touched his arm. "Lorrie, we're a family."

Lorenzo sprang from his chair. "Don't contradict me *in front of the boy!*"

Angela scooted into a corner, her eyes bright and eager.

Frank moved closer. "If you're lookin' to hit someone, I'm over here."

"Frank, don't provoke him. Lorrie, he doesn't mean it. He's just a boy. Let me talk to him."

"Jesus fucking Christ! Doesn't anyone think I know what I'm doing?" He started pacing. "Doesn't anyone think I know how to run my own family, my own farm?" He pointed his finger at Frank. "I don't need your money. I don't need your help. But by God, I will have your respect." He wheeled around. "That goes for all of you!"

"Daddy?" Angela whispered from the corner.

"Not now."

She shrank into a tight ball, her knees clasped to her chest.

He turned to Frank. "I am the head of this household. Not you, you self-centered little prick." He turned to Arlene. "And not you, always sticking up for your boy, putting him ahead of me."

"Lorenzo, I'm sorry. It's not his fault."

"It's *always* his fault!" He stood in the center of the room. "I spent six years fighting that old bastard on how to run this farm. Six years! Pellegrinis have always farmed. It's in our blood, it's a fire in our heart. But he never listened. It was always Virgil's way or the highway. Well, he finally blew himself to Hell, and now it's *my* turn." He turned to Frank. "You don't want to be part of it? Fine. I don't need you." He pointed to his mother and Angela. "They don't either. This outfit would run a lot smoother without you."

Frank scoffed. "You can't run this farm by yourself."

"Just watch me. Once I sell the north field to the Woolvines, it'll be a snap."

"That's the best bottom land in the county. It's our biggest yield."

"It's a pain in the ass with that trestle running through it. Lose it and we cut the work in half."

"You couldn't farm this land if you cut it to forty acres and a mule. Not with a fleet of tractors and ten hired hands."

A light dawned in Lorenzo's eyes. "You sent him, didn't you?"

"Who?"

"That faggot cowboy. Thinks he can just waltz in here and show me how to do things."

"He just wanted to help, Lorenzo," Arlene said.

"Get it through your thick head, woman, I don't need help." He turned to Frank. "You sent him, didn't you? Virgil's old hand, the one that ran off."

Frank scowled. "Jim Newton's in Colorado."

"Oh, now I'm imagining things, am I? I just *imagined* he showed up here, uninvited, asking all kinds of questions, implying he knew better, offering to look after things." His dropped his voice. "You'd like that, wouldn't you? You're just his type."

"Oh!" Arlene covered her face and ran from the room.

Lorenzo watched her leave, his face pained, then turned to Frank. "You are going to pay for this. You are going to pay for every tear she sheds. By God you will." He followed her. The door to his parents' room slammed.

Frank looked at Angela. "What the hell? Was Jim out here?"

She sneered. "Don't bother hanging around. You won't see me cry."

He drove back to town. Jake's porch light was on as he rapped on the door. He was still worked up. As soon as Jake let him in, he started in on him. "Where were you? I thought you said come over."

"I did." Jake clutched the top of his head. "I had to take Virginia to the hospital. She's getting worse. Which means . . . Oh hell, I don't know what it means." He slumped on the sofa.

Frank exhaled, trying to let his fear and anger go. He sat beside him. "What happened?"

"She can't catch her breath. Joanie thinks I should tell Randy. Virginia keeps saying it's not that serious, but I think it is. It messes up everything." He leaned against him. "I can't do this again." Frank put his arm around him and Jake looked up. "Sorry. You got troubles of your own. Is your stepdad after you again?"

"Yeah. He wants to kick me off the farm, cut me off. I worked that land more years than he ever did, but it don't matter. He wants me gone."

"That sucks."

Jake's ribcage felt solid against his. "He pretty much called me a fag right in front of my mom."

Jake's fingers slid between the buttons of his shirt. If he did nothing, their mouths would be roaming soon. "Did you send Jim Newton out to my place?"

"He's back?"

"Lorenzo thinks so."

Jake shook his head. "I mean, you talk about him, but I don't even know what he looks like."

"Well, someone must've told him what was goin' on. He came out to check up on me."

"Oh shit. Mr. Anderson."

"That fat fairy?"

"Hey, he's a friend."

"Yours, not mine.

"I told him what was going on. About the whippings."

Frank stood up. He had to put distance between them or bust. "What'd you do that for?"

"I had to do something. He said he knew someone who could help. And Virginia said she'd help too, if you need it, though that's messed up now. And Mrs. Oldfield said you could stay over here if things got rough."

"Christ! Bring the whole damn town in on it. Take out ads. Broadcast it on the radio."

"You were getting hurt. I couldn't let that go."

"What goes on at my house is my business." Lorenzo's words in his mouth stopped him. He shook his head. "It's private."

"Pain isn't private. It shouldn't be. Not in a good world."

"You think this is a good world? Don't be a sap."

"Okay, it's a crappy world. The world sucks." Jake got up and went to him. "Your granddad blew his brains out. My dad smeared himself halfway across town." He put his arms around him. "But that's them, not us. You aren't what your stepdad thinks of you. I'm not what Andy thought of himself. We aren't the worst the world makes of us. We're the best we make of each other. That's love."

Frank squirmed but not enough to break free. "Love is what people say to get what they want. Truth is, everyone's alone. Because everything ends, Jake, everything good. My dad, your dad. The world tears it out and throws it away. One by one, until all that's left is you. And then it tears you out, too."

Jake searched his eyes. "You don't really feel that way, do you?"

"All I really feel right now is you. I can't be around you without wanting you in me, on me, all over me. I don't care what you call it. I want it. Everything else can go to hell."

In the bedroom, in their heat, with the rhythm driving them closer and closer, Jake paused and put his lips to his ear. "I am in you. You are in me. Nothing can tear us apart."

"Shut up. Keep going."

When he got back to the farm, the front door was locked. So was the kitchen. Frank tried his key, but it didn't work. He backed away from the porch and looked up. The top and bottom sashes of the dormer were shut. He climbed up anyway. The sashes were locked, too. He sat on the roof and looked into the night. Locked out of the house, looking down on the farm, he was suspended, not part of one world or another. All the warmth he'd soaked up from Jake seeped away.

It wasn't cold enough to freeze to death, but you wouldn't need to freeze, would you? Just slow everything down till it stopped. It would be faster if he were wet, but the horse trough was down by the barn and he'd have to climb down and then back up. It hardly seemed worth it. It was probably empty, anyway. His eyes slid over the barnyard.

A fan of light spread out from the tack shed.

He was off the roof and at the door before he could think. He yanked it open. "Jim?"

The room was empty. The bed was made. His clothes lay folded in neat piles on the shelves. The chaps were gone.

He sat on the edge of the bed, his vision blurry. It made starbursts and rays of everything shiny in the room. The lamp, the heater grill. There was a bucket with a towel over it to use in the night. There was a plate with a knife and a fork. In the corner, cleaned and oiled, was his grandfather's shotgun.

If Lorenzo left it, it meant one thing. *They'd be better off without you.* If Arlene left it, it meant something else.

Granddad always kept the ammo locked up because of Angela. Lorenzo probably did, too. It didn't matter. He knew where to find three shells.

Dear Randy

I wanted to write you sooner but Jake said I shouldn't but I think I should so here goes.

Your mom is in the hospital. They found a cancer on her lung and they're going to operate. I thought you should know.

I don't even know if this is the right address for you. I had to copy it from a letter I stole from Jake. Maybe there's some kind of deal going on, and maybe where you are is supposed to be some sort of big secret, but I don't care.

Come home.

—Joanie

Corners

I f you want your past to stay buried, you shoulda made plans not to have one." Virginia lay propped up in her hospital bed, an oxygen tube under her nose. She had to catch her breath now and then, but Joanie thought her color was better than when she first got here. "It always comes back to bite you. And Ada's Memorial has one hell of a past."

"Well, we've got *The Croy Evening Call* behind us at least," Joanie said, "though there's lots of letters to the editor against it."

"And there's only the one panel so far," Jake said.

"I'm going out to Adam Jameson's this afternoon to look at it. And Daddy's going to talk to the rest of the library board about re-installing it."

"It wasn't ever installed," Virginia said. "They just kinda hoisted it on cranes. So folks could take a look." She smiled. "That was Jed's idea."

"We don't know where the Soldiers Panel is," Jake said. "Or The Goddess of Prosperity. We're hoping Miss Lancaster can help."

Virginia looked thoughtful. "You should ask Jed. That's Mr. Tucker to you. Or Sunny. They were kinda close back then." She smiled crookedly. "You could ask Harry if you can find him. Which thank God nobody can. Percy Owen is still after him for breaking out of Atoka."

"We'll track the panels down," Joanie said. "We promise."

Virginia squeezed her hand. "Thanks, kiddo. It would

mean the world to me if you did. Especially the Goddess. I'd like to see her one last time."

She took a sip of water from her glass. While her face was turned aside, Joanie mouthed, *One last time?* to Jake. He mouthed back, *What the hell?*

"So, how's the band?" They both snapped back before she could see the looks on their faces.

"The dance went well," Jake said. "The kids seemed to have a good time."

"Everyone loved Jake's song."

"You write songs now?"

Jake shrugged. "Just the one so far."

"Andy wrote lots of songs. All about Jesus, but catchy just the same. So what's next?"

"We're looking around. We're tired of the vets hall, and the Teen Center doesn't pay."

"Belle's getting them a gig out at The Corners," Joanie said. Jake shot her a look.

Virginia frowned. "You can't spend the night in a bar."

"Belle says she's got something figured out."

Virginia pointed a finger at him. "You can *not*. Spend the *night*. In a *bar*. I will rise from this very bed and haul you back myself."

"Okay. I'll tell Belle."

Virginia nodded and leaned back. Her eyes closed.

Out in the parking lot, Joanie said, "It's not right. First Al, then Mr. Craddock, now her. All in one year. I think there's something fishy going on, a cancer cluster or something."

"Joanie, not everything is a news story waiting for you to crack."

"I'll bet if I could search the records . . . maybe at the pharmacy."

"Just skip it. We've got enough mysteries to solve without making ones up." He looked up at St. Joseph's. "I don't like what she said up there. 'One last time.' She shouldn't think like that." He turned to her. "And you shouldn't have upset her by mentioning The Corners."

"I didn't know it would upset her. She's probably been there dozens of times herself."

"That's not the point. She's supposed to be resting, getting her strength up for the surgery. Besides, it's not even a sure thing yet."

"When it is, will you tell her?"

He shook his head and got into his car. "You just can't keep anything to yourself, can you?"

Not if it's the truth. "I'll catch up with you later."

The Jamesons lived almost all the way to Napier Corners, several miles past the infamous bar and grill that straddled the Conlan County line. *Kids who live out here must spend hours on the bus just getting to and from school.* She passed the site of Marcus Garvey High School, a flat concrete pad slowly getting eaten by the prairie. *Still, it's better to have one school district instead of two.*

Adam Jameson met her at the front door and led her around back. "We keep it in the carriage house. It's too big for inside."

The carriage house was like a small barn. A running horse weather vane topped its white-trimmed cupola. "Do you keep horses?" she asked.

"My grandfather did. He was a hostler back in the day. A farrier, too. Zach wanted to start that up again."

"What happened?"

There was a glint in Adam's eye. "He burned down the forge."

"How's he doing?"

Adam stopped, his smile gone. "He's over there now. It's as if they couldn't ship him out fast enough."

"But things are quiet, I hear. The fighting has almost stopped."

"That's just monsoon season. Once the rain stops, the killing and bloodshed will start again. Did you hear Del Longacre got killed?"

"No, that's awful!"

Adam shook his head. "Dr. King was right. It's a rich man's war, but a poor man's fight." He slid open the door and they entered. The peaceful light inside reminded her of a chapel. A large trapezoidal wooden frame sat just under the rafters, draped in a tarp. Adam started untying the ropes.

"I passed by Garvey High on the way out here," she said. "It's just weeds now."

Adams fingers worked swiftly. "My grandfather started that school. Named it, ran it. Then my father."

"But it's worth it having just one district, isn't it?"

He faced her. "Getting up in the deep cold of winter to catch the school bus. Getting home way past dark. An hour and a half each way. It better be worth it." He threw over the tarp.

Joanie gasped. "Oh my God."

"Dramatic, isn't it? That's my grandfather there, holding open the door to the storm cellar. And those figures in the background are The Salvagers. They supplied the town with victuals when everything else was in ruins."

"It's amazing." She leaned forward, intending to touch it, but Adam tensed so she stepped back. Then the shape of it struck her. So familiar.

"It's been at Garvey High this whole time?"

"Yes. That's quite the family legend, how they got it out there in the middle of the night. Of course, it's only one corner of the whole sculpture. Nobody knows where the other corner is, or the center panel."

She felt a prickling in her brain. "The frame—did it come like that?"

Adam shrugged. "It's what they used to get it to Garvey, and what we used to bring it here. We never throw anything out. Why?"

The prickling ran from her brain to her skin, raising goose bumps. "I've seen one just like it, reversed." She folded her arms and stared intently. "I know where the other corner is."

Belle led the band through the door of The Corners like she was walking into an ice cream parlor. The gloom inside blinded Jake. Frank bumped into him from behind.

"It kinda smells," Beau said.

Jake nodded. "It's definitely a saloon."

"Rough crowd," Frank said, looking at the guys at the bar.

Belle scoffed. "Those guys? A bunch of pussycats."

One of them detached himself and sidled up to Frank. "Hey farm boy," he said. "Show us your dick."

"What?"

Belle stepped between them. "How about I show you mine?"

The man sneered. Belle stepped closer, grinning. He turned and went back to his drink.

Belle smiled. "See? Pussycats."

A short man in a Western shirt came up. "Who are these kids, Belle? You know they can't be in here without an adult."

"This is the band I told you about."

"You didn't say they was kids."

"It's all right, Marion," said a voice in the dark. "They're with me."

"A little young, Sammy, even for you."

"You can kiss my ass Marion."

"You wish."

"And you hope. But in vain."

Jake listened to this exchange open-mouthed, peering into the gloom. "Mr. Anderson?"

Anderson's large frame, seated at a round table with a tall glass in front of him, gradually resolved itself. "Jake, sweetie. How about you and your friends sit here while Mr. Bowles and I have a little chat?" He and the other man moved off and talked in low voices.

As they sat, Belle nudged him. "Why didn't you tell me you knew her?"

"Who?"

"*Her*. Sister Many Agonies. That's her talking to the owner."

"That's Mr. Anderson. We've been friends for years. Who's this Sister person?"

"That's his drag name. He's the star here Friday nights."

"Huh," Beau said. "Neat."

"Randy told me things were different on Fridays. I guess that's what he meant."

"I don't like any of this," Frank said.

"We're going to be his opening act. If we can pitch it to Marion. Mr. Bowles, that is."

"How do you know all these guys?" Jake asked.

"I work in the kitchen. Have for a year." The guys looked at her. "Okay, I'm a dishwasher. But they've been wanting a lead-in for the drag show for months."

"We're gonna be backup for a bunch of fairies?" Frank asked.

Belle started to explain, but Mr. Anderson joined them. "Jake," he said, smiling. "I already know Belle. And this would be Frank, I'm guessing. And you are?"

"Beau. Beau Hamilton. *Very* pleased to meet you, sir."

"Same here. And just call me Sammy. Now." He folded his hands on the table. "What in hell are all y'all doing out here?"

Belle took a breath. "You've been looking for a warm-up to your show. And we're it. We can do rock, we can do country western, we can do R'n'B, and—"

"No."

She stopped short. She looked at Jake.

She wants me to play the friendship card. "We're really pretty good Mister—um, Sammy. We won the talent show, we've played at school dances and the Teen Center—"

"That's all kids' stuff. The guys here are hard core."

"And the VFW, the Elks, and the Odd Fellows' Hall," Belle added. "They all like us."

Anderson shook his head. "Look Jake, you know what your mother would say."

"Sure. You can't spend the night in a bar."

"But we can play in the back bar," Belle said. "Marion doesn't open that up till your show starts anyway."

"But the bar *does* open when I start. If it didn't, I'd be lip-synching to an empty room."

"But we'd be playing *before* you opened. It'll draw folks in. You'll start with a warmed-up crowd instead of guys just trickling in."

"What do you lip-synch?" Beau asked.

"Streisand mostly, some Diana Ross. And a Julie Andrews, but let's stay on topic. The Corners is just an old barn, even if Marion has divided it up for, let us say, geopolitical reasons. It's one building."

"So's the VFW," Frank said. "We've played there plenty of times. The bar's upstairs, the dance hall downstairs."

"And your folks are okay with that?"

Frank shrugged. "As long as I bring home the take."

"Beau?"

"My folks have even come watched a couple of times."

"I know your situation, Belle."

"Which leaves me," Jake said. "I know you and Aunt Margaret had a falling out over me, but you and Mom were always close."

"At one time. It's been years."

"I think she'd be fine with this, so long as she knew you were here. She'd be okay with this place."

Anderson looked around. "She might at that. It wouldn't be the first time." He shook his head. "Okay, I'll speak to Marion."

"Yay!" Belle's yell turned heads at the bar.

Anderson raised a finger. "But your set ends *before* the bar opens, got it?"

Belle grinned. "We'll have it all broken down and stowed away before they pour the first shot."

"What's your band's name, anyway?"

"The Quirks," Beau chirped.

Anderson nodded. "Figures."

"Mr. Anderson, Sister, um—"

"Just Sammy, Beau."

"Sure. Sammy. Once we're done and everything . . ."

"Yes?"

"Can we stay and watch?"

Jake and Joanie had a lot of catching up to do. "You won't believe it," she said over the phone.

"Neither will you."

They agreed to meet at Herman's, but when they got there, a sign read, "Closed For Remodeling."

"Maybe they're finally going to add an indoor bathroom," Joanie said. "I mean an *indoor* indoor bathroom. Not just some tacked-on shed."

"It won't have the same cachet."

"We can hope."

They sat at one of the outdoor picnic tables, the wind scooting catalpa and sycamore leaves around their legs and making Joanie's hair fly up. "You first," she said.

"We got the gig at The Corners."

She raised her eyebrows. "And Virginia?"

"It'll be okay. Mr. Anderson will pitch it to Susan and she'll okay it with Virginia. And he'll be there with us the entire time."

"Wow, he's really going to bat for you guys."

"Actually, we're doing him a favor. We bring in the

crowd just before he starts his act." He grinned. "He's the star of their Friday night show. He's a drag queen."

"A what now?

"He dresses up in women's outfits and does jokes and sings. He's a big hit."

"And people pay for that?"

"There's a cover charge. His best bit is Sister Many Agonies. He puts on a nun's outfit and cracks jokes about the Catholic church."

"I'm not sure what Virginia would think of that."

"You mean you're not sure what *you* think of it."

"Oh no, I'm pretty sure what I think. But it's none of my business. The Corners has always been kind of a free-for-all." She looked at him sideways. "Is that something you'd do?"

"Naw. But it's fun to watch. And Beau is enchanted. It's like he's found a home. At least on Fridays."

"Personally, I wouldn't be caught dead at The Corners *any* night. But, like you said, 'There's got to be a place for everyone.' I suppose that applies even in Oklahoma." She cocked her head. "So, how'd Mr. Anderson do in Norman?"

"Oh. Not so good. The archive was a microfiche of a Xerox copy. He could make out most of the words, but the pictures were all blurry and useless. He couldn't see any details."

"Well, we have plenty of details here. We have the originals."

Jake frowned. "I thought all the articles and photos were missing."

"Who needs articles and photos when you've got the real thing? The Jamesons have the original tornado panel, and it's in great shape. And I think I know who has the soldiers' panel."

"Who?"

"Mr. Tucker's uncle, the one who lives in Pesogi."

"Uncle Crazy Head?"

"You aren't supposed to call him that."

"But that's cool! That's two out of three."

"Two out of three what?" a figure behind them said. They turned, then leaped up and hugged him.

"Randy!" Jake cried.

"I knew you'd come!" Joanie said.

Jake pulled back. "What?"

"I knew you wouldn't write him, so I did."

"But you said you wouldn't!"

"No, you said *you* wouldn't."

"Yep," said Randy. "It's good to be back."

The angry man was angry. It had been going on for several minutes now. Listening ears didn't have to strain to hear.

"I followed my boy out there to see what sort of place it was. It's sick! I saw it with my own eyes."

"Can you say which side of the tavern you were in, sir?" the deputy on desk asked.

"What do you mean?"

"Was it the front bar or the back bar?"

"What the hell difference does that make?"

"It's a slick deal they got out there. Two bars, front and back. Straddles the county line. We come in the front door, everybody scoots to the one in back. Conlan County boys come in the back, everybody scoots to the front. It's like trying to catch a greased pig."

The man snarled. "I tell Percy Owen I've got a man out at my farm making threats, and he says it's a county thing. Talk to the sheriff. I talk to you boys, even tell you where to find the faggot, and you hem and haw and make excuses. You're both a bunch of useless peckerwoods."

"Is there anything else we can do for you today, Mr. Pellegrini?"

"I doubt it, but there's some in this town as will. There's some in this town who fear God and respect a man's right to protect his family. The rest of you can go to hell."

The door slammed.

"And a good day to you, too, you fucking wop."

All this was duly noted by *Bucky Firestorm and All His Friends*. They heard the deputy muttering as he left the dispatch room.

"What's a wop?" whispered Rafe, lying across the rafters above the dropped ceiling.

"I think it's a kind of dago," Kyle whispered back. "They should do a coordinated raid. Our guys from one side, Conlan County from the other. Bam!"

"But why?"

"You heard him. They're doing drag races."

Rafe nodded. "Like that movie on TV? Where they go over a cliff? I'd like to see that."

"Me too."

End of an Era

The Quirks finished their first set at The Corners and took a five-minute break. Jake sought out Randy in the crowd. He was leaning against a wall, foot propped behind him, nursing a bottle from the front bar.

"How was it? How'd we sound?"

"Buford, if you can get cowboys to dance, you must be doing somethin' right."

Jake looked around. There were couples, mostly men but some women, and sets of three or four scattered around. The easy way they touched each other and laughed made him giddy. "So, none of this bothers you?"

"I'd be bothered if it *did* bother me."

"Can you believe the way some of these guys dance? It's like two egg beaters mating."

"Well now, that's a picture." Randy put his beer on the rail behind him. "I gotta go."

"You should stay. You haven't heard Frank on 'House of the Rising Sun' yet."

"If I have another beer, my kidneys'll burst."

"So stop buying."

"Who says I'm buying?" He hitched his belt. "Anyways, I wanna check on Virginia. Bobbie's gonna pull some strings and sneak me in."

"She's looking good, don't you think?"

Randy's eyes shifted away. "Sure. Hey, tell the rest of the band they're great. And who knew Belle could sing?" He disappeared into the cigarette smoke of the front bar, turning heads as he passed.

Jake laughed. *Shoot. He's not going to hear my song. Maybe I'll play it for him later*. He looked around. *Where's Frank?*

Frank saw Jim Newton staring at him from a corner of the bar during their first set. He didn't look in that direction the rest of the evening. As they were breaking down at eleven, he looked around but didn't see Jim anywhere.

He was waiting for him out by his truck.

"You sound good."

"Thanks." He loaded his guitars into the cab and strapped his amp in the back. He didn't look up or say anything.

"You doing okay?" Jim asked.

"You got any right to know?"

Jim was quiet a while.

"Nope." He was silent a bit longer. "See you around." He walked way.

When he was sure Jim was out of earshot, he slammed his hand against the hood. He hated the feeling he had inside. He hated that burning knot of hope.

Belle looked up sharply at the metallic sound of someone slapping a car hood, but she couldn't make out anything in the unlit parking lot. She was responsible for depositing the band's check each night so it could be divvied up once it cleared. But this was the first time there'd been a tip jar. She counted the cash in disbelief. It was almost twice Marion's check. She had a vision of herself flying down the highway, hair wild to the wind, the Mexican border a mile ahead. *Shit girl, that's one crazy-ass dream*. But the band was booked for next Friday, too. That would be a week before Christmas. The place would be packed. "Bigger tips," she told herself. *Bigger dreams* whispered a voice inside. She screwed the jar shut. "Where the hell is Beau?" she demanded of the night.

Beau was with Mr. Anderson—Sammy—hanging out in the converted closet he used as a dressing room. The big man took up a lot of space but seemed perfectly at ease sharing it with him. While Sammy transitioned into Sister Many Agonies, they chatted about the crowd and how the band had played, but that wasn't really the point of his being here. He was finally getting to meet his real family.

"That's a nice camisole you've got on," Sammy said.

Beau grinned. "You can't even see it."

"I can see it in the way you carry yourself." Sammy smiled at him. "You know, it's safe in here. And it's safe out there." He nodded at the noise from the bar. "But only on Friday nights."

"I know."

"I wouldn't want you to get caught out."

Beau shrugged. "That's already happened."

"And?"

Beau looked at the floor.

"I'm so sorry, sweetie," Sammy said. "It happened to me, too. Cops raided a bar where I was performing. Cost me my job, my home, some of my friends. Most of them, actually."

Beau looked up. "But you're back."

"I am indeed." Sammy pulled his hair taut with a band and examined the effect in the mirror. "Who knows for how long? But you build a home here, you build a home there, pretty soon you know how to build one anywhere." He turned to him. "But it takes time. And caution. Especially out there, you know what I mean? The *real* out there."

"I know."

"I'm not saying anything about your folks. They seem really nice. Lovely people."

"You've met them?"

"Oh, sweetie, I talked to all your folks before agreeing to let you perform out here. And you're folks are real gems." He turned back to the mirror.

Beau knew an artful pause when he heard it. "But?"

Sammy put down his Max Factor. "But they'll never get it. They'll love you and support you and say they understand you, but they'll never get *it*. They'll never have to consciously choose who they are. They're born and society says, 'It's a boy!' or 'It's a girl!' And they're done. It fits. For us—it doesn't fit."

"I used to think I don't belong anywhere," Beau said. "I didn't fit the labels. But that's not it, is it? The labels don't fit me."

Sammy nodded. "The world is full of them, full of lines and labels separating people. Black, white, straight, gay, Communist, American. But they aren't real. We made them up. Once you realize that, the world has no boundaries. For some people, that's freedom. For others, it's terrifying."

"What's it for you?"

Sammy picked up his pancake. "For me, it's the work. Once you know who you are, once you make your choice—when you realize you *can* make a choice—your just keep on choosing. It's not a one-step process. You keep on, and then the work," he regarded himself in the mirror, "becomes a dance." He turned to face him. "It's a tricky dance, being yourself and being careful at the same time. But you'll find it, your rhythm, your place, your home." He rolled his eyes at the dingy walls. "But probably not this place. What a dump."

Beau shrugged. "Probably not any place."

"Don't give up, Beau. There is a home for you even if you have to build it yourself."

"Thanks, but what I meant was, it's not likely to be some *place*. It's likely to be some *one*."

Sammy patted his knee. "You're way ahead of me."

Randy sat beside his mother's bed and watched her breathe. Her eyes flicked back and forth beneath the lids. Her hair was pushed to one side.

The loose feeling the beers gave him began to wear off and he started seeing the room, the machines, and his mother's face with more clarity than he liked. He left and went to the Claremont and ordered a beer and stared at it.

"Well, if it isn't Croy's prodigal millionaire," a young woman said, taking the stool beside him.

He looked up and smiled. "Candy. It was never a million. And if you remember, Mr. Prodigal returns broke and worn out."

"Well, I hope it was fun."

"It was a learning experience."

"Sounds dreadful." She took out a cigarette but didn't wait for him to light it. "Sorry about your mom."

"Thanks."

"How is she?"

He looked around. "Let's take a booth. Can I get you a drink?"

"I'll get it."

She joined him with a Coors and a glass. "It's like homecoming. Everybody's coming back."

"Oh? Who else?"

"Red Conner. And Del Longacre, though he's coming home in a box."

"The hell."

"Maybe two. They say he was blown clean in half saving somebody's life over there. The VFW is going to throw him a to-do, and Red's going to speak."

Randy shook his head. "Red. Did you know we had a bet once that I could get a date with you?"

"Just a date?"

He smiled and picked at the label on his beer.

"You are a pair of assholes."

"No argument there. It was stupid, even if I did end up with the girl."

"You didn't end up with the girl. You and the girl ended up in the same room, that's all. So, did you ever collect?"

"No. I never told him."

"You tell anyone?"

"I told Jake. I didn't have to tell Joanie."

"She's one sharp cookie." She took a drag on her cigarette. "I don't like her, but I admire a girl who knows what she's after. She's really onto something with this sculpture thing. It gets my parents' panties in a twist, so kudos for that."

"What's that all about?"

"You haven't heard?"

"I've only been in town a couple of days."

"Well, you know the Memorial Library?" He raised his eyebrows. "Oh shit, of course you do. Well, the town paid for a sculpture out front, only it was never made, but then it was, and now Joanie, bless her heart, is trying to drum up support to have it installed."

"How's that related to your parents' panties?"

"It's supposed to be obscene. Or something. My folks don't really care. They're just jumping on the Reverend Mathers bandwagon. The Committee of Like-Minded Saints said they'd boycott any business that supports it. So, it's all letters to the editor and pickets and speechifying. I wish I could call it hypocrisy, but it's not even that. They don't really believe the Devil's at work in Croy. Mathers just says that because his damned ego cathedral is losing money hand over fist. But he's found a rich pond of cash, and he's gonna keep pumping till he sucks it dry. Makes good business sense." She took a drink. "Sorry. Got wound up there. Back to your little bet with Red. Did I ever tell you why we ended up together that night?"

"I guessed. To get back at your dad for showing you off like that."

"Sharp cookies all around."

"Not back then. Back then I was about as sharp as a wet noodle. Took me a while to put it together."

"Your noodle was okay, as I recall. Anyway, my little scheme backfired. My mother put me on the pill. Can you believe it? What a great Catholic she turned out to be."

"We weren't such great Catholics either."

She looked at him steadily. "I used you to get back at them. Sorry."

He shook his head. "I was livin' the dream. Also, kinda drunk most of the time."

"I noticed. What changed?"

"Lubbock. Death and destruction. My dad."

"I'm just gonna sit here and wait for you to unwind all that." She tapped her cigarette in the ashtray and waited.

"I must have still been plastered when I agreed to go down to Lubbock and help those folks. But all the varsity jocks were going, so why the hell not? It was different once we got there. The stench alone. And then my dad shows up, head of the rebuilding crew I was on."

"Wait. Your dad? But he was wanted or something, wasn't he?"

"Escaped felon. Broke out of McLeod Correctional."

"By himself?"

A smile tipped his lips.

"Sweet Mother of Jesus, who were you back then? All I got was this kinda sweet, kinda dumb, sorta hot stud."

"Well, thanks for throwing in 'stud' there at the end."

"I don't remember you being this interesting."

"I don't remember you being this hard."

She narrowed her eyes at him a moment, then her face relaxed. "I've had to make some hard decisions. Right ones, but hard. Worth it. Jesus, I sound like my parents. All calculations and bottom line. They wanted me to marry you, you know."

"Well, that's just crazy."

"Gee, thanks."

"No, I mean—aside from the sex, what did we have in common?"

She shrugged. "You were rich and Catholic. That was enough for them. And our kids would've looked terrific."

"Well, thank God there's none of that. What a mess that would have been."

"Think of it. I'd have married you. We'd have had a kid."

"Or two."

"Yeah, right. Then Harry would have been captured and you would have been arrested."

"And out of cash."

"And in jail." She smiled wistfully. "Oh, that would have been sweet. But not worth it."

He raised his bottle. "Here's to not worth it."

She raised her glass. "Amen."

He went back to the hospital the next day, nursing a hangover. Virginia smiled like she'd just awoken from a good dream. She waved one of her IV lines. "You look like you could use some of this."

"Does it kill the pain?"

"No. It just sets it in a corner. Where you can keep an eye on it without it bothering you." She tilted her head. "What was the occasion?"

"Candy."

"Oh." She reached for her bedside table, then laughed. "Damn. I still do that. How are the kids?"

"Who?"

"Joanie? Jake?"

"Oh. Joanie's on a tear because the O.S.U. people said they can't use her notes because the Memorial Library isn't a Carnegie."

"I coulda told her that. They turned Lerner down flat. Not Carnegie, some other outfit. Said it was too elaborate. Too ambitious for a town the size of Croy. He'd turn purple every time he mentioned it."

"So now she's bugging Coach Tucker for Sunny Sohi's address so she can talk to him."

"You know, I don't really give a damn about that memorial."

"What?"

"Really. I just told Jake and Joanie to go looking for it to give them something to do. I didn't want them moping around here all day. And I thought, if the two of them spent more time together, maybe—" She shrugged.

"Mom, Jake's not going to change."

"How do you know? It's possible. Harry did."

"What? Is this the drugs talking?"

"I just thought, years from now . . . But that's a stupid thought, isn't it? Years from now. Who's got time for that?"

"Mom, that's a helluva lot to take in."

"And the band—what is it, the Kinks?"

"The Quirks. What you said about Dad—"

"Was Sam Anderson watching the whole time? I told him to, but I don't know about him." She rubbed her forehead, eyes screwed tight.

"I wasn't there all night."

"Didn't you stay to make sure?"

"I had drinks with Candy at the Claremont."

"Oh, yeah. You said."

"And I came here. To see you."

She frowned. "I don't remember that. Damned morphine."

"No, you were asleep. I think you were dreaming."

"Oh yeah? You know, I think I do remember."

"You remember me being here?"

"No, the dream." She looked across the room at something. He turned to see it, but there was nothing there.

"You ever been to San Francisco?"

"No, Mom. Nothing west of Denver, and we only drove through it." He winced. *Best she not know I was traveling with Pop.*

But she was lost in her recollection "Harry and I went once. It's just the strangest place. When was that? It couldn't have been our honeymoon. We didn't have one."

"You never told me this."

"Or did we? I guess it doesn't matter. You know, they have streets there that aren't streets at all. They're just stairs."

"That's crazy."

"Stairs that go right up a hill where a street should be. Only no street *can* be, on account it's so steep. So they put stairs instead. It's the strangest thing. You should go sometime. It's quite the sight."

Her eyes were fixed on the distance. Randy looked around. *Should I call a nurse?*

"Anyways, I dreamed I was there again. And Harry was with me. And then he wasn't. And I was at the top of one of those streets that's nothing but stairs. And it was dark and cold and wet. It gets that way. The fog goes right through to your bones. It hurts."

She was quiet a while. She was so still he wondered if she was falling asleep with her eyes open. She took a sharp breath.

"I was on top of a hill. And there were these narrow stairs going down. All gray. I could see all the way down. And there was no one down there. It scared me."

"Mom, are you okay?"

She shook her head, smiling. "But then the sun came up over the bay. I turned my face and it warmed me right up. It was beautiful, the light on the bay. Have you ever seen sunrise in San Francisco? Oh, of course not. Stupid Ginny."

"Don't say that."

"But the thing of it was, when I looked around, the stairs weren't dark anymore. And they weren't narrow, either. They were wide and golden-colored. From the sun, I guess. And there were people on them. Not many, but some. Nicely dressed, too. Coming up and going down. And I thought, *I wonder what's down there, down these beautiful stairs?* And I was kinda looking forward to it." She turned and looked at him. "I'm sorry, kiddo."

"Sorry? About what?"

"I'm not getting out of here."

"Of course you are. They're doing the surgery as soon as they can. And then you'll get better, and then you'll come home."

She shook her head. She pulled down the top of her gown, showing the start of a long scar and stitches. "They already know. They opened me up and took a look. There's nothing they can do."

Christmas Lights

Frank woke with cold air blowing across his face. Angela was standing in the open door to the shed, her arms crossed. "Chrissakes Angie, were you born in a barn? Close the door."

"At least I don't live in one."

"Come in or go away." He emerged from double blankets fully dressed. Cold penetrated his socks the minute he touched the floor.

Angela stuck her head in and sniffed. "It stinks in here."

He nodded toward the house. "It stinks in there, too." He plugged in the hot plate and started a pot of water for coffee. "Have you moved into my bedroom yet? There should be a nice view from that window of all the land that won't be ours soon."

"Daddy's gone to town."

"What's that to me?"

"Mom says there's hot breakfast in the kitchen if you want."

"The usual mush?" He shook his head.

Angela glared at him.

"What?" he said.

"I hate you."

"Get in line."

"Come back. Mom needs you." She ran off, leaving the door open.

Angela wasn't in the kitchen when he entered. A steaming bowl sat with a knife and spoon on one side, a fork and napkin on the other. There was a glass of milk and a glass of orange juice and a cup for coffee. The napkin had holly leaves and berries on it. It looked like a place setting from Randall's Diner.

"There's bacon, too, if you'd like," his mother said, facing the stove. Its salty-sweet smell filled the room.

"Yes ma'am, thank you, I would." The mush was better than he remembered. His bones relaxed.

Arlene poked strips of bacon around the skillet with a wooden fork, warming them up. She shook her head. "Ma'am. Is that what I am to you now? Ma'am?"

"I'm just tryin' to walk a respectful line here."

"And that's all I get? Respect?"

"Mom—"

She turned and slid the bacon onto his plate. "I expect more from you. I deserve more."

"You deserve better."

She shook her head. "I'm not divorcing him. I couldn't bear the humiliation."

"He humiliates you every day. In front of me, in front of Angie."

"He's my husband."

"I'm real sorry about that, Mom, but there's nothin' I can do." He wrapped the bacon in his napkin and rose. "I need to catch up on things before there's a hard freeze. Thanks for breakfast."

Joanie put her hand to her mouth. "No!"

"Are you sure?" Jake said. "She's looking much better."

Randy shook his head. "No, she isn't. You guys can't see it. You've been here all along. I saw it the minute I got back."

"She can't give up."

"She's not giving up. She's fighting. But she's got less and less to fight with."

Joanie hit him. "Don't say that!"

Jake looked around the Edoms' kitchen. He had spent so many hours here, listening to Virginia's stories, sharing laughs, learning to like coffee. "It can't just end. People don't just end."

"She won't." Joanie wiped her face with her palm. "There's Ada's Memorial. We can do that for her."

Randy shook his head. "I think you should give up on that."

"What? No. We're so close."

Jake took her hand. "Joanie."

"Oh, don't look at me that way, you two! It's what she asked for. It's what we promised."

"There's no money, Joanie. Even if we found it all, where would it go? How would we pay for it?"

"You have money. You have that bequest or trust fund or whatever the heck it is."

"I'm going to need that for the hospital," Randy said. "Mom doesn't have insurance."

Jake felt sick. "Shit."

"And not just the hospital. She hasn't paid her taxes. And I got to the gas and electric just in time, or we'd be sitting here in the cold and dark." Randy rubbed his mouth. "Jake, you've been through this before with your grandfather. I'm gonna need help."

"Sure, sure."

"I can help, too," Joanie said.

"Great. Can you contact Dunbar's? I've got to make arrangements."

Joanie stood. "No. It's too soon."

"The doctors said—"

"I don't care what the doctors said. She just needs a boost, something to live for. I'm not giving up." She left, shaking her head and muttering.

"I should go after her," Jake said.

"Leave her be. She has her own way of facing things."

Jake shook his head. "I don't think she can face this. I don't think *I* can."

"We don't have a choice." Randy leaned forward, cradling his head. "Why the hell did I go away? What the hell was I thinking? I should have been here. I could have seen what was happening. I could have stopped it."

Jake put an arm around his shoulder. He wanted to be there for Randy. He wanted to be his support. Instead, he felt miles away and completely alone. *I can't do this again.* He wanted someone to wrap their arms around him, comfort him, make it go away. He wanted Frank.

Joanie hated the Christmas lights at the Rexall. They blinked cheerily as if the world weren't coming to an end. The store was packed with short-tempered customers and cheerful customers and customers who couldn't make up their minds. She hated them all.

Her parents were no help. Her mother just shook her head. "Just like poor Amelia Jacobs," she said sadly. Her father refused to take her suspicions of a cancer cluster seriously. She had to sneak in her call to Sunny Sohi using the store phone or risk being blocked at home. She would figure out how to explain the charges later.

"Mr. Sohi?" she said, simultaneously ringing up Mrs. Armbruster's five boxes of Christmas cards.

"Yes? Who's calling please?"

"You don't know me, but I'm Joan Tibbits, from Croy, Oklahoma. I'm doing a series of articles for *The Croy Evening Call* on our local landmarks, and I was wondering if you could give me any information on the figures you created for the Memorial Library here." She mouthed "Thank you" to Mrs. Armbruster, who gave her a funny scowl and walked away.

There was silence on the other end.

"Mr. Sohi?"

"Joan Tibbits? From Croy?"

"Yes sir. I'm a reporter for *The Croy*—"

"Related to John Tibbits?"

"Yes sir. He's my father." She bit her tongue. *That's not what a real reporter would say!*

"Well, I'll be damned."

"There's great interest in having the panels restored."

"They're gone."

"That's what everyone thought, but we've located two of them."

Mr. Sohi muttered something away from the phone, something like "mucking Jedediah," only Mr. Sohi didn't say "mucking." In full voice, he said, "Look, this is all ancient history. Why would anyone still care?"

"There are plenty of people in town who remember it, Mr. Sohi. My father, for one. And . . ." How was she to refer to Mr. Tucker's uncle? ". . . and Virginia Edom."

"Ginny? Ginny Alquist? How is she?"

She swallowed. "She's not well, I'm sorry to say. There's a movement afoot to try to install the panels before she— While there's still a chance she could see them." She felt dirty, playing a card like that, but if it got him to talk . . .

"I'm sorry. I can't help. Goodbye."

"No! Mr. Sohi, please don't hang up."

"I'm not part of that world. They gave up on it, I gave up on them. That's it. That's the end of your story."

Kyle burst into the store and ran up to the counter. "Joanie! Joanie! You gotta help!"

She covered the mouthpiece. "Not now!"

"But—"

"Mr. Sohi, the library board is meeting next week to finalize plans. They're hoping you can help."

"How?"

"You could tell us where to find the third panel. The middle one. The Goddess of Prosperity."

"I never knew. I never wanted to know."

"Joanie!"

She glared Kyle into silence. "But do you have any drawings of what it looked like? Or details how to install it on the library?"

"That was Harry's department. And he had his doubts. Look, it sounds like you've got your hands full over there. I'm sorry, Miss Tibbits, but there's nothing more to say."

The line went dead.

She turned to her brother ready to blast him for ruining her best lead, but she saw tears running down his cheeks. "What's wrong, Bean?"

"It wasn't my fault. He slipped."

"Who?" He was trembling. She came around the counter and held him. "Shh. It's all right."

"They're going to do it, just like I said they would. Rafe wouldn't believe me, so I took him up there."

"Up where? They're going to do what? You're not making sense."

"Can you take me to the hospital? That's where they'd take him, isn't it?"

"Who?"

"Rafe. He fell through the ceiling at the sheriff's office. He's going to be all right, isn't he?"

"Daddy!" she called over her shoulder. "Call the Hamiltons! Something's wrong with Rafe." She got into her coat. "Where is he, Kyle?"

"The sheriff's office."

"What?" her father said. People in the store were staring.

"Something's gone wrong at the sheriff's office, something to do with Rafe." She pulled her brother with her out the door, bending over him. "Tell me on the way."

Lorenzo Pellegrini stood against the wall beside the Christmas tree in The Corners' front bar. He could see through its scrawny branches to the back bar where his stepson's band was making a noise like Hell's accordion. They wore shirts with frilly fronts and purple pants. He crushed his cigarette on the floor in disgust.

The band was up against the back wall on a raised platform by the entrance to the kitchen. Some of the boys would come in that way when they got his signal. The rest would come in the front. This freak show would end tonight.

He could have called them when he saw men dancing together, but he wanted to catch Frank at something. So far no one had served the boy liquor or even come up and said anything except that interfering bastard Newton. He was hoping the queer would make a move on him, but Frank had ignored him.

Dancing faeries weren't enough. He would catch Newton and Frank both. Then Arlene would see he was right. He lit a cigarette and thought about ordering another beer. He could wait all night if he had to.

They finished the last set and packed up their guitars. Jake started taking down the mikes and coiling the cords. Beau came up, all smiles. "Sammy's going to show me how to tuck!"

"Great. But help me out with the equipment first, huh?"

Belle tugged his arm. "Let's get the tip jar and drums out to my truck."

"Just a sec."

"I wanna get out of here."

She seemed agitated. "What's up?"

"There's a weird vibe here tonight. Can't you feel it?"

He looked around. Beau was talking to Sammy, Jim was talking to Frank.

"I liked the outfits last week better," Jim was saying.

"You shoulda seen me in chaps," Frank said. "I'd a worn them tonight but some asshole took 'em."

Jim walked off, his face tight.

"We're tired, is all," Jake said.

"Frank?" Sammy called. "Come with Beau and me."

"I gotta stow my gear."

"That wasn't an invitation, sweetie. Come." Beau and Frank followed Sammy to his dressing room.

"Oh Christ," Belle said. "Now we'll never get outta here."

"Come on," Jake said, picking up Frank's amp and Belle's bass pedal. "Let's get started."

All the Christmas lights in the bar were red—the ones in the tree, in the garlands, over the entrance, wrapped around the bottles behind the bar. Jake laughed.

"What?" Belle snapped.

"It's more cathouse-y than Christmas-y."

Belle shook her head. "Where's Marion?"

He was on the pay phone next to the main bar.

"We're packing up, Mr. Bowles," she said. "Can we have our check, please?"

He waved them away and spoke loudly into the phone, "This is a bar, miss, not an answering service."

"Screw it," Belle said and headed for the door.

When they finished stowing her drums, she said, "I'm not going back in there."

"Aw jeez, Belle, there's the mike stands and the rest of the amps and—"

"We got over three hundred dollars from the tip jar. That's in cash. I want to drop it in the night deposit tonight."

"I'm parked right by the back door. It won't take but a second."

"I'm not leaving the money out here in the truck and I'm not going back in there with it stuffed in my pockets. We can come back for the check tomorrow."

"Fine. I'll do the rest myself."

"And tell Beau to get his ass out here. I'm not standing out here in the dark for half an hour like last time."

"Sure, sure." He made his way back through the bar, his mood spoiled. *They still think of me as their roadie. I'm as much part of the band as anyone. Things have got to change.* As he gathered the rest of the equipment, he heard two men arguing, but the argument in his head was louder.

"Are you going to show Frank how to tuck, too?" Beau asked. Frank felt boxed in by the tiny dressing room. Sammy eyed him up and down. It made him squirm. "That would be a task of epic proportions, but no. Frank, I called you in here to say something I didn't want Jim to hear. He wouldn't want me to say it."

"So don't say it."

Sammy sat down at a tiny table with a mirror propped against the wall. It didn't make the room any less cramped. "I know there's history between you, and that's none of my business."

"Damned straight."

"But there's something you need to know about Jim Newton."

"He can't keep his promises. That's all I need to know."

"Did he make a promise? Because that would be news."

Frank looked away.

"I've known Jim for more years than either of us like to admit. And he's got his shortcomings."

Frank laughed. "Is that what you call it? Is that what you call it when people say they care about you, say they'll look out for you, and then cut and run? He knew what my grand-dad was plannin'. He saw it comin' and left. He's a coward."

Sammy colored. "Jim may be many things, but he's not that. You'll never pin him down to one place or one person—or, hell, even one sex. He's basically a screwing machine. But once you're his friend, you're his friend for life. And he'll always, *always* have your back."

"Unless he's not there."

"But that's just it, sweetie. He *is* there. He came back for you. Can't you see that?"

Frank clenched his jaw. "You done?"

Sammy sighed and shook his head.

Beau turned to the door. "What's all that yelling?"

"Christmas at The Corners. It's always a riot. I'm not wise, Frank. I'm just old. And I'm telling you, you can't afford to throw friends away. No one can."

"I need some air. There's too much bullshit in here."

He stepped back into the bar. There was a commotion by the tree. He started toward the stage to help Jake when he saw his stepfather and Jim facing off.

"I saw those boys go in that back room," Lorenzo sneered. "I know what goes on in there."

"You're in the wrong bar, mister."

"Is that how you get your kicks? Fuck up a kid and then sell him off to some fat fairy?"

Frank pushed through the gathering crowd.

"I've had it with assholes like you," he heard Jim say. He cleared the ring of bystanders in time to see his stepfather flick his cigarette toward the tree. He knew it was a feint, a trick. "Jim, he's got a knife!" he yelled as Lorenzo whipped it from his back pocket.

His stepfather whirled around, slashing out with the switchblade, slicing Frank at the shoulder. He fell to the floor as Jim leaped, pulling Lorenzo's arm away before he could strike again. They both went down. The crowd cheered.

The tree burst into flames.

Beau and Sammy came running from the dressing room as the tree roared to life. "Christ!" People where running everywhere. Frank was on the floor, bleeding. The crowd surged toward the kitchen, knocking over mike stands and tripping over amps. "Jake!" Sammy yelled.

Beau fought against the crowd to get to Frank. Smoke billowed across the ceiling in waves. He could barely see, but he heard Frank's screams and groped until he felt his shirt. He pulled him to his feet. "This way!" he yelled, and they lurched through a door.

Jake was unconscious, knocked over and trampled by the panicked crowd. Sammy scooped him up and looked around. A clot of people jammed the entrance to the kitchen. The only way out was through the front bar, past the blazing tree. He nearly collided with a couple as he ran, crouching, tucking Jake under him as he dove through the flaming archway.

Belle saw people running out the door before she realized what was going on. There was yelling and car engines starting and horns blaring. Spinning wheels threw up clouds of dust. Smoke poured from the front of the bar as she ran toward it.

Mr. Anderson came out, dragging Jake. His shirt was smoking. She pulled them back to her truck, where they collapsed. Jake coughed and sputtered to life. "Where's Beau?" she yelled over the noise.

Jake's eyes went wide. "Frank!"

"Shit!" Mr. Anderson looked around. "You kids get out of here before the cops show up." He ran back into the building. Jake tried to follow him but fell in a heap, coughing.

"Stay here!" Belle screamed. "Stay here! I'll sit on you if I have to."

Flames churned through the windows.

Jim had seen Beau and Frank run into the men's room. He kicked himself free of Lorenzo and chased after them, slamming the door shut to cut off the smoke.

"Where are we?" Frank cried out. "Where are we?" He held his bleeding arm to his side.

Beau looked at Jim. "This isn't the kitchen. There's no door and the window's stuck."

Jim grabbed a metal waste can and battered the transom until the glass gave way. "Up!" he yelled. He grabbed Beau and hoisted him up and pushed him through.

"What's happening?" cried Frank.

He grabbed him as well and boosted him up. But Frank grabbed the window frame and turned around.

"Jim! Come with us!"

"Fuck it!" Jim punched him in the face and pushed him through. The door blew open behind him and he fell to the floor.

"Oh thank God. Oh thank God," Belle said over and over as Beau and Frank stumbled around the corner of the building. Sirens approached from the distance and more cars seemed to be coming than going.

"We have to go back," Frank said. "We have to go back. Jim's in there."

"Did you see Mr. Anderson?" Jake yelled. "Beau, where's Sammy?"

Beau raised his voice above the roar of the fire. "Everybody calm down. We have to leave."

"No!" Frank said.

"Belle, you take Jake in your truck. I'll follow in Frank's."

"You can't drive."

"I'll follow real close. Guys, we gotta move. It's getting too hot."

The building was fully engulfed.

"The mikes," Jake said. "The amps."

"Belle! Take Jake."

She grabbed him then hesitated. "Take him where?"

"His place. We gotta get Frank patched up. Let's go. Now!"

Frank was sobbing.

"Frank." Beau moved Frank's hand to the slash on his shoulder. "Frank! Listen to me. You've got to press down on that wound. Do you hear me? We're going to get you help." Frank continued sobbing. Beau guided him into the cab of his truck and got behind the wheel. Belle pulled out ahead of him. He could barely see her taillights. "Fucking glasses," he said and ripped them from his face.

They stumbled through the door of the granny house. "Have you got a first aid kit?" Beau asked.

"Why's his nose bleeding?" Belle asked.

"I don't know," Jake said, "I don't think so."

"Mrs. Oldfield, then. Belle, get me a wet towel. Frank, can you take off your shirt?"

"No, not her." Jake reached for the phone.

"He's dead, isn't he?" Frank said. "He's dead."

"Belle, please?" She handed Beau the towel. "Lie back, Frank." He gently pulled Frank's shirt off and laid the towel on his forehead. "Put something under his feet."

"Joanie? Come over, quick. Something bad's happened. Bring a first aid kit."

"And bandages," Beau said. "Maybe big ones."

But Jake had already hung up. "Should I call back?"

"Oh good lord!" Mrs. Oldfield exclaimed from the doorway.

"Mrs. Oldfield, thank goodness you're here," Belle said. "There's been an accident and Frank needs bandages. And maybe some Mercurochrome. Do you have any?"

"Certainly. What kind of accident? Why do you all smell of smoke?"

"It would be a great help."

"I'll call the doctor."

"There's one on the way. Can you get us the bandages, please? Frank's cut his arm." Belle hustled her out and closed the door. She turned around. "What the fuck are we going to tell her?"

"Just what you said," Beau said. "It was an accident."

"It warn't no accident," Frank said. "He did it deliberately. I saw him."

"Did either of you see Sammy when you got out?" Jake asked. "Did anyone see Mr. Anderson?"

Beau shook his head.

"The last we saw, he went back for you guys," Belle said.

They were quiet. A siren cut off abruptly in the distance.

Tires scrunched to a hasty stop outside and Joanie bustled in. "I've got rubbing alcohol and bandages and ointment. What's going on?"

"There was a fire at The Corners," Jake said.

Frank sat up. Blood oozed from his arm. "They're all dead."

"Let me look at that," Joanie said. She knelt beside him. "Not too bad. I've seen worse tonight. We wash it, sterilize it, and wrap it. I don't think it needs stitches. What happened to your nose?"

Mrs. Oldfield arrived at the door but could barely squeeze in. "Is the doctor here yet?"

"I don't think one is needed, Mrs. Oldfield," Joanie said. "It's not as bad as it looks."

She set her lips. "So, you didn't call one after all." She looked them each in the eye. "You will tell me what is going on. You will tell me now or I will have each of your parents on the line before you can say Jack Robinson."

"There was a raid out at The Corners," Joanie said, "while the band was playing."

Jake looked at her, mouth open.

"I tried to warn you," she told him. "The guy on the phone wouldn't listen."

"And there was a tussle," Belle said.

"And the tree caught fire," Beau said.

"The whole place went up," Jake said.

"It was planned," Frank said. "They did it on purpose."

"Frank's in shock, a little," Beau said.

Mrs. Oldfield shook her head. "It's a miracle none of you were killed. Virginia was a fool to let you perform out there. Let me look at that." She inspected Joanie's bandaging. "Well, that should hold up. Is anyone else hurt?"

Jake's head throbbed and he was becoming aware of an ache in his ankle, but he shook his head. The other kids all mumbled they were fine.

"We can thank the good Lord for that," Mrs. Oldfield said. "The county's well rid of that hellhole." She smoothed out her bathrobe. "Now all y'all go on home. Your parents must be worried sick."

"I'm staying," Beau said.

"That's actually a good idea," Joanie said. "Your parents have their hands full tonight."

"What now?"

"Rafe broke his leg. I'll explain later." She turned to Mrs. Oldfield. "I'll tell them he's staying over with Jake."

"And you?"

"I'll go home."

"Frank?" Jake asked.

"Should I call your parents to come get you?" Mrs. Oldfield said.

"No fucking way."

Mrs. Oldfield pursed her lips. "Young man, there's no call for—"

"He's the one gave me this!" He pointed to his bloody arm. "He's the one set the place on fire with me in it." He stood and turned his back. "He's the one done this."

Mrs. Oldfield sucked in her breath.

"I'm staying, too," Belle said.

"No." Mrs. Oldfield was firm. "The boys can stay, but you can't stay here in a house full of boys."

Jake shook his head. *There's no way she'll understand how silly that sounds.*

"I'm not leaving them," Belle said. "We went through this together. We'll face it together."

"She'll be fine, Mrs. Oldfield," Beau said.

Clara Oldfield set her shoulders. "No. You children think you have everything in hand, but I still have some sense left. You'll stay with me, Belle. Come along." She didn't wait for agreement. She turned and left.

Belle stood at the door with a stricken look.

"It's better than kicking you out," Jake said.

"I can handle that, but—"

"Her bark is worse than her bite," Joanie said.

"I'll wake up smelling of talc!"

Joanie slipped an arm through hers. "I'll walk you up."

"Leave me an Ace bandage," Jake said. "I think I twisted my ankle."

Belle looked past him. "Look after him, will you?"

He turned. Beau was leading Frank down the hall. "I will."

He watched the two girls walk up the lawn then closed the door and started limping to the bedroom. The door was ajar and he pushed it open. Frank lay on his side, his bandaged arm dangling over the edge of the bed. Tremors shook his body. Beau wrapped himself around him and rocked him slowly, humming. He looked at Jake in the shaft of light coming from the hall. Jake nodded and closed the door. He limped back to the living room.

Pulling out the hide-a-bed was painful. Every time he put weight on his injured ankle, he lost his balance. He skipped making the bed and just pulled down the afghan and turned up the thermostat. He was barely able to get his shoe off the injured foot. "This sucks big wet weenies," he said as he wrapped his ankle. He lay back and immediately felt the support rod beneath the mattress. *How did Randy ever do it? I'll never get to sleep.* He fell asleep.

At four minutes past midnight, a stillness passed through town. It began north of the city when silence opened a hole in the night above the White Horse River. The silence widened at Post Street when a whistle did not blow. Dogs raised their heads as the stillness passed, sniffed the night, and returned to their dreams of prairie grass and jack rabbits. The hole in the night began to close at Choctaw, where signal lights did not flash and the crossing bell was silent. The hole emptied itself, closed, and was gone. The exhausted children slept and did not notice.

Ashes

The next morning Belle rapped on the door and stuck her head in. "Brace yourselves. She's making waffles."

The four Quirks entered Mrs. Oldfield's kitchen and faced a breakfast of waffles, toast, preserves, maple syrup, sausage patties, and scrambled eggs laid out on a checkered tablecloth. Strong tea brewed in a cat-shaped pot. A radio tuned to KROY played gospel music in the background.

This is all so normal it's weird, Jake thought. *And it smells delicious*.

An announcer interrupted the program as the kids sat themselves around the table. "This is a KROY News Update on the fire at The Corners Bar and Grill. The five-alarm fire started just before midnight last night. Despite quick response by local fire departments from both Kennsing and Conlan Counties, and help from a dozen volunteers on the scene, the blaze completely destroyed the local landmark."

"Hmmph!" Mrs. Oldfield said.

"It is not known if there were any casualties, or if the fire was arson or accidental. Authorities are combing through the rubble this morning for answers. We will update you as information becomes available." The station went back to recorded music.

Mrs. Oldfield turned down the volume. "They usually broadcast 'The Tremblin' Hour' now, but I guess other things are more urgent. You children go ahead and eat. There won't be any news for a while." She shook her head. "There's some would say I'm committing the sin of scandal, letting you off the hook for your bad behavior. That I'm a foolish old woman. But who else is there?"

She's worried about Pastor Mathers. "Some say the foolish are chosen to shame the wise," Jake said offhandedly.

She raised her eyebrows. "And others that the Devil can quote scripture. Eat your waffles."

"They're fantastic," Beau said.

"Belle helped."

"I brewed the tea," Belle said with a smirk.

Frank didn't touch his plate.

"We need to think how we can restart the band," Jake said, taking seconds.

"Are you serious?" Frank asked.

"We got the drums to my truck before the fire started. And one of the amps," Belle said.

"Frank's. Did anyone get their guitars out?"

"I don't think so," Beau said. "What about the mikes?"

Jake shook his head. "I was packing them up when I got knocked over. That's when I twisted my ankle, I think. We got back-up mikes in my car, but they aren't as good."

"Are you guys kidding me?" Frank said. "People died out there, and you're talking about the damned mikes?"

Jake glanced at Mrs. Oldfield, but she faced the stove and pretended not to hear.

"We don't know that," Belle said. "Everybody could have gotten out."

"Sammy was staying at Mrs. Chisholm's, wasn't he?" Beau said. "We should call over and ask."

"Hush a moment." Mrs. Oldfield turned the radio up.

"Kennsing County authorities confirm two bodies have been found in the wreckage of The Corners. The fire marshal said—"

Frank ran from the kitchen.

Beau and Jake followed. Frank got into his pickup and sat behind the wheel, not moving. "I don't know where to go. I don't know where he's staying." He pressed his fingers to his forehead. "Sammy would. They're friends. Where did you say he lived?"

"Mrs. Chisholm's," Beau said.

"Where's that?"

"Stonewall and Broad, across from the train depot."

Frank started his truck.

"Wait!" Belle came down the porch steps. "Frank, wait."

"I ain't got time for this," he muttered.

She came up to the cab. "They just announced the name of one of the victims. They know who one of them is."

Frank squeezed his eyes shut.

"Is it Mr. Anderson?" Jake whispered.

Belle shook her head. "It's Lorenzo Pellegrini. Frank, it's your stepdad."

They looked at Frank. He shook his head, his eyes still shut. "Shit." He struck the steering wheel with both hands. Then he opened his eyes, dead calm. "I gotta go home. Mom's gonna fall apart. And Angela . . . shit."

"Did they identify the other body?" Beau asked.

"No."

"It could be Sammy."

"Or—"

Frank shook his head. "It doesn't matter. I gotta go."

Beau reached in and squeezed his hand. "I'll check at Mrs. Chisholm's. Maybe she's heard something."

"Thanks."

"Belle and I will go out to The Corners," Jake said. "Maybe we can ask the folks there."

Frank spun gravel as he left the alley. Beau, Belle, and Jake crammed themselves into the cab of Belle's pickup. Beau was in the middle, practically riding the stick shift.

"What's the scramble?" Randy called from his back porch.

Jake leaned out the window. "Can you give Beau a ride?"

Beau looked at him. "Drop me off at Chickasaw. I can walk from there."

"It's faster if we split up," Jake said.

"Sure. Let me out."

Randy walked up while Beau got out and they rearranged themselves. "A ride where?"

"Mrs. Chisholm's," Jake said.

"If it's no bother," Beau said.

"No bother a-tall. It's on the way to St. Joe's. What's up?"

"Beau can fill you in. We gotta go."

Randy and Beau watched them tear down the alley and up Front Street.

"Holy Hannah," Randy said. "Where's the fire?"

Beau told him.

The blackened shell of The Corners was still smoking when Belle and Jake arrived. A volunteer fireman stood by, laying down water from a pumper and smoking a cigarette.

"Where's your car?" Belle asked.

"Near the kitchen."

They parked in front and walked around to the back, Jake limping and leaning on Belle. A car sat by the blackened kitchen entrance, but it was a charred hulk. Jake shook his head. "So ends the Dream Machine."

"So ends The Quirks."

"Don't say that."

"Well, what have we got? You guys lost your guitars. Our back-up equipment was in that car. Even with the money from tips, we don't have enough to replace it all. And I don't think Marion's going to be writing us a check anytime soon."

"There's got to be a way—"

"You kids shouldn't be out here," the fireman called. "It's still dangerous."

Belle walked up to him. "Were you here went it went up?"

"Yep. Went like a torch. About the only thing that burns faster than a bar is a church."

"I hear they found a body."

He shook his head. "Two of 'em."

"Do they know who it was?"

"One was a local farmer. Forget his name."

"What about the other guy?" Jake asked.

"Unidentified."

"Well, was it a . . . a large man or a small man?"

"Not even sure it was a man." He tossed his cigarette into the weeds. "What's your interest?"

"Thanks mister," Belle said, pulling Jake back to her truck.

"So, we still don't know," Jake said.

"Maybe Beau's having better luck." She crossed her arms. "You shouldn't have palmed him off on Randy like that."

"Like what?"

"You can't keep ignoring him."

"I'm not ignoring him. I'm being nice."

"Nice? You call that being nice?"

"Jesus, Belle, I can't handle riddles. Not after last night."

She looked like she had more to say, but she changed her mind. "Let's head back to town."

Jake said nothing on the way back. His car was gone. His guitar, too. And all the mikes and mike stands and cables and amps. Except Frank's.

And maybe Frank was gone, too. Jake *had* been nice to Beau this morning. Kind, even gracious after the little sneak climbed into bed with his boyfriend. *It should have been me there, comforting Frank, rocking him to sleep, sharing the night. But I haven't said a word about it.*

Neither has Frank. Did he even miss me?

Can this day get any worse?

He got an answer as soon as Belle dropped him off. Waiting for him inside the granny house was his aunt Margaret.

There was a strange car in the drive when Frank arrived at the farm. The front door was unlocked, and as soon as he entered the living room, BT Crawford rose from a chair. "Frank! Thank the Lord you're all right."

Arlene gave a short cry and ran up and hugged him. He smelled alcohol on her, but didn't see a glass or bottle. *Of course. She put it away when the pastor's son arrived.*

"BT," Frank said, "thanks for coming by."

"I was at the Woolvines when I heard the news. I came right over."

"Thank you, Robert," Arlene said, wiping her nose with a handkerchief. "That was very kind of you."

"Mrs. Woolvine said if there's anything you need, you be sure to ask."

"That's so kind of her, what with all she's got on her plate."

"Where's Angela?" Frank asked.

"She won't come out of her room. Your room. Upstairs."

BT headed for the door. "My father will be in touch directly."

"Thank you, dear. Tell him we'll make arrangements, same as last time with Daddy. A service, a viewing at Dunbar's—"

"No, Mom," Frank said. "No viewing."

"Oh. Of course." She sat on the sofa and stared at the table.

"Every sorrow shall be comforted," BT said.

"Sure. Thanks." Frank held the door for him.

BT leaned forward. "Your mother's a little fragile. You know—" He made a drinking gesture with his hand. "If you need help—"

"Thanks. We'll manage."

As soon as the door closed, Arlene leaped up and pounded him on the chest. "I thought you were dead! Where were you? Why didn't you come home?"

"Mom, stop it. Are you all right?"

"Well what do you think? You go out there, he goes out there, neither of you comes back. And then the fire. Oh!" She sat again. "They aren't going to make me look at him, are they? I couldn't stand it if I had to look at him."

Angela stood at the foot of the stairs. "You're a complete mess."

Frank looked down at his torn and bloody shirt. He knew one of his eyes was swelling shut, too. "I am at that."

"But you made it back. You did, he didn't."

"Angie." Frank shook his head. "I'm sorry."

"Did you do it? Did you burn him up?"

"Angie," Arlene said, "not now."

"He was there, wasn't he? Daddy went to get him."

"Please, Angie."

"No, Mom," Frank said. "She has a right to know. Yeah, your father was there, but I didn't know it till the fight broke out."

"Fight?" Arlene said. "The sheriff didn't say anything about a fight."

"He and Jim Newton got into it."

"He did it, didn't he?" Angela said. "He killed Daddy."

"I knew it!" Arlene exclaimed.

"Will you two quit and let me explain? No. It was the other way around. Lorenzo pulled his knife on Jim—"

"And you started the fire to save him," Angela said.

"Christ! Lorenzo started the fire with his fucking cigarette."

"Frank! We don't use such language."

"What the hell does it matter? They're both dead."

They were silent.

"They said there was two bodies," Arlene said quietly. "I thought for sure the other one was you."

"It's Jim. I'm pretty sure."

"I knew you were going to run off with that man. Lorenzo was right to stop him."

"Jim saved my life, Mom. He pushed me through a window and saved my life."

"Did he give you that black eye or was that Daddy?" Angela asked.

"It was Jim. I wanted to pull him out. He wouldn't let me."

"What about Daddy?"

Frank shook his head. "I didn't see him after the fight started. Lorenzo cut me and I went down. I didn't see after that."

"What?" Arlene frowned. "Lorrie wouldn't do that. He went there to save you."

"Then what the hell is this?" He pulled down his shirt and showed them the bloody bandage.

Arlene shook her head. "No. No, that's wrong. Lorrie wouldn't do that."

"Yes, he would," Angela said.

There was a knock at the door.

"If that's Betty Woolvine with a hot dish, I'm going to choke her." Arlene went to the door. As soon as she opened it, she cried out and backed into the hall.

"I'm terribly sorry, ma'am," a man's voice said, "but I come to check up on Frank. Is he here? Did he make it home?"

Frank ran into the hall and leaped into Jim's arms. He wrapped his legs around his waist and kissed him full on the mouth.

"Guess that answers that," Jim said. There was a soft sound behind them. "Your ma's fainted."

"Yeah. She's had a rough morning."

Angela stood in the hall, her hands on her hips. "You're a sicko."

Frank grinned. "And you're a psycho."

"She needs to be put to bed." She grabbed one of her mother's legs. "Well, are you going to help or not?"

The three of them got it done.

Jake was lying on the couch with his foot up when the phone rang. He tried to get to it first, but Aunt Margaret was quicker.

"Yes?" she said. "Who's calling?"

It's Beau. Or Frank. Jake didn't know who he wanted to hear from first.

"He needs to rest," Aunt Margaret said.

"No, I don't."

She covered the mouthpiece and gave him a stern look.

"Is it Beau? Let me talk to him, please. He was going to check up on Mr. Anderson."

Her mouth turned down. "I might have known he'd be mixed up in this." She uncovered the receiver. "Just a few minutes, young man. Malachi needs a good scrubbing and a long nap. He's had too much excitement for one day." She handed over the phone. "It's Beau Hamilton."

Jake took it eagerly. "Beau?"

"Who is that witch?"

"Yes, that's my Aunt Margaret."

"And I thought Mrs. Oldfield was scary."

"Oh, pretty much the same. Maybe more."

"She's standing right there listening, isn't she?"

"Yep. All the time."

"That's heavy, man. I'm sorry."

"Thanks. I'm sorry, too. Have you heard anything?"

"Yes. Sammy wasn't at Mrs. Chisholm's, and she hasn't seen him since last night, so I went home. It's crazy here. Rafe's in a cast with a compound fracture. You wouldn't believe—"

"Uh-huh, uh-huh. And Mr. Anderson?"

"Oh. My mom suggested calling the hospital, and sure enough, he's there in the burn ward."

"Oh, Jesus."

Aunt Margaret scowled.

"They won't let me see him, but I got to talk to him. He's a little messed up, but he'll be all right. I'm going to ask Bobbie to check up on him. She's a Candy Striper there."

"Yeah. Have you heard from Frank?"

There was a pause on the other end. "No. But Sammy said Jim, Frank's friend, made it out, too."

"Oh. That's great. So he's fine."

"Jim was going to Frank's to check up on him. That's what Sammy said. Do you think everything's all right out there? I mean, not all right, how could it be? But with his mom and sister and all."

"Frank would call me if there was a problem." *Or maybe he wouldn't.* "They still haven't identified the other body, have they?"

Aunt Margaret reached for the phone. "That's enough."

"Just a minute please, Aunt Margaret. There's something I need to ask Beau."

"Jake?" came Beau's voice from the receiver.

"Beau, I gotta know. Are we all right?"

There was quiet on the line. Finally, Beau said, "I'm really shook up. I can't breathe sometimes, and sometimes my heart gets going real fast. Is that what you mean?"

"Yeah, that, and— I want to know we're all right, you and me."

"We'll be fine, Jake. It's awful, but we'll be fine."

Aunt Margaret moved her things into the bedroom that evening, exiling Jake to the sofa for the duration, which—more bad news—would be until his mother arrived. *Virginia could handle this with one arm tied behind her back. Now it takes three of them just to make sure I take a shower and get to bed on time.*

He lay on the comfortless mattress, his head buzzing with the past twenty-four hours. *Sammy's okay. Well, maybe not okay, but not dead. Beau says we're okay, or will be. What about Frank? He should have called about Jim. Or should I have called him about Sammy?*

It was getting close to midnight. Half a moon slanted through the window, cold and distant. He wondered if Frank would start their ritual when he heard the train. He gave himself a few trial tugs. The mattress frame jiggled but didn't squeak. Aunt Margaret would not be alerted to what he was doing.

He listened for the train. He didn't hear it. Had he heard it last night? He couldn't remember. He twisted around to see the glowing clock in the kitchen. It was ten past midnight, yet there was no sound from the river. He started anyway, imagining the train crossing the trestle at Frank's farm. It approached the town, going faster. It passed the cemetery with Andy's grave, the fatal crossing at Post Street. Closer, harder. It passed the railroad buildings with their faded lettering and boarded up windows and padlocked doors. Marcus Longacre whispered in his ear, "Some boys is wily."

He sat up so fast the couch nearly folded beneath him. "Holy Goddess of Prosperity!" He knew exactly where to find her.

Saving Croy

To the Editor:

Recently, these pages have lamented the loss of our town's heritage. I was appalled to read that some people regard the destruction of The Corners in this light.

A good man died in that fire trying to save his son from the debauched influence of so-called "entertainers" and defilers of God's plan. Are we to throw away his sacrifice?

Now we learn the library is contemplating the installation of an offensive statue rejected years ago by the good people of this town. Does the Library Board think themselves above the will of the people? Or above the will of God?

If we allow corrupting images and ideas to flow unfiltered through the minds of our children, Mr. Pellegrini will have died in vain. We may as well burn the cross of Calvary and eat the ashes.

This paper published an editorial titled, "Saving Croy for History." If we do not save Croy for Christ, our history will not matter.

—Mrs. Cal Littledeer

Red's Return

R ed Conner stepped off the Trailways bus on the corner of Stonewall and Broad and looked at his former hometown. Little had changed. The Santa Fe depot across Broad Street had been restored. Its barrel-arched Romanesque windows were no longer boarded up, and a sign beside the entrance proclaimed it the Kennsing County Historical Society and Museum. Hours were posted. It was currently closed.

Farther up Broad was the Conoco sign for Longacre Brothers Auto and Service Station. "Excellent Prices For Excellent Service," a hand-lettered sign read. He hefted his duffel bag over his shoulder and headed in that direction. He supposed he ought to book a room at Mrs. Chisholm's, but he needed to talk to someone first.

He used a cane and favored his left leg. The closer he got to Longacre Brothers, the harder it got to move his feet. When he reached the driveway, he stopped and turned his back on the station and looked across the rail yard. He lowered his duffel to the sidewalk. A crew was dismantling one of the buildings, carefully pulling away planks and piling them on a flatbed rail car hitched to a truck whose wheels had been amputated and replaced with steel. *They're just train wheels*, he told himself. His heart pounded.

Beyond the rail yard, he could see the houses along Front Street. Del's house, and next to it, Marcus's. The hair on the back of his neck prickled. *He's coming. All smiles and innocence with death in his hand.* A stone skipped on the pavement behind him. He gripped his cane.

"Boo!" a voice said.

He swung the cane and knocked the little bastard to the ground. The kid cried out. Red raised his cane again, intending a killing blow with its knobbed head. The air was on fire and buzzed with insects.

"Holy crap, Red," said the figure sprawled on the ground. He rubbed his arm where Red had struck. "Is that any way to treat your old buddy?"

Cool air washed Red's face. The jungle pulled back to the edges of his mind. "Marcus," he said. He extended his hand and pulled him up. "We need to talk."

They entered the service bay of the station, Marcus heading for a low fridge in the alcove that passed for an office. "I suppose it's my uncle you're wanting to see," he said. "Big homecoming party for his boy Delbert."

Red lowered himself onto a bench seat pulled from a truck and laid his cane on the concrete floor. His duffel bag slumped against the open bay. "The VFW asked me to speak. I don't want to, but I kinda owe it. But it's you I gotta talk to first."

Marcus grinned. "Do tell." He pulled two beers from the fridge and waggled them. "Like old times. Uncle Rusty would pitch a fit, but he's busy getting plastered at the Wayland."

Red took a bottle. "Thanks. Some special occasion?"

"You might could say that. We got a foreclosure notice from Eli Brown and the good folks down at the S&L."

"It's like a family tradition with the Browns, ain't it? Tossing people out on their ass."

Marcus looked around. "They want this grease pit, they can have it." He took a swig from his bottle. "So you came back for that thing for Del down at the vets hall?"

Red nodded, keeping his eye on him.

"Quite the hero, ain't he?"

Red shook his head. "The whole hero thing is bullshit. A guy they call a hero is just some schmo who looked out for you more than himself. A Silver Star is what they give his folks so they don't know what an idiot he was." He put the bottle down. "But there was something Del wanted me to pass on. To you, not to his dad or the vets or the rest of the town. Just you, his cousin. He wanted to say sorry."

Marcus sneered. "I heard all that before."

Red narrowed his eyes. "When?"

"I'm sorry," Del said.

Marcus continued walking across the backyard, toward the train tracks. He could hear his mother wailing in the house behind him, hear his uncle Russell trying to console her.

"What for?" he said. "He was drunk. You didn't put that bridge there. He found it all by himself." He was passing the shed where they kept the lawnmower. He gave it a kick. "Now we're out a car, too."

He glanced back at Del. In his cadet uniform, he was dressed sharper than him, but he looked more tore up by the funeral. "You got some weed?"

Del looked back at the house. "Let's go behind the shed."

They lit up. The autumn sun was sliding behind the Conoco station across the tracks. "They'll have to change the name now. Longacre Brothers. There's only one left." He laughed. "One Brother Auto and Service. How lame is that?" He giggled and looked at his reefer. "Shit, this is strong shit." He handed it back to Del.

"It's my fault. With your dad."

"Fuck that." Marcus pulled away from the shed and walked through dry weeds to the tracks.

Del came up behind him and put his hands on his shoulders. Marcus felt stiff and confined in his suit. He yanked his shirt tails out and stretched for the sky. Shadows stroked his stomach.

Del reached around and pulled him in. "Hey."

Del was bigger, but that didn't scare him. Marcus knew

he had the power here. He relaxed and leaned back. Del slid his hands under his shirt. Marcus sucked in his gut and Del slipped his hands beneath his belt. "Well shit," Marcus said.

"Del? Marcus?" a man's voice called from the house. "Where the hell you boys at?"

Del's hands snapped back as if on wires. Marcus turned and opened his mouth. "Don't!" Del whispered, his eyes frantic.

Marcus smiled. "Out here Uncle Rusty. We'll be in directly."

"We was more careful after that. Used the old Santa Fe buildings, just like you and me did later. So if that's what old Delbert was sorry about, forget it. He got his and I got mine. Excellent weed for excellent service."

Red nodded soberly. "Yeah." He rested his elbows on his knees. "That's just the sort of shit I don't want to hear from you."

Marcus scoffed. "Because you're both supposed to be such big heroes?"

"No, fuck that. Because he saved my life. So no more talk like that about Del."

"Or what? You'll hit me with your cane again?"

Red snatched it off the floor and drew back his arm. Marcus cringed, but Red threw it across the bay. It clattered against the tool bench on the opposite wall. "I don't need no cane."

Marcus shook his head. "Stupid fucker."

"I know you played Del like you played me. But he never told you the whole story, did he?"

"That *is* the whole story."

"Tell yourself that if you want." Red picked up his beer. "But I think you know different." He looked at him down the barrel of the bottle as he took a long pull.

Marcus shook his head. "This is like talking to a woman. You have something to say, say it."

"'Sorry about your Dad. It's my fault.' That's what he told you, right?"

"Something like that."

"Only he never told you why. Once you started your little arrangement, he didn't think he could talk to you about it."

"We warn't much for talking."

"But he talked to me. We were both wasted on ganja, or he wouldn't have spilled it. And I wouldn't be telling you now except I know you. Your sly looks, your little words, dropped here and there. Del doesn't deserve that."

"Del don't deserve shit. Uncle Rusty always talked him up, always compared me to him, and I'd always come up short. Now Del's this big martyr with a medal."

"The medal's for them. It's for your uncle and the vets and the folks in town. They've gotta have something, or it's all just a fucking waste. This is for you."

Red took another swig before diving in. "You've been out to The Corners. You've taken a shit out there, the men's room. That hole between the stalls? You know what that's for. Del was out there one Friday night, horny as hell. Usually, he just sticks his dick through and soon enough someone comes along."

Marcus snickered.

"But this night—this night the guy gives him a few licks and turns around. And Del's fucking the guy through the wall. Clumsy as hell, but it feels great. Then, when he finishes up, the guy turns around and sucks him clean. And the guy says, 'That's one fine cock,' and Del says, 'Uncle Ray?'"

Marcus's sneer froze on his face.

"And your dad takes off like a bat outta hell. Del figures he wants to get back first so he can deny everything if Del shows up. Only Ray doesn't make it."

Marcus was staring at him, thumbs hooked in his overalls.

"Del thought if he hadn't said anything, your father wouldn't have driven hell bent for leather through an ice storm straight into a bridge abutment. Me," he picked up the bottle and took another slug, "I figure the abutment was just convenient."

Marcus rose and walked across the bay. He looked down at Red's cane lying on the stained concrete. "This is you getting back at me, ain't it? For what we did back then. Throwing it in my face."

"This has nothing to do with me," Red said.

"Then why tell me all this bullshit?"

He shrugged. "Maybe it's bullshit. Maybe it's not. Del was pretty fucked up when he told me, and I was as far gone as I could get. He said he loved you, Marcus. And that wasn't bullshit."

Marcus turned around. "It warn't never love."

"No, not for you."

His cocky sneer returned. "And I'm supposed to believe this? The two of you just happen to find each other in the middle of the jungle? And then what? You become butt buddies?"

Red inhaled. Flies the size of bats knocked around inside his skull, trying to get out. He pushed them away. "You keep trying to make this about me. That ain't gonna work. I never liked it. You know that. And you know what?" He leaned forward. "You never did, either."

Marcus's shoulders slumped. He looked at the floor, shaking his head.

Red lowered his empty bottle. "Uncle Rusty got more of these?"

"It was just us," Marcus said quietly. "Del and me. Two rats growing up side by side, playing in the dirt. He was always the bigger one, faster. Two years older. Big man at baseball. He could outrun, out throw anyone. But I was the wily one, the smart one." He laughed. "Not smart. Clever."

He walked over to the fridge and took out two more bottles. "When Del made Eagle Scout, his dad lorded it over my dad. I never made it past second class. Fuck, who'd want to? Who needs all those knots and Morse code and shit? But I could feel it, the heat of his jeering. It made it all the way inside our house." He sat opposite Red and handed him a bottle. "So I made me a little plan. I bet Del he couldn't start a fire with two sticks, like the manual says you can, and he said he could, and I said, 'Show me. Show me out by the shed.' There was lots of dry wood back there, weeds, dead flowers and shit from his mom's garden. And Del takes the bet, so we head out there and he starts drilling away, rubbing the stick between his hands. I made some dick joke and he laughed and it threw him off. But soon enough I see smoke coming from the bottom stick and that's when I sprang my trap."

He took a long swig from his beer. Red nursed his, letting Marcus take his time.

"I'd brought some kitchen matches, see? And I stuck one in there and *whoosh!* It caught and flared up. And the weeds caught. And the dead grass. And soon we had us a real bonfire."

He leaned forward, his teeth and eyes glittering. "But here was the clever part. I'd timed all this so it was just as my dad and Uncle Rusty were coming home from the Conoco. Just as they were crossing the tracks. *Whoosh!* And it looks like Del's set the whole shed on fire.

"Rusty bellows and comes roaring at us like a bull. I take off for home but stick around outside to see what happens. And Del starts running around his house, his dad's chasing him, and he makes it around a couple of times, and then his dad— His dad catches him." Marcus shook his head. "He must have let his dad catch him. Del could outrun anybody." He took a drink. "And Rusty? He grabs Del around the middle, yanks his pants down, and bends him over his knee and starts smacking him on the ass. Del is sixteen, man. Sixteen, and he's being paddled like a five-year-old, his butt in the air. And his dad is yelling and cursing and all red in the face. And Del's mom comes out, and his two sisters, and my mom comes out, and God knows who else in the neighborhood. And Rusty's face is red as a beet and Del's ass, too, and it's almost comical except it ain't 'cuz you know Uncle Rusty's lost it, and if there'd been a bat or a crowbar handy he'd have beat Del to death."

Marcus stopped, the beer in his hand forgotten. He stared, but he wasn't seeing Red or the Conoco station around them. "He only stopped because he got winded. He dumped Del off him like a sack of garbage. And all this time, Del doesn't make a sound. And he's left there on the ground, alone, his pants around his knees, until everyone goes back inside. And then he gets up, his face blank and loose, and he pulls up his pants, and he walks back to the house, where his dad who just beat him is, and his mom and his two sisters who watched. And he walks inside." Marcus looked up and met Red's eyes. "And do you know what my dad did? After all that?"

Red shook his head.

"Nothing. Not a word. Del's dad never gave him a bit of regard. Del wasn't his kid. He was his weapon. Against my dad, his brother. Against me. And the weapon failed. It misfired. So Rusty sent him off to military school to make sure that never happened again.

"Me? I'd have welcomed a beating. But my dad didn't have a scrap of time for me. He always found a reason to be somewhere else. Like he couldn't stand to be in the same room with me, so he could pretend I wasn't even there."

He took a drink, still looking at the wall or at nothing. "So, when Del got back and he paid attention, and we started messing around? I thought, Well, shit, at least it's something. Finally, somebody looked at me like I was there. I got used to that." He shook his head. "Love? Fuck, no. He never said nothing about that. And when he left for Nam he never said goodbye, neither. Fucker."

Red watched quietly as Marcus finished his beer. "So, what are you going to do?"

"About what?"

"About what I just told you."

Marcus scoffed. "About The Corners? About my dad and Del? It's just a story. Yours or Del's, it don't matter. The only two who know for sure are dead."

Red finished his bottle. "Well, Del wanted me to tell you. Wanted you to know he's sorry and why. Now I've told you. I ain't telling nobody else."

"Quiet as the grave, eh?" A thin smile curled his lips.

"If you want."

He laughed. "Want? When have I ever gotten what I want?" He stretched his arms over his head and leaned back. "One way, Del stays a hero. T'other, well, we're just the field rats we always been." He shook his head again. "Who'd listen to me anyway? A grease monkey in a bankrupt filling station." He got up and went to the fridge. "'Nother?"

"Sure."

"Keep this up, you'll need more than a cane." He turned around, grinning. "Oh, man. The Corners. Wait till you hear."

Hidden Resources

Randy pounded on the granny house door. "Jake? You home? Virginia needs us at the hospital."

Aunt Margaret opened the door. "You will cease that racket at once, young man."

Jake pushed past her, fearing the worst. "Is it Mr. Anderson?"

"I beg your pardon, ma'am. No, it's not Mr. Anderson. But Virginia called and said she wanted to see you and me and Joanie right away."

"You haven't had breakfast yet," Aunt Margaret objected.

"I'll grab something in the cafeteria."

Jake couldn't wait to get into Randy's car. "What is it? What did she say?"

"She said, 'The circus is in town and these are your monkeys.'"

"How did she sound?"

"Pissed off."

"Seems normal."

"I need to find out what's up. I called Joanie. She'll meet us there."

Beau lingered in the hospital waiting room, hoping for a chance to visit Sammy.

"You may as well go home," Bobbie told him. She adjusted the waist of her Candy Striper pinafore. "They won't let anyone in except family."

"He doesn't have family. I'm the closest he's got."

"You're not related in any natural way, and that's that.

They're already on edge about all the people in Mrs. Edom's room. Any more rules being broken, and they'll call security, and that'd be a pretty mess." She lifted one shoulder, then the other, a look of discomfort on her face.

"The darts aren't right," Beau said, pointing to the front.

"It's a uniform. It's supposed to be . . . uniform."

"But you aren't. I could fix that for you."

Jake, Randy, and Joanie came down the hall. Without looking in their direction or stopping at the nurse's station, they headed for Virginia's room and went in.

"Oh, for heaven's sakes!" Bobbie said, marching after them.

This was his chance. Beau checked up and down the hall then slipped into Mr. Anderson's room.

His bed was cranked up so he sat nearly upright. His head was bandaged and gauze covered his upper left arm and shoulder. He looked like he had a ferocious sunburn. He smiled as soon as Beau entered.

"This is a surprise. How'd you evade the basilisk?"

"Dragons no guard."

Sammy looked thoughtful. "Hmm. Not quite right. The *u* is in the wrong place."

He bowed. "Dr. Awkward, at your service."

Sammy chuckled. "I am going to miss you and your palindromes."

He pulled a chair up to the bed. "Miss me? Why?"

"St. Joseph's Spa and Sanitarium is fully booked. They need my room."

"But you'll still be in town, right?"

Sammy shook his head. "My room at Mrs. Chisholm's was week to week, and it's been more than a week. I'm out."

"But that's not fair. She must know you're in the hospital."

"Oh yes, she knows. And she knows why. Apparently the other lodgers don't approve."

"But you saved people."

"One person. Maybe two. Jim might have gotten out without me."

"You came after me and Frank."

"That doesn't count. I thought I saw you dodge into the men's room. I went looking but—*pfft!*—you were gone."

"Still, you were pretty brave."

"I was pretty stupid. At least now no one can object when I wear a wig." He mimed patting his coif and smiled.

Beau tried to smile back. "Or a wimple."

Sammy sighed. "I fear Sister Many Agonies perished in the blaze. Dust and ashes are all that's left of her habits— except the nasty ones. Do you know how hard it is to find plus sizes in religious wear?"

Beau reached out to touch him but pulled short of the bandages. "You'll be all right though, won't you? I mean, for real."

Sammy dropped the cheerful act. "I've lost some range of motion in my left arm, but with a little physical therapy, it should come back."

"What if it doesn't?"

"Then I'll simply learn to flourish with my right." He demonstrated.

It brought tears to Beau's eyes.

"Don't worry about me, sweetie," Sammy said. "I have hidden resources. But I may lose my book contract if I don't hop out of this bed and start spitting out chapters. It's time to move on." He reached out and clasped Beau's hand. "Besides, there's more important things to worry about. Right here in Croy."

Beau looked at their hands. "The band is dust and ashes too."

"That's not what I mean."

"I know what you mean. I know who."

"Jake is still trying to find out who he is. You're ahead of him, that's all."

Beau let go of his hand. "Thanks, Sammy."

"He'll catch up, sweetie. You just have to give him time."

He looked him in the eye. "What if we don't have time? That's what the fire taught me. Things can change in a flash."

Sammy shook his head. "It's no good me telling you to take it slow, is it?"

"It surely is not."

Randy halted just inside Virginia's room. Jake bumped into his back, and Joanie nearly did the same to him.

"Pop?" Randy said, his voice up a register.

Harry Edom stood against a wall, out of sight of the door. "Close that, would you son?" he asked.

"Pop, what are you doing here?"

"That's just what I asked," Virginia said. "Who do I have to thank for this?"

Randy and Jake looked at Joanie. "I had nothing to do with it," she said. "This time."

A second man rose from a chair in the corner. "I did." He extended his hand to Randy. "Sunny Sohi, an old friend of your parents."

Joanie whispered, "Whoops." Jake hoped Randy didn't hear it.

Sunny continued, "When I heard you were sick, Ginny, I contacted Harry."

"Well, that was stupid."

"Hey, I've always been good with stupid," Harry said.

"You'll get yourself arrested," she said. "Again."

"You can't stay," Randy said. "It's too risky."

"I'm sorry," Bobbie Littledeer said from the doorway, "but there are too many people in this room."

"Who's saying that?" Sunny said. "I can't see you."

Bobbie edged her way through the visitors. "I am. I'm the Candy Striper for this ward."

"Not the nurse, then," Sunny said.

"No."

Harry shrugged. "Well then."

"How many is too many?" Virginia asked.

"All y'all. Nearly. There's only two that *could* be allowed to visit, and one of them isn't supposed to be here at all."

"Is this the room with the party?" Susan called out.

"Susie-Q?" Virginia's face lit up.

"Lord, give me strength," Bobbie said. "I'm stepping out and closing the door. Not one more person!"

"Excuse me," Jedediah Tucker said, squeezing in.

Susan Jacobs leaned over Virginia and kissed her on the cheek.

"Well, that tears it," Virginia said. "I'm dying for sure. Nothing else could drag you back here."

"None of that," Susan said, taking Sunny's chair. "I'm back for a short spell because a certain Mr. Someone can't seem to keep himself out of trouble." She looked around for Jake, but he shuffled behind Coach Tucker.

"I got hold of Susan through Vince," Sunny said.

"What?" Jake said. "How do you know Vince?"

"There you are," Susan said. "You and I need to have a chat."

There was a knock on the door. Harry ducked behind a folding screen, which caused everyone to shift. "Ow!" Joanie cried.

Jake shushed her.

"Somebody stepped on my foot!"

Jed Tucker opened the door a crack. "Yes?"

"I just saw the nurse leave her station." Bobbie said. "I think she's getting security."

"God, I need a cigarette," Virginia said.

"Thanks." Jed closed the door.

"Pop," Randy said. "Time to move."

"I'll stop by tomorrow for a proper visit," Susan said, rising. "Jake, you're coming with me."

"I don't have a car, Mom. It got— I don't have a car."

"Jed will take us, won't you Jed?"

"No, I'll take Sunny."

Jake saw a look pass between his mother and Sunny. It was not friendly in either direction.

"There's no need," Sunny said. "I'm staying at the Claremont."

Unguarded, Tucker's expression slid from open and hopeful to lost and hurt. It looked out of place on his usually stony face. Jake recognized it with a jolt. *That's how Beau looked when he figured out about me and Frank.*

"Jed," Harry said, "maybe you can give me a hitch?"

Coach Tucker snapped back to himself, his face neutral again. "Sure. Where?"

Harry looked around the room. "I think I better not say."

"Right." Jed opened the door and checked the hall. "Ready?"

Harry nodded.

"Pop?" Randy said.

"Don't follow me."

"I won't, but—"

"You'll see me again before I leave." He and Jed slipped out.

"I'll be going, too," Sunny said, picking up his hat and a cane that leaned against the wall. As he turned, he smiled at Joanie. "Miss Tibbits, I presume?"

Joanie blushed. "Yes sir."

"I want to talk to you later. At *The Evening Call* offices, perhaps?"

Her blush deepened. "No sir. Actually, you can find me at the drug store."

"Ah. Yes. I know where that is." He turned to the hospital bed. "Ginny, you've never looked ghastlier. It's great to see you."

"Sunny, it's great to be seen."

He tipped his hat and left.

Virginia sighed. "Finally, there's some air in this room."

"Mom," Randy said, "I swear I had nothing to do with this."

"I'm so sorry, Mrs. Edom," Joanie said.

"Yeah, yeah," Virginia said. "That's all very nice. Now all y'all just go away, will ya? A gal's gotta get her beauty rest."

"Let's go, kids," Susan said and ushered them out of the room.

Randy and Joanie whispered furiously to each other as they walked down the hall. "Well, how was I supposed to know?" Joanie said. "He never said anything to me. In fact, he hung up on me." Randy stormed away, brushing off Bobbie Littledeer as he passed her.

"Uh-oh," Susan said. "Trouble in paradise."

"What? Oh, no. They're not seeing each other anymore."

"Really? You could have fooled me. I was hoping to get a ride with Randy, but I guess that train's left the station." She put on her gloves. "I don't suppose Joanie drove."

"Wait, Mom. There's someone else you should see."

"What? Here?"

"Mr. Anderson is just down the hall."

His mother hesitated.

"He saved my life, Mom."

She nodded but still didn't move. "Is he— Is he badly injured?"

"Beau says he's a little messed up, but he'll recover."

A frown creased her forehead. "Who's Beau?"

"He's in the band with me. The Quirks."

"Ugh! That name."

The door to Mr. Anderson's room opened, and Beau came out. "That's Beau now. Come on, I'll introduce you."

Beau looked downcast but brightened as Jake and his mother approached. "Beau, this is my mom, Susan Jacobs."

"Gosh!" Glee and awe rippled across his face. "This is great, Miss Jacobs. I'm a big fan. I've seen every episode."

"Thank you very much. It's people like you who keep us on the air. Jake tells me you are in the band with him."

"It's really Beau's band," Jake said.

"No, it's all of ours. Jake writes the songs."

"Really?"

Jake didn't want the attention on him. "How is Sammy today? Can he take another visitor?"

Beau checked down the hall for Bobbie or the nurse. Bobbie was talking to Joanie. The nurse was back at her station and paying them no mind.

"I wouldn't want to tire him," Susan said.

"No, he'll be glad to see you," Beau said. "Go on in."

Susan rapped softly on the door and opened it a crack. "Peek-a-boo."

"Susan!" Sammy's voice boomed out.

She smiled and slipped inside.

"Gosh," Beau said. "Your mother. The Witch Evangeline. Here."

"She came to visit Mrs. Edom. They're old friends from high school. Drama Club or something."

"Thanks for introducing me. I should have gotten her autograph."

Jake almost laughed. He looked away and saw Joanie

waving him over. She was still talking to Bobbie. "I gotta go. Maybe I'll come by later, okay?"

"Okay."

Beau waved to Joanie and Bobbie as he passed. Joanie smiled but Bobbie glowered. "He shouldn't have sneaked in like that," she said. "Your mother, either. I don't care if she is a celebrity."

"Never mind that," Joanie said. "Tell Jake what you told me."

"People will know," Bobbie said.

"About what?"

Joanie lowered her voice, "About, you know," she whispered, "*Mr. Huckleberry*."

"There's no point in pretense," Bobbie said. She looked at the nurse's station. "She just went for a break. She didn't recognize him. But still, he mustn't come back. You need to tell him that."

"She's his wife, Bobbie," Joanie said. "A family has a right to be together at . . ."

"At the end," Jake finished for her.

Bobbie nodded. "You have my solemn word it won't be from my lips, but people will talk." She looked around. "There are some in this town who would rather be right than Christian."

"I'll tell him," Joanie said. "Randy, that is. If he ever speaks to me again."

"I have other duties to perform," Bobbie said, "but there's one more thing, and this is for you, Joanie, because I think we're friends."

"Well, yes, of course."

"My mother didn't write that letter to the editor."

"I kind of thought not."

"It's pretty obvious who wrote it," Jake said. "Sounds just like him."

Bobbie looked grim. "Yes. Anybody can tell. I asked Reverend Mathers about it, and he told me, 'Your mother stands in for the voice of the people.' But it's not her voice. It's his. Her signature on that letter is a lie, right there in print. But instead of being ashamed of it, they're congratulating each other." She shifted inside her uniform. "I needed to say that to someone. Someone who would listen."

Joanie touched her shoulder. "I'm sorry about this, Bobbie."

She shook her head. "Sorry isn't enough. There's going to be a reckoning." She walked away.

"She means it," Joanie said. "I'd better track down Randy."

Susan came out of Sammy's room looking dazed. Jake bid Joanie goodbye and joined her. "How is he?"

"Cheerful." She shook her head. "And heartbroken. He has to leave, but he really likes you kids. All the kids in the band."

"All the Quirks."

She looked at him. "Yes. You and Beau."

"And Belle and Frank."

They started down the hall. "I haven't met them yet, have I?"

"No."

"Beau seems a nice young man." They walked quietly. "Was he . . . wearing perfume?"

Jake nodded. "Estée Lauder. Youth-dew, I think."

"I thought so." She stopped. "Oh dear, Joanie's gone. I was hoping to ask for a ride."

"It's only a couple of blocks to the Claremont."

"Oh, I'm not staying there. I'm staying with you."

All Things Must Pass

B eau reverently held up George Harrison's new album with both hands, soaking in the jacket art. He was glad he had the house to himself for a change. He was just cuing up the first disc when the doorbell rang. He sprang up, hoping it was Jake. *It'd be great to hear this for the first time with him!* He bounded to the front door and flung it open, but it was Susan Jacobs who stood on his porch.

"Good afternoon, Beau," she said smoothly.

Beau's heart thumped. *She's more elegant than before!*

Her look turned quizzical. "May I come in?"

"Oh my goodness! Of course you can, Miss Jacobs."

He showed her to the living room. "Can I get you something?" *What do TV stars drink? How do you make coffee?* "My parents aren't home. Dad's at work and Mom's taken Rafe, that's my brother, to the doctor to check on his— well, you don't need to know about that. And Sophie went with them because they're twins, and I guess you don't need to know that either. Can I get you some coffee?" *Please say no.*

"I'm fine, Beau. Is your brother all right?"

"Oh, he's fine. He just has to wear a cast, but it's not forever."

"I'm glad to hear it. I really came to see you."

"Huh." He sat in the chair across the coffee table from her. "What about, Miss Jacobs?"

"You can call me Susan."

"Really? Cool."

"Any friend of Sammy's is a friend of mine."

"Sammy's great."

"We've known each other for years. I wanted to thank you for visiting him today. He doesn't have many friends. At least not here in Croy."

"He's probably the one person in town I can really talk to. Adult person, I mean."

"I'm sure your parents are lovely people."

"They surely are. But they're my parents, you know? You can only say certain things to your parents. If you try to talk about other stuff, they get all parenty."

She nodded. "My father was a minister. There were things I could never say to him. But he knew anyway."

"There was this doctor person I was supposed to talk to, but he was kind of a dick. Oh, sorry."

"Don't be. I know exactly what you mean."

"Sammy was much better at it. Still is."

"He told me you and Jake started The Quirks. That's the name of your band, isn't it?"

"Yeah. We dreamed it up right here, out on the front porch. It was just a thing, you know, to do. But then Jake started writing songs, really good ones, and we really clicked."

She smiled. "His father wrote songs, too. Do you think the band will continue? It's all Jake talks about."

"I don't know Miss— uh, Susan. We haven't met since the, you know, the accident."

"The fire."

"Right. We lost all our sound equipment and most of the instruments." He worried he sounded like he wanted her to do something about it. It embarrassed him. "Would you like some water?"

"No, I'm fine. Do you think Jake would mind if you played me one of his songs?"

"Um, I don't have the Fender anymore, but I still have the Gibson." He dashed to his room and brought it out with a sheet of lyrics. "This is called 'The Midnight Train.' Some of it's a little low for me, but here goes." Susan sat silently, her eyes distant as he sang. "It's really better with slide guitar," he said when he was through. "That was Frank's part."

"No, it's beautiful. May I?" She reached across the table and took the lyrics. "Could you sing it again, please?"

He felt more confident the second time, imagining they were back before an audience, his voice floating out over the crowd.

She let the silence hang after he finished. "Andy wrote a song for me once," she said at last, "just in my register, to show off my voice. We sang it at Mt. Hermon, the old one a few blocks from here. We had the choir, a soloist—that was me—and Andy at the piano. Nothing more."

"Jake didn't write this for me. It's really for Frank."

"Frank is one of the Quirks?"

"Yeah. He has a great voice. He does the verses, and I do the chorus. And he's amazing on lead. Or was. I don't know what happens next."

Susan sighed. "Change, I suppose. Mrs. Oldfield tells me they're selling the old church. Everything's at that monstrosity out on the highway now. Amplified sound, stage lighting, television cameras—it's more elaborate than our studio in New York. I don't know what my father would think. They're even dropping the name, changing it to New Life Christian Church." She looked at the lyrics again. "Can I have a copy of this?"

"You can have that one. It's not like anyone's asking us to play anywhere."

"Would you add the chords, please? I really liked the color they added."

"Sure." He took the sheet and started marking chords. "I'll trade you. Guitar arrangement for autograph. Deal?"

Susan smiled. "Deal."

There was a sound at the front door. "That's mom and the kids. Prepare for a noise attack."

Susan rose, but instead of his mom, his father walked in. He stopped in the living room doorway, his briefcase still in hand. "Good God," he said. "Susan Jacobs."

A genuine smile broke over her face. "Scotty? Scotty Pritchard?"

Beau retreated to his bedroom and lost himself in Harrison's vision of the world. He separated the stereo's speakers and lay on the floor between them and closed his eyes. Hours later, his mother knocked on the door and peeked in. "Jake's here to see you."

"Cool!" He got up. "He's got to hear this."

"Don't you think you could give that album a rest? 'My Sweet Lord' isn't all that sweet the umpteenth time around."

"Just once more. I want Jake to hear it."

Jake came in, twitching his basketball from hand to hand. "Thanks, Mrs. H.," he murmured. He still had a slight limp.

"Not the whole album, hon," his mother insisted.

"No. Just this song. Maybe one more."

"Volume down?"

"Way down."

"And door closed, please." She turned as she was leaving. "Jake, would you like to stay for supper?"

He was all smiles. "That would be swell, Mrs. Hamilton." But as soon as Beau closed the door he dropped to the bed with a groan. "Saves me having to sit through the pow-wow up at Mrs. Oldfield's."

"What's the deal?"

"My mom and Mrs. Oldfield and Aunt Margaret are deciding my fate. The Three Fates. The Three Hags."

"Your mother's no hag. She just plays one on TV."

"It's worse than last summer. I think they're going to send me back to New York with her. I'd rather join the Marines."

"She came by today."

"Who?"

"Your mom. Turns out she and my dad were in the same choir at Mt. Hermon. Isn't that weird? And she knew my mom, too, though not as well."

"So, she came to visit them?"

"No, me. She wanted to know if the band was getting back together. I told her it was up in the air."

Jake leaned back and tossed the ball at the ceiling. "Up in the air." He caught it. "Down to earth. The moon goes up, the moon falls down."

He's not in the mood. Beau moved the tone arm back to its rest and turned off the player. "What's going on?"

"She's staying at my place. My mom. In my bedroom. So I get to sleep on that torture rack in the living room. Aunt Margaret is staying with Mrs. Oldfield, which will probably start World War III, which would be hilarious if it were happening to someone else. I've got half a mind to sleep over at Randy's. Serve him right after all the times he's slept over with me."

Beau sat beside him. "You could stay here."

"Naw. Your folks don't need another broken-winged bird to look after."

"All my wings are intact."

"I was thinking of Rafe." He stopped tossing the ball. "So, what's this song I gotta hear?"

Beau started the turntable and dropped the needle in the first groove, remembering to turn the volume down. "It's called 'What Is Life.'" He got back on the bed, looking for signs that Jake's mood was lifting. *This song should do it.*

But Jake frowned throughout. At the end, he said, "It's 'What Is *My* Life,' not 'What Is Life.'"

"That's the title."

"But that's not what the lyrics say."

"Let me try another."

He flipped the disk and cued up the second track. Harrison's guitar soared through the opening to "My Sweet Lord." Beau grinned. "Can you picture Frank doing that?"

"I'm having trouble picturing any of it. What's with all the orchestration?"

But Beau could tell he was getting into it. The mix of eastern and western music and imagery gripped him. When the final chorus switched from *Hare Rama* to *Hallelujah*, he sat upright, his eyes sparkling. "Wow. That's genius. East, west, ancient, modern. It's all one, it's all whole. And it's not just an idea. He makes it *real*."

Beau slid the vinyl into its sleeve, careful not to touch the grooves. "How do you think that would go over at the vets hall?"

Jake laughed. "They'd think we're a bunch of Hare Krishnas."

"Belle's always had a thing for Kali, goddess of destruc- tion."

"Which one is she?"

"Bloody tongue, scimitar, necklace of skulls."

"She probably has all that in her hope chest." Jake leaned on his elbow. "Do you think we'll ever get back together?"

"All things must pass." He held up the album jacket. "Says so right here."

Jake groaned and lay back, his feet on the floor. Beau sat cross-legged on the mattress beside him.

"You really kept your cool out there at The Corners," Jake said.

"I've had practice. Outside, smooth and soothing, a pond of serenity."

"Or a babbling brook."

"Thanks. Inside, it's more like a mudslide. Or sometimes a lava flow. With orchids on the fringes."

"I get it. Fierce, but lacy."

"Only the fiercest wear lace."

"If you hadn't kept your head, we'd probably still be standing in the parking lot, shell shocked. Or rounded up by the cops."

"Yeah. Where'd they all come from, anyway?"

"Joanie said they were planning a raid. That would have been a nifty finale to our set." Jake spun the basketball in his hands. "Frank hasn't called or come to town. He spends all his time out at the farm. Joanie says he's dropped out of school."

"That would be stupid."

"Frank is not stupid."

"Okay, then it would be very, very . . ."

"What?"

"Frank."

Jake laughed, then stared at the ceiling. "I told him I loved him."

Beau stretched out beside him and let that sink in. It didn't hurt as much as he thought it would. *How would I feel if he said that to me? I'm not sure anymore.* He turned to look at him. "Did you say that so you could hear him say 'I love you' back?"

"That's a helluva thing to say." Still, Jake paused, like he was thinking it over. "Do *you* love him?"

"*That's* a helluva thing to say."

"You spent the night together, that night."

"He was just a kid, y'know? I felt like a mother with a baby. A *big* baby, but . . . I sang him a lullaby."

"Which one?"

"I couldn't really think of one, so I sang 'The Coventry Carol.'"

"Oh jeez, Beau! King Herod's slaughter of the innocents? Real soothing."

"Well, it was seasonal. Besides, I couldn't remember the words so I just did *loo lee loo li*. It seemed to be help. He stopped twitching and fell asleep."

"He did seem less crazy in the morning."

"Huh."

"Well, less crazy for Frank."

"Maybe love isn't what he needs. Maybe he just needs someone by his side."

Jake pulled a face. "You've been listening to that album too much."

"You're probably right." He sat up. "It's still light out. Wanna shoot some hoops?"

Jim was settling his stuff on the shelves in the shed when Frank entered. "Come for my boots," he said.

"Yep," Jim replied.

He picked them up and lingered, looking at Jim's back, his wide shoulders, his crow-black hair. The chaps hung on the wall again. "It gets cold out here."

"No worse'n roughin' it on the trail."

"The heater works, if you need it."

Jim faced him. "It'll be spring soon enough."

"We could run a water line out here. Sink for dishes, toilet."

"I'll expect a mint on my pillow next."

Frank didn't know what to say. It was Jim's turn.

He took it. "You back in the big house, then?"

Frank's chest unclenched. "Angela's keeping my old room. I get granddad's."

"Any ghosts?"

"Not any more. Bein' out here a month taught me the value of a hot shower in the mornin'."

Jim laughed and sat on the bunk. "I remember hosing you off when that manure spreader tipped. I never seen such a sight."

Frank sat beside him and put his boots on the floor, toes pointing in. "I thought I'd die. You had me strip down. Even with the hose on me, I got a hard-on. I thought you'd rag on me, or give me a whuppin', or tell granddad. But you didn't. You stood and stared."

"It was quite the sight. You were all pale and rigid, like some mushroom sprung from the earth."

"You remember what you said?"

"Nope."

"'Damn.' Drawn out. *Day-yum*."

"It was somethin'." Jim looked at the boots, then turned his eyes on him.

Frank swallowed. "You stayin'?"

Jim put a hand on the small of his back. "You know how I am."

"I do now."

"I won't be here forever."

"Sure."

"But I won't leave you and your mom to fend for yourselves. I'll see to it."

"That a promise?"

Jim dropped his hand. "I don't use those words. Love. Promise. Tried it once. Watching someone's heart break nearly tore me in two. I'm nobody's hero, Frank. Heroes need victims, and you're no victim. You're a survivor like me. So, no promises."

Frank took a deep breath. "Good. Then there's nothin' to break."

"You okay with that?"

"It's just what I need." He swung his leg over and sat on his lap facing him. "It's just what I need right now."

Jim's eyes flashed blue fire.

Three Hags and the Moon

First is the hag who comes in the day.
Her vision is black, she has something to say.
"His death is the light and the truth and the way."
  And what have they done with my love?

Next is the hag who comes around noon,
Gibbering jabbering notes like a loon.
She says, "It will end," but she doesn't say, "Soon."
  And what have they done with my love?

Last is the hag who hovers at night.
Her eyes are ablaze and her hair is a fright
For Mother knows best, and Mother is right.
  And what have they done with my love?

I am the moon who cradles you whole
Who holds you aloft in the night and the cold
And knows to grow new you first must grow old.
  And where have you gone, my love?

The Dismissal of
Miss Ida Lane Lancaster

I 'd like to go to the library board meeting with you," Joanie told her father. "I'm going to report on it for *The Clarion.*"

"These meetings are pretty tame affairs," John Tibbits said. "This one will be particularly dull stuff."

"But it's about the vandalism, isn't it?"

"Yes, and other kinds of damage and how to protect our holdings."

"I was there when Miss Lancaster discovered it. That is, when Mr. Anderson reported it. And I was there when Jake found out all the pictures of his father had been cut out. I can tell the board what that feels like to a student and a library patron. If you could have seen the look on Jake's face—"

"I don't think feelings will come into it. It's mostly technical, about converting materials to microfiche, and the budget we need to do that. Miss Lancaster has come up with a reasonable plan."

She looked at him, clutching her notepad and pencil.

"Okay, come along if you want. But don't blame me if you fall asleep."

The first thing she wrote in her notepad was who was who on the board. There was her father, of course, a pharmacist and member of the Chamber of Commerce. He was going to introduce Miss Lancaster, who would detail her proposal. Mr. Carl Smalley, a supervisor at the paper products plant, was president of the board, though that was a rotating position. Joanie recognized Mrs. Marjorie Douthitt, American History teacher and head of girls' P.E. at the high school. Mrs. Douthitt, a newcomer to Croy and a civic enthusiast, also chaired the Community Chest Drive. The board was rounded out by Mrs. Elena George, a member of the Kennsing County Historical Society, and Mr. Eugene Swofford, owner of Swofford's Lumber Seed and Supply, also a member of the Chamber of Commerce and past commander of the American Legion post. Besides herself and Miss Lancaster, the only other member of the public present was Reverend Joshua Mathers, which she thought was curious.

Mr. Smalley gaveled the meeting to order and turned it over to Mr. Tibbits.

"I've asked Miss Lancaster here this evening to address an issue at the library. As many of you know, some of our periodicals have been mutilated, articles and photos cut out. Miss Lancaster has a proposal that will help preserve them and reduce the cost of storage and maintenance as well. Miss Lancaster?"

Miss Lancaster took a seat at a table facing the board and opened a manila folder. "Gentlemen and ladies of the board, thank you for allowing me this time to speak to you on this matter. Over the years, the cost of preserving and maintaining an archive of our local periodicals has increased, slowly but steadily, as has the space needed to store them. Recently, the safety of the materials from random vandalism—"

"Excuse me, Miss Lancaster," Gene Swofford interrupted, "but my understanding is that the vandalism, if that is what it was, was not random, but targeted."

"The damage that was reported, first by Mr. Anderson, a visiting researcher, and then by a local high school student, was targeted at articles about a specific topic and person.

Once it was brought to my attention, I began a search of all archived copies of *The Croy Evening Call* to see if the damage is more widespread."

"And is it?"

"That remains to be seen."

"Pardon me, Gene," John Tibbits said, "but perhaps we should allow Miss Lancaster to present her proposed solution, which is not just about damage, but storage and maintenance as well."

Swofford shrugged, and Smalley nodded for her to continue.

"If we adopt a system of microfiche storage and retrieval, we will save considerable space, and we won't have to keep some items in temperature and humidity controlled rooms."

"Won't conversion be costly?" Mrs. Douthitt asked.

"In the short term, yes, but in just a few years, the savings will overtake the cost."

"What sort of items?" Smalley asked.

"Initially, only the most vulnerable, which is currently locally produced periodicals, such as *The Croy Evening Call*."

"But eventually other periodicals as well?"

"Eventually, all of them. We will keep physical copies going back three years, but each year, the oldest will be converted to microfiche."

"And that includes periodicals that advocate anti-Americanism and include anti-war propaganda?"

"Carl?" Tibbits asked. "Where are you headed?"

"There is concern about some of the material in the library."

"Concern about what? Raised by who?"

Swofford answered for him. "The Americanism Committee of the American Legion has published a list of periodicals and books of concern."

Miss Lancaster cleared her throat. "The proposed solution includes all periodicals to which the library is currently subscribed."

"That includes *The Nation* and *The National Review*, does it not?"

"It does."

"There are other concerns, too," Mrs. George said. "I've asked Reverend Mathers here this evening to express them."

"We have a proposal before us," Tibbits said.

"Not yet," Smalley said. "Reverend Mathers, if you would?"

Joanie saw her father whisper something to Smalley, who shook his head. "Perfectly acceptable. This is a public meeting. Mathers is a member of the community just like anyone else."

There was only one chair at the table in front, so Miss Lancaster closed her folder and yielded to Reverend Mathers.

He smiled. "Thank you, Miss Lancaster. Mr. Smalley, Mr. Tibbits, and other members of the board, this won't take but a moment. It has come to my attention, or rather the attention of some of my parishioners, parents of young children and teenagers, that the library contains materials that may not only be, as Mr. Swofford indicated, conveyors of anti-Americanism and anti-democratic propaganda, but also rife with questionable moral content. Since these materials are readily available to any library patron, including young, impressionable minds during their most formative years—"

"Now just a minute," Tibbits objected. "This is getting pretty far afield. Miss Lancaster is here to propose a very reasonable solution to a very particular problem. She hasn't come prepared to defend the entire contents of the library's holdings."

Smalley smiled. "Miss Lancaster knows the library like the back of her hand, don't you, Miss Lancaster?"

She folded her hands in her lap. "I am prepared to answer any question you have about the catalog."

"Questionable moral content is a rather broad brush," Tibbits said.

"I can be quite specific," Mathers said. "A committee of concerned citizens has compiled a list of one hundred and thirty-one titles containing or discussing scenes of moral degeneracy. These materials would subvert the healthy mental and moral development of our youth."

"Again, 'moral degeneracy' is a vague term."

"It isn't to me," Mrs. George said.

"But what is it based on?"

"That will be made clear if I may continue my report," Mathers said.

Tibbits turned to Smalley. "Mr. President, this matter was not on the agenda, and Reverend Mathers—excuse me for saying it, Reverend, but it's true—has no standing to bring it up. We have procedures for a reason."

"Then I'll bring it up," Smalley said. "Reverend, if I could have that list, please?" Mathers passed it up, and Smalley put on his reading glasses.

"Who came up with that list?" Mrs. Douthitt asked.

Swofford spoke up. "It was compiled by private individuals on their own time and of their own volition, using public records available at the library, specifically the card catalog."

"Using what criteria?"

Smalley cleared his throat. "It's pretty clear. Perhaps, John, you might ask your daughter to leave the room?"

Joanie held her breath.

"Joanie is capable of thinking for herself."

"Very well."

"May I see that?" Tibbits asked.

"It will be included in the minutes of this meeting," Smalley said. "The criteria—" He looked directly at Joanie— "is that these are books whose subject card catalogs include the terms 'homosexuality,' 'bestiality,' 'lesbianism,' or 'invert sexuality.'"

"I beg your pardon, Mr. President," Miss Lancaster said, "but other than homosexuality, none of those are legitimate card catalog terms. Furthermore, homosexuality is but one subcategory under the general subject of the study of sexes in society."

Smalley frowned. "The study of sexes in society? Why isn't it under mental derangements or abnormal psychology?"

"The study of sexes in society is thought a more neutral wording of the topic."

Swofford huffed. "What is there to be neutral about? It's deranged, disgusting. A mental disorder."

"That is a matter of debate—"

"In New York or San Francisco, maybe, where they parade their perversions for all to see. Not in Croy."

Miss Lancaster smiled tightly. "As I was going to say, a matter of debate among experts."

"Miss Lancaster," Smalley said, "you've never married, have you? You've never had children of your own to care for."

Mrs. Douthitt sat upright. "Just a minute, Carl. I have never had children, either. But I oversee the mental and physical education of young women every day. I am perfectly capable of understanding the risks and the care I need to take."

"That is not the point."

"It is *exactly* the point," Tibbits said. "Miss Lancaster conducts the children's reading hour every Saturday and has for decades."

Swofford raised his voice. "In the same library that contains these volumes of filth! What if one of the children gets ahold of 'em?"

"The care of children—" Mrs. Douthitt began.

"Permit me, Mrs. Douthitt," Miss Lancaster said. "Mr. President, members of the board, I am here in a professional capacity as your employee. I am not prepared or inclined to answer questions about my personal life."

"An employee for now," Swofford muttered.

"For heaven's sake, Gene," Tibbits said. "Personnel matters are not discussed in open meeting. You know that."

"Then maybe we should ask Miss Tibbits to leave."

"And Reverend Mathers?"

Smalley raised his hands as if separating boxers. "That won't be necessary. This is not about personnel, but about library policy and whether it reflects community standards."

Swofford and Tibbits settled back in their chairs. Smalley smiled at Joanie. "Perhaps if Miss Tibbits could put away her notebook?"

Joanie swallowed. "Is that an order, sir?"

"No." He looked at her father. "You're sure about this, John?"

"I'm glad she's here. I wish more people were."

"Very well. Reverend Mathers, if you could retire to your seat? And Miss Lancaster, if you could return, please?" He picked up Mathers's list. "I have in my hand a report compiled by a committee of concerned citizens. It lists one hundred and thirty-one books of moral degeneracy or questionable moral propriety, and an additional sixty books and circulating periodicals that promote anti-Americanism and contain anti-war propaganda."

"Again, I'd like to see that list."

"It will be in the minutes, John, just like I said. Now,

Miss Lancaster, I'm asking you to remove from the stacks all the books on this list whose subject catalog entry includes the word 'homosexual.' Can you do that for us?"

"Permanently?"

"Until the controversy cools down."

Mrs. George scoffed. "When will the promise of eternal damnation ever cool down?"

Miss Lancaster regarded her coolly. "It is always possible to stir people's anger. To frighten them, to get them to hate. It is harder to get them to think. But there should always be something in the library for them to think about."

"The Community Chest campaign begins in a few weeks," Mrs. Douthitt said. "Aren't you concerned that word of this matter will cut into your donations? And if those donors turn away, won't that hurt other causes as well?"

"You could always say the books were lost," Smalley offered. "Or that you've sent them to the bindery."

"Why stop there? I may as well say we don't have them at all and never did." Miss Lancaster gathered herself. "A library is either a library or it is a tomb, a depository for dying ideas too weak to stand up to contradiction. And how would you pick which ones to cut away? How can you pluck one bead from a strand without the whole thing unraveling in your hands?

"Every catalog slip, every book, pamphlet, broadside, newspaper, and periodical has its place, and each reflects on all the others. Should we censor the Readers Guide to Periodical Literature? Black out the words we don't want people to know someone's written about? Then what? Would you remove words from the dictionary? To what hope? That the words would never be spoken again? Perhaps there are words that should never have been spoken in the first place, but they were, they were uttered, they came out of people's mouths with the breath of their life. Should we then cut away those lives as well? I suppose that's what some people wish. But it is an idle wish. Lives and ideas and words and books do not vanish without repercussions. That's why there are libraries. We may forget from time to time. Tribes may be vanquished, peoples disappear, empires collapse in ruin or be overrun, but as long as one person remains, one curious, courageous person remains and reads, those lives are restored to us. As long as there are libraries, we can always bring them back."

"Back?" Swofford said. "Why bring them back?"

"So we might know the truth, the whole truth about ourselves."

"Oh, this is all high and fancy. The simple truth is—"

"The simple truth, Mr. Swofford? There is no simple truth. There is, perhaps, a simple-*minded* truth that we are all wicked and weak and need to be protected from ourselves. Or the awful truth that we are all lust-filled and self-indulgent and need to be held in check with an iron rod. I don't believe in either of those truths. Nor in the 'high and fancy' truth you allude to, that we have the stuff of angels inside us, just waiting to be set free. The library shelves all these truths, but the library alone, intact and unabridged, tells the whole truth: that we are, at best, a mixed blessing on this earth. Forget that, and we will all vanish without a trace."

Board president Smalley leaned back, shaking his head. "This is getting us nowhere. If you won't remove the books, will you remove the cards with the offensive words from the card catalog?"

"No sir, I will not."

"Will you remove the books from the general stacks and place them in a locked cabinet?"

"No sir, I will not."

Swofford leaned forward. "Will you keep a record of the people who check out these vile books and make such records available to any duly appointed officer of the law, or citizens' committee, or judicial officer?"

"No sir, I will not."

"Oh, for heaven's sake, Miss Lancaster. I know you keep records. We all know you keep records. How else could you collect on overdue books?"

"I do indeed keep records. But they are for the library's use alone. A person's reading list should be as private as his thoughts."

"But if there is no wickedness in those thoughts, why conceal them?"

"If there *is* wickedness, why pry it out? I'm sure most people wouldn't care to hear it."

"A man's life should be an open book."

"Should a man's life be judged by the books he's opened or by the principles he chooses to follow? I trust my patrons to find those principles for themselves. I will not cripple the process by offering them only a handful of curated ideas. Moral fiber is not developed in a warm bath of ease. Good judgment requires exercise. Removing that exercise and putting it in the hands of a select few—a council, a citizens committee, a judge, or even a librarian—robs the mind of vigorous argument and leaves it flabby."

Smalley rapped his gavel. "This board is now in closed session. Spectators and guests, please clear the room."

Joanie followed Miss Lancaster out. Reverend Mathers bid them both a cordial good evening and walked away smiling.

"I'm going to publish this entire travesty in *The Clarion*," Joanie said. "People have a right to know what went on in there."

"That's admirable, Joanie," Miss Lancaster said, "but you should clear it with Mrs. Taylor first."

"That's prior restraint. It's unconstitutional."

"Those freedoms don't apply to young people. I wouldn't want what's happening to me to happen to Mrs. Taylor."

"Why? What's happening to you?"

"Grown men do not like being contradicted in public, especially by an unmarried woman." She looked at the closed door of the board room. "We needn't live in fear, but neither should we live as if we had nothing to be afraid of. I suspect I will no longer have my position come tomorrow morning."

"Daddy won't let them do that."

"There were enough votes on that board to do what they set out to do."

"But that's just the board. It's not the whole town. You're librarian for all of us. Those people in there are a minority."

"A small cadre can get ample power to do what they wish when no one is watching."

"But that's so small-minded!"

"Indeed. The smaller the better."

As soon as her father got home, Joanie pounced on him. "What happened? Is Miss Lancaster still librarian?"

"I tried my best, Princess."

"Oh no! They fired her?"

"No. They did worse. They passed a resolution requesting the city council take jurisdiction over all library acquisitions and materials."

"But she keeps her job?"

"Not for long, I'm afraid. And I won't be on the board for long, either. They're giving the council the power to appoint a new board, and the new board can select a new librarian, which they probably will."

There's got to be a way to stop this. "What was the vote?"

John Tibbits sat down with a sigh. "Three in favor, one against. Mrs. Douthitt abstained."

"So, just three. We just need to convince two and it's all over."

He shook his head. "There's something more, Joanie."

"It can't get any worse, can it?"

"When the city council takes control of the library materials, that will include the panels. That's what they're really after. They're after Ada's Memorial."

The Storm

R andy built a ramp leading from his back porch to the yard. He'd been able to complete it in peace, out of sight of the granny house and Mrs. Oldfield's. He didn't want kibitzers or critics. Doing something physical and solitary focused him on the immediate task and kept him from thinking about what lay ahead.

When he finished in back, he brought his tools and the lumber around front. The ramp here would be shorter since the porch was nearly at grade. He was extending the railing when he saw Clara Oldfield cross the alley. *I knew it was too good to last.* "I'm almost done, Mrs. Oldfield," he called out as she approached.

"So I see." She stopped a few feet away. "That looks good and solid."

"Virginia wants to be able to get out. She says outside air is more alive."

"She's right."

"I'm remodeling the kitchen, too, so she can get around. Widening some doors."

"You may as well build a new house."

"It may come to that."

"When does she come home?"

"Monday, if the doctors say."

"For how long?"

Randy looked off. "For as long as she can. That hospital is killing her." *I promised not to think about that.* "Not physically, you know, but her spirit."

"I know. A hospital is no place for a soul." She looked at her house. "I took care of Gerald entirely at home. It's no small undertaking."

"That doesn't matter. She's my mom."

"It does matter, Randy. It will take fortitude, patience, forbearance, and forgiveness."

He looked at the ground. "I'm no saint, Mrs. Oldfield."

"Oh, don't worry. I'll not mistake you for one. But you'll need help. Don't be ashamed to ask for it or to accept it."

"I won't."

She stepped closer and examined at the ramp. "You're obviously planning for a wheelchair. Do you have one?"

"There's a medical supply store in Daggs Valley. If they don't have one, I may have to zip up to O. City."

"I still have Gerald's. Let me get it for you."

"You don't have to do that."

"Now what did I just say about accepting help? You're going to have your hands full come Monday and plenty to do till then. You don't need to be gallivanting all over the state to boot." She ran her hand along the railing. "You picked up some important skills this summer."

"Thank you ma'am."

She looked at him narrow-eyed, as if uncertain he meant it. "Hmm." She headed back across the alley. "I'll bring the chair directly."

Mrs. Taylor did not approve the article on the library board meeting for the upcoming issue of *The Clarion*. "Can I at least write an editorial about it?" Joanie pleaded. "No one else covered the meeting. People have a right to know."

"Why don't we discuss it with Mr. Boyd and Mr. Maxwell?" Mrs. Taylor proposed.

They met in the school superintendent's office, but it wasn't much of a discussion. "It's not school news," Principal Maxwell stated flatly.

"But these are important issues to lots of kids," Joanie pleaded. "Many of us use the city library for research. We've come to depend on it."

"We have a fine library here at school," Maxwell answered.

"But it's small and limited."

"This is not an issue for young people to decide or even discuss," Superintendent Boyd said. "It's a city matter. Why don't you do another piece about the trophy case, like you did last year?"

Mrs. Taylor put her hand on her arm to keep her from answering. It probably kept her out of detention as well.

The city settled the matter quickly. At the request of the library board, the council enacted a new ordinance. The old board was dissolved and a new one installed. Their first action was to fire Miss Lancaster. Mrs. Craddock, recently retired from the high school, was hired as interim librarian while a search was conducted for a permanent replacement.

Joanie next saw Mr. Smalley at the Rexall. He and her father seemed to have patched up their differences. *Well, what did you expect? They're in the same clubs together.* But the chilling effect of city politics on her year as senior editor still stung. When Smalley come up to the counter with a bottle of aspirin, she remarked mildly, as if inquiring about the weather, "I notice Mr. Mathers' list of books didn't make it into the minutes."

"I beg your pardon?"

"The one hundred and thirty-one youth-corrupting texts and the sixty anti-American periodicals. They aren't in the minutes for the last library board meeting."

"Joanie," her father said, "would you come here a minute?"

"That's all right, John." Smalley smiled at her. "The issue of the list is moot since the board it was presented to is dissolved, and a new board has been seated. They operate under different rules."

"Do you still have it?"

He took his aspirin and receipt. "Good day, Miss Tibbits."

Her father pulled her behind the pharmacy stacks. "If you can't treat our customers with courtesy, perhaps you shouldn't be behind the counter."

"Perhaps I shouldn't."

"It's not helpful, Joanie, stirring things up."

"Miss Lancaster is leaving today. Did you know that? They're saying goodbye to her at the library. Perhaps I can be more helpful there."

Miss Lancaster was offered a position at Oklahoma State University, the same institution that was gathering data on Oklahoma's Carnegie libraries. She did not hesitate. She put her small cottage up for sale and packed her belongings. There remained a few items of sentimental value at her old office in the Memorial Library, and with Mrs. Craddock's consent, she went there to collect them.

A small group of high school students and a few adults gathered in the rotunda to say goodbye. Jake was there, and Beau and Adam, and the kids from *The Clarion* and the yearbook staff. Joanie was surprised to see Randy there too, and Red Conner. Among the adults were Mrs. Lila Armbruster and a few other members of the Historical Society, but not Mrs. George. Mr. Frye from Croyen Top Clay was there, and the editor-in-chief of *The Croy Evening Call*. Sunny Sohi stood off to the side, his linen suit glowing in the indirect light. He stared up at the dome and smiled. No one who worked at the paper products plant attended.

"I'm not one for sentiment," Miss Lancaster said, "but I thank all of you for coming. My way forward is clear, and I take it with no regrets, though I am sorry to leave you. I am most sorry that I will not be able to attend the hearing to discuss the fate of the panels, now that the council has possession of them. That will have to be in your hands."

Mrs. Craddock cleared her throat behind the circulation desk.

"Yes. Goodbye and good luck to you all."

The adults shook her hand and left one by one. Mrs. Armbruster was among the last. "I'm so sorry, Ida," she said.

"We did our best."

"They're safe in the museum for now, but for how long?" She shook her head. "Already some members are complaining they take up too much space. There isn't room for them side by side, even in the waiting room, so they're in separate rooms."

"They were meant to be elevated and seen together," Mr. Sohi said, stepping forward.

"Oh, Sunny," Lila Armbruster said. "You haven't been by to see them yet, have you. Would you like me to arrange a viewing?"

"Not really."

"Mrs. George says the Society should be compensated for storing city property, but I doubt the council will consider it."

"That's exactly her point," Sunny said. "Miss Lancaster, you have been a champion." He took her hand and kissed it. "The times are drawn like knives against us. May you cross this sea of troubles to more pleasant shores." He turned and walked out, his cane clicking on the terrazzo floor.

"Well, he hasn't changed," Lila Armbruster said.

"Not a whit."

"Goodbye, Ida. Stay in touch."

"I will, Lila."

Everyone had left except Randy, Jake, and Joanie. Miss Lancaster picked up a cardboard box from the circulation desk. Mrs. Craddock didn't acknowledge her, and Miss Lancaster didn't bid her goodbye.

"Can I carry that for you?" Jake asked.

"It's just down the steps to my car, but thank you, yes." She took a moment handing it over to take a deep, shaky breath.

When they passed through the front doors, they saw a crowd of people, larger than had been inside, walking a picket line in front of the library. Many carried placards. "God Sees All!" and "No Filth With Public Funds!" Bobbie and Al were among them. Reverend Mathers stood a few steps up the library stairs, exhorting them in his calm but firm voice.

"Who are these people?" Randy asked.

Jake shook his head. "Matherites."

"Look at this, children," Miss Lancaster said. "Look at this and remember."

"I thought it was just a few people on the board," Joanie said. "This is more. This is too many."

"No, it isn't." Miss Lancaster turned her back on the protest and squared her shoulders. "People who have nothing to lose get nothing done. It's the folks who risk everything that move mountains.

"Jake, put down that box. You three, give me your hands." They stood in a circle. "Think of what it took to rescue and conserve those panels. We had almost no warning." She looked at Randy. "If your mother hadn't called that night, they would have been dumped at the confluence of the White Horse and Little Bushy Creek. She had very little time to act. She was going into labor. But act she did."

She turned to Jake. "Think of Mrs. Armbruster, negotiating with her husband to use the rail yard to store the biggest panel, the one you so cleverly discovered. It's large and heavy. She certainly couldn't have shifted it by herself. Who helped?"

She faced Joanie. "Think of the Jamesons, driving their

flatbed truck through town in the middle of the night to get to Garvey High, risking their lives to save a sculpture. Did they have an escort?

"And Jedediah Tucker and his uncle, driving up that twisting road to Pesogi, a difficult road in good weather, and it had recently rained. But they got it there without a hitch or a hoist. And Jed the whole time wondering if Sunny would live or die.

"All those people kept the memorial alive. For whom? For you. Don't you forget them. Don't you give in."

She picked up the box and walked down the stairs, passing Reverend Mathers without a glance. The picket broke before her, but as she approached, a man spat across her path. Joanie gasped. But Miss Lancaster did not waver. She crossed the line and got into her car.

Joanie was so focused on her she almost missed a movement at the edge of the crowd. Bobbie Littledeer placed her placard face down on the sidewalk and walked away.

The hearing before the city council on the disposition of the panels was merely for show. Joanie, Jake, and Adam Jameson listened from the gallery as the words swirled around the hearing room. Randy stayed home to look after Virginia, but made them promise to give him a full report.

The mildest controversy centered on the Goddess of Prosperity, which the council promptly renamed the civic pride panel to avoid any whiff of idolatry. Nevertheless, a council member raised a concern.

"What about the damage? There is a significant chip on the lower right along the base."

Mr. Frye from the brick works approached the public mike to respond. "That's Croyen Top Clay in those panels. Tough as concrete and as impervious as glass."

"But isn't there a danger the damage will spread and

weaken the whole panel? That could become a liability for the city."

Mr. Frye puffed up. "No sir, not at all. I'd stake my reputation on it. Why, the entire town's water and sewer lines are made of Croyen Top Clay. Made, fired, and installed right here in Croy. It will last a century or more."

They moved on to the soldiers' panel. The mayor appeared to head off controversy by stating, "We are not, I repeat, *not* going to entertain public comment on the alleged salaciousness of the figures in the foreground. There are ample celebrations of the human form in public art, and an honored tradition of it in the representation of military figures. We should be proud of the sacrifice depicted here, not embarrassed by it, and certainly not ashamed of it."

"That'll quash the Matherites," Joanie muttered to Jake.

"Looks like Andy's getting resurrected," he replied.

But the Matherites were prepared. They didn't attack the bare-chested soldier or the nude body of his dead comrade. Instead, they went after the images behind them, depicting the 45th Infantry's liberation of Dachau.

"Why is a swastika included?"

"Nobody shoots left-handed. That left-handed lieutenant is a coded message. We can guess for who."

"Besmirching the reputation of our fighting boys weakens America. Anything that weakens America strengthens Communism."

Red Conner rose to defend the panel. Using information from vets he had met at the VFW, he explained the two insignia of the 45th, a swastika before the war and a thunderbird during it. "Both are included in the panel," he pointed out. "They represent the Native American heritage of many vets of the 45th. The thunderbird is—"

Councilman Sullivan interrupted. "Mr. Conner, I thank

you for your service and am relieved you have returned to us. But may I ask on whose behalf you are speaking?"

"I'm here representing the VFW."

"Not the VVAW? The Vietnam Veterans Against the War?"

"Sir?"

"Didn't you participate in the Winter Soldier Investigation? An effort to smear the honor of our boys in Vietnam with accusations of war crimes. Those lads are heroes."

"They wouldn't agree sir, I assure you."

"You don't think they're heroes?"

"They're soldiers, sir, doing a soldier's job."

"So you weren't in Detroit last January? Isn't that where you really got your alleged injury?"

Councilman Brown interrupted. "I fail to see what Mr. Conner's activities out of state have to do with us. This is a local matter."

Red stood at attention. "I will gladly answer any question Councilman Sullivan has about my injuries and personal activities. I will do so outside, in person, and with embellishment."

Sullivan sat back in his chair. "I think I have my answer."

"Mr. Conner?" the mayor asked.

"I have nothing further to say."

"I have." Sunny Sohi rose and took the mike. "This communist innuendo nonsense is just that, nonsense. The soldiers' panel isn't a signal to secret fifth-column cells. It was designed specifically to *fight* communism."

The councilman who worried about cracks spoke to the mayor. "I don't think we're interested in the word of an outsider on this matter."

"Sir, I am a native of Croy," Sunny replied, "born right here on a farm you can see from the belvedere atop the county courthouse. But you don't have to take my word for it. Look at your own records. I had in mind another design entirely for that panel. The council approved it, then changed their minds. They chose *this* design instead precisely because it *was* anti-communist. Read your own records! You can read, can't you?"

Jake groaned and covered his eyes. "And that buries Andy."

The objections to the tornado panel were even more far-fetched.

Mrs. Elisa Welmut rose to read from a sheet in her hand. "I am the mother of two children who attend Croy Consolidated High School, and the wife of William Welmut, owner and manager of the IGA on Broad Street. I am concerned about the figures depicted in the tornado panel. The large Negro man in the foreground appears to be a representation of Marcus Garvey, a notorious Black Nationalist and exploiter of the poor, who spent much of his life in England, France, and Russia. He is not representative of local history at all, and certainly not of local values."

The crowd rumbled with concern.

"That isn't true," Adam muttered.

"Ever since we consolidated with Marcus Garvey High School, the insidious influence of this notorious man has been indoctrinating our children. We have a right to control what goes into our children's minds."

Mrs. Oldfield rose to her feet. "Elisa Welmut, don't be a fool. That figure is no more Marcus Garvey than I am."

Mrs. Welmut planted her hands on her hips. "Then why has it been hanging in Marcus Garvey High for nearly twenty years?"

"Ladies, please," the mayor said. "One at a time. Mrs. Welmut, you have the floor."

"I've said my piece. Let Clara Oldfield say hers."

Mrs. Oldfield approached the mike. "Cecil Jameson saved Gerald Oldfield and myself that day, the day the TriCounty Twister struck. He stayed behind to hold the storm door open for us rather than seek shelter with his own family. That's who's on that panel, Elisa, not Marcus Garvey."

"Liar," someone said just loud enough to be heard.

The mayor rapped his gavel. "Is there anyone who can verify this account? Mr. Sohi?"

Sunny rose. "Mrs. Oldfield is correct." He said nothing further and sat down.

"Anyone else?" the mayor asked.

Jake looked at Adam, but Adam shook his head. "Not on your life," he muttered.

In the end, the city council declared the tornado panel and the soldiers' panel unsuited for display on tax-funded public property. The civic pride panel might be displayed, perhaps in the library rotunda, but only after further study determined it was structurally sound and safe for public viewing.

"As if a glance would shatter it," Mr. Frye said in disgust as he left the hearing.

In their final action, the council decided the panels would stay in the Kennsing County Historical Society Museum for now. They allocated enough funds to reimburse the society for one month of storage.

Joanie, Jake, and Adam sat on the steps of the Memorial Library, watching people stream out of the town hall.

"Well, that was a shitshow," Jake said.

Adam nodded. "A true *circus cacatus.*"

"What are we going to tell Randy?" Joanie asked. "I don't know where to start. He'll never believe Mrs. Oldfield rose to our defense."

"Yeah, she was a surprise." Jake picked a pebble off the steps and looked down the block. Red Conner was talking to Candy Sullivan. "Red was kinda cool. And Mr. Sohi. I guess Miss Lancaster was right. We have more allies than we thought."

"Not enough, though." Joanie sighed. "The Matherites packed the hearing."

Jake looked at Adam. "Why didn't you speak up about your grandfather?"

"How many colored people did you see in that chamber?" Adam said. "I counted three. Mr. Sohi, Eli Brown, and myself." He shook his head. "The folks in there would rather rip their own history to shreds than admit there was ever a time when they were weak, afraid, or alone. Or just plain wrong about who they thought they were. And they'll tear apart anyone who gets in the way of that happy, perfect vision." He stood to leave. "My father told me the memorial was supposed to celebrate the *entire* town, its whole history. It would be a bridge to cross our divides and show us our community is one. But the only panel people will see, if they see any, is the civic pride panel—the one panel without a single African American or Native American on it."

Jake pitched his pebble across the walk. "I can imagine what Zach would say to that."

"Oh, so can I."

"What?" Joanie asked.

"Minus the profanities? 'You can't cross a bridge if you ain't got legs.' People in this town wouldn't know if they were missing a limb, and most wouldn't care to find out."

Sunny Sohi came down the town hall steps and extended his hand. "A valiant effort, Mr. Conner."

Red extended his but inwardly drew back. *The same eyes, the same skin.* No, they weren't. He pushed the image farther back in his mind and forced a smile. "Until I lost my temper."

"Daddy had it coming," Candy said. "He practically accused you of being a Commie agitator."

His smile flickered. Sohi's hand was warm and firm. Social convention saved him. "Oh, my manners. Mr. Sohi, I'd like to introduce you to Candy Sullivan, the councilman's daughter. Candy, this is Sundar Sohi, the man who made the sculptures."

Sunny bowed and kissed her hand. "Pleased to meet you, Miss Sullivan. Most people call me Sunny."

"Charmed. And call me Marsha, please."

Sunny indicated Red's cane with his own. "Nice stick. Hefty knob."

"Maybe too hefty. I nearly clobbered somebody with it."

"Well, if we choose our battles wisely, we live to fight another day." He tipped his hat and walked off.

"I'm really sorry about your father," Red said. "I can be a bit of an asshole sometimes."

"More than a bit from what I hear."

"So, word got around."

"It's Croy. Word didn't have to go far."

He rubbed his chin. "I could use a beer. Can I buy you one at the Wayland?"

"It's a little early for me."

"Can I buy you lunch, then?"

"Sure. Randall's?"

"Sure." He looked around and laughed. "That's funny. I don't remember where it is."

"It's just across from the police station, where it's always been."

"Of course." He wondered why he was sweating. "I guess some things never change."

"Oh, you might be surprised."

Passenger of Infinity

Virginia enjoyed two beautiful, difficult weeks at home as winter thawed into spring. Jake helped Randy get her in and out of bed and did the yard work. Joanie brought hot meals cooked by her mother and a squad of other women. Father John visited, but only after promising there would be no anointing with oils or muttering of rosaries. Mrs. Oldfield showed up one afternoon and stripped the beds and did the laundry "before it shamed the town." But in the end, just as winecups were showing in the fields and daffodils opening in the garden, Virginia had to be readmitted to care. Randy knew if he needed to talk to her about anything, it had to be soon. He looked around at the remodeled kitchen, the widened doorways, the ramp, all unlikely to be used again. *It was worth it.* He left for the hospital.

He walked in on his father giving his mother a kiss. Harry stood quickly and stepped away; Virginia wiped her mouth.

"That's it," he said, "you're both grounded."

"I just—" Harry started. "I was just saying goodbye. I'm heading out tonight. Things are getting hot."

"I'll say."

Virginia shifted against her pillow. "Watch it. I'm not so far gone I can't rise from this very bed and smack you."

He smiled, but the truth was she didn't look like she could lift a finger. "I'm glad I caught you, Pop. There's something I gotta ask you, but I gotta ask Mom first."

"No," Virginia said.

"I haven't asked it yet."

"If it's something you can't do unless I say yes, then it's no. That's a rule."

"I'm gonna ask anyway." He pulled up a chair. "Did you mean it when you said you really didn't care what happened to Ada's Memorial?"

"I said that?"

"Yeah, a while back. Thing is, they've got the panels, and they're probably going to ditch the whole thing."

"Who is?" Harry asked.

"The city council and a bunch of nutjobs."

Virginia cleared her throat. "Same difference."

"But I can stop them. I'm going to buy the panels from the city. That'll take it out of their hands. I don't know where I'll put them but I'll find someplace that's not city-owned, and eventually we'll build a frame or something for them and install them. That's where you come in, Pop. I'll need the plans for how they were supposed to be mounted on the library. Do you know where they are?"

"With the rest of Lerner's papers, I guess. I don't know where those are, though."

"Hold on, hold on. Wait your turn, Harry." Virginia sat more upright. "Kiddo, if there was a question in there for me, I missed it."

Randy pressed his hands together. "There's still a quarter of Granddad's legacy left, held back to encourage me to go to college."

"Yeah, but you didn't."

"But I could. Or VoTech. Anything post-secondary."

Virginia chuckled. "A seminary." The chuckle turned into a cough that fed on itself.

Harry glanced at Randy. "Ginny, should we call the nurse?"

She waved her hand. "Ask. Ask the question."

"Granddad wanted the sculpture destroyed. You said you didn't care. If I go back to school, I'll get the rest of the money. But I won't use it for school. I'll drop out as soon as I have it and use it for this."

Virginia didn't say anything.

"Is that stupid? Is it a waste?"

"Harry?" Virginia said.

"It's your money, son. Your future. How you spend it is up to you."

Virginia started picking at the IV in her arm. "Get this thing off me."

Harry touched her hand. "Is that a good idea?"

"And get me out of this damned bed! That's all I am to them anymore. This damned bed. I want out."

Randy stood. "I don't know, Mom. The doctors—"

"The doctors don't give a shit. They say I'll never leave this room. To hell with them. Help me up."

Harry detached the IV line, and he and Randy got Virginia to her feet. "Harry, bring the oxygen," she said.

"We going on a road trip?" he joked, but Randy could see the fear in his eyes.

"Downstairs. Out the back. Gotta show you something."

With one of them under each arm, they got her to the door.

"Check the hall," Harry said.

Randy checked. "Clear."

It took them forever to cross the hall and get down one flight of stairs to the exit. Randy grew more frightened with each step. "This is crazy, Mom. Just tell us what you want us to see."

"It's right there," she said. "Just open the door. Just let me step one foot outside this goddamned prison."

Harry pushed the panic bar and they stepped out onto a concrete loading dock overlooking the parking lot.

"Shit," Virginia said.

The town was enveloped in thick fog. Cold wet condensed on their cheeks. They couldn't see more than a block. Virginia raised her arm. "It's over there."

Randy squinted. "Where?"

"We can't see a thing, Ginny."

"The Armory's over there somewhere. Is that what you mean?" Randy asked. "Should I keep the panels there?"

"No. Across from it."

Harry and Randy peered into the milky void.

"There's nothing there, Ginny."

"*Now*. There's nothing there now." She drew a breath. "God, that air tastes good." She nodded toward a dark shape that could be the Armory. "Used to be a Cities Service station over there. Across from the parade grounds. I got steady rent from it. Gone now. Poisoned the earth. I never could sell it."

She turned to Randy. "You look like her. Lerner always said I looked like him, and that was my bad luck. But you look like her. I'd like to see her again, Randy. I'd like people to see her." She pointed into the fog. "Put it there. Otherwise it's useless." She turned slowly. "Okay. Back in."

They got the door open but she stopped at the foot of the stairs. "I can't do that."

"No problem." Harry scooped her up. "Randy, take the tank."

Randy climbed the stairs ahead of them, carrying the oxygen tank tethered to his mother.

Virginia chuckled in short gasps as they exited the stairwell and crossed the hall. "Harry. You weren't this romantic on our wedding night."

Randy grinned and opened the door to her room.

Police Chief Owen stood in the middle of the room, his

hands on his hips. "Harry Edom, I'm arresting you on a warrant for escaping from McLeod Correctional Center."

"Fuck you, Percy," Harry said. "Help us get her back in bed."

As soon as they laid her on the mattress, Owen faced them. "Let me see your hands, Harry." He pulled handcuffs from his belt.

"Jesus, have a heart!" Randy cried. "Not in front of Mom."

"Are you going to give me trouble?" Owen asked him.

"Let it go, Randy." Harry held out his hands.

"How'd you get to Texas?" Owen asked, snapping the cuffs in place.

"I hitched."

"It's illegal to pick up hitchhikers outside of McLeod Correctional Center."

"What can I say? Southern Oklahoma is awash in lawless Samaritans." He smiled at his wrists. "This must be a first for you, Percy. Getting an Edom in cuffs without shooting him first."

"There's still time."

Randy turned away in disgust and looked at the bed. His mother's color had changed. "Mom?" She didn't answer. "*Mom?*" He turned to his father. "Pop!"

"Ginny!" Harry lunged for the bed.

Percy put his hand on his holster but didn't draw. He watched the three of them for a bit, then stepped into the corridor and spoke calmly. "Nurse? When you get a minute."

◈

A cold rain drizzled on the mourners in the Catholic section of the cemetery, adults and high school students and people in between. Father John said his words of blessing over the coffin, but Jake tuned them out. He knew them by heart now. His grandfather, Frank's grandfather, now Randy's mom. *Pentecostal, Methodist, Catholic. When it comes to funerals, the words are all the same.* Jake wanted to make Virginia's special. He set an Emily Dickinson poem to music and meant to sing it over her grave when the religious part was over, but when the time came, he choked.

"Joanie? Could you?" He handed her the music.

She shook her head. Tears fell from her cheeks.

Belle took it. "Here, let me."

> *To the staunch Dust we safe commit thee;*
> *Tongue if it hath inviolate to thee—*
> *Silence denote and sanctity enforce thee,*
> *Passenger of Infinity—*

She sang it twice. The mourners drifted away, Belle and Beau holding hands, Joanie hugging Randy before standing off to one side. Red and Randy stayed at the grave, Randy staring at the coffin. He flinched when Candy Sullivan kissed him on the cheek. As the adults began to file away, Susan wrapped her arms around him. "I'm so sorry," she said.

"Harry should have been here," Randy said. "They should have let him come."

Susan nodded, then she and Aunt Margaret left with Joanie.

The last adult to leave was Mrs. Oldfield. Standing alone in the soft rain, she almost looked like a memorial pillar herself.

Jake thought everyone had gone, but Frank stood by the low stone wall that divided the Catholic from the Protestant part of the cemetery. There were separate roads and entrances for each. You couldn't get to one without leaving the other.

"Thanks for coming," Jake said, joining him.

"I didn't really know her, but she was important to you."

"She was my mom-away-from-mom." He leaned against

the stones. "At least there's a good solid wall here. Aunt Margaret wouldn't want good Catholic dust mingling with lesser stuff."

Frank looked to the other side. "There should be a wall over there too, separating Lorenzo from Granddad. That's going to be unsettled ground for some time."

Jake hung his head. "Sorry I didn't come."

Frank hiked himself up on the wall and sat. "It was a zoo. Mathers' people showed up, spoutin' off."

"About what?"

"The Devil. End Times. They were rather particular about me. Seems I'm going to hell. And not alone. The whole band, too."

"They said that to your face? At a funeral?"

"They didn't care. Having somethin' to holler about was more important. They made Lorenzo out to be some kind of warrior for God. Finally, Angela—*Angela*—said, 'Come on, Mom, let's get away from these kooks.' We left the lot of them standin' around yellin'."

Jake wondered what he would have said if he'd been there. *Should I say something now? Maybe I'm not that close to him anymore.* But he had to say something. "I don't think you're going to hell. I don't think I am either."

"Hell would be a breeze after life with Lorenzo."

"I don't think he was out to kill you."

Frank knocked his heels against the wall but said nothing.

"He was out to kill failure. In himself. It was all going downhill. You, the farm, your family. But The Quirks were a success. You were a success. So he had to put a stop to that or look a fool."

Frank stopped kicking. "Naw. He made a stupid mistake and it killed him. That's all."

They looked at Virginia's grave. Only Red and Randy were left. Randy was kneeling.

"Are you coming back to school?" Jake asked quietly.

Frank shook his head.

"Are you coming back to the band?"

"There won't be time. Things are tight at the farm. We'll be lucky to make it."

"You're running it yourself?"

"Me and Mom and Angela."

"And Jim."

"And Jim."

And there it was, the real reason. "I guess I was just filler."

"No." Frank hopped off the wall. "You're right. It warn't Lorenzo was after me. It was me. I come close, too. Granddad shootin' himself nearly did it. I knew we'd lose the farm. I felt I was slidin' away, nothin' to hold onto. But you were there, with your high words and your forward look. There was always somethin' better comin'." He took Jake's hand. "You warn't filler. You're why I held on." He held his hand a moment longer, then let go and leaned against the wall. "The band was filler."

Jake almost objected. The band hadn't been filler for him. *I learned guitar. I wrote songs. I sang in front of people. Things I'd never done before.* And it wasn't just the band. He looked at Frank. This guy had roamed his body like fresh territory, crossed borders, shown him sights he'd never imagined. *I want more. I want to keep going. But Frank—all the while he was fighting to stay in one place, to get back what he'd lost, to get back to Jim.* The difference between them couldn't have been more solid than the wall they leaned on.

Frank brought him out of his reverie. "Who's that with Randy?" He nodded at the gravesite. "The guy with the cane?"

"Red Conner."

"That's Red? He looks different."

"He nearly got blown up. They say Del Longacre saved his life."

Randy knelt on the wet grass and sobbed. He felt Red's hand squeeze his shoulder. "I know, I know. Act my age." He tried to pull back his tears.

"I would never say that," Red said quietly, then sighed in exasperation. "Where's Joanie? Where's Mally? They should be here for you."

"That's him over there with Frank."

"That's Mally? He looks different."

"He calls himself Jake now."

"And Joanie. Where's she?"

"My knees are soaked. Help me up." Red gave him a hand. "She's working on a speech or something."

Red shook his head. "I been gone less than two years, and this is the best they can do?"

"They were here for the hard part. That's over now. She's not sick anymore." Randy wiped his nose and pointed to his grandfather's headstone. "Two dates and a quote. She deserves more than that."

"There's rows and rows with less."

"Sorry, Red. Didn't mean any disrespect."

"Oh hell, man, don't listen to me. I've been an jerk since I got back."

Randy smiled despite himself. "A pissed-off jerk."

"Anger keeps even the dead moving."

"Why'd you clobber Marcus?"

Red shifted on his cane. "He knew things about Del. Things that shouldn't get back to his father. So we had a chat, cleared the air." He shook his head. "I still can't believe Del tackled that fucking kid with the grenade. How'd he even see him? And to save my ass? Stupid." He wiped his eyes. "Christ, now you've got me bawling."

Randy hung on his shoulder. "They deserve better." He looked up. The rain had stopped. "They're going to get it, too. Virginia, Del, all the pissed-off ghosts. Lerner chief among them." He faced his friend. "What d'ya think my chances are of getting into a seminary?"

Red laughed. "Squat."

"Yep. And you can't build squat with squat. But I'm going to do it. I'm going to build Ada's Memorial. It's going right where she said, across from the Armory. For her, for Del, for the folks lost in the TriCounty Twister. I don't give a rat's ass what the city council says. It's going up."

Guardian Angels

When Jake got back from the cemetery, Susan was in the bedroom, folding her black dress into her suitcase.

"You're leaving?"

"Just finding a place for things. This house is unbelievably small."

He looked around. "Bigger than our apartment in Greenwich Village."

"Thank God those days are over." She latched the suitcase and slid it under the bed. "But I'll have to leave soon. The network won't hold my place in the cast forever. I sent them a little project to fend them off, but it won't last. The question is, are you coming with me?"

Jake sat on the bed. "I graduate soon. I turn eighteen in July and start college in the fall. Isn't it time I tried life on my own?"

"You've been on your own since Virginia got sick."

"And I've done okay. I'm graduating with honors, I got accepted at Boulder, I have a job at Tibbits, and The Quirks were really catching fire." Susan raised her eyebrows. "Maybe I shouldn't have put it that way."

"You almost got killed."

"You took a chance when you started out too, didn't you? Earning a living and raising a kid on your own."

"I had help. I had Aunt Margaret and Sammy."

"I've got help, too. A whole mess of folks. I'm just beginning to figure that out."

She sat next to him. "That's what Sammy said. He was

beginning to see you find yourself. He wished he could stay to see it."

"I don't need a guardian angel."

"But someone has to be there."

"Will you be there if I come to New York?"

"Of course I will."

"And if they offer you another movie?"

"You'll come with me."

"So, I'd move again."

She sighed. "Well, who then? Ginny is gone, Sammy is leaving, Mrs. Oldfield is too old, Aunt Margaret—"

"Is a no."

"Well, I agree. She was completely wrong about Sammy. So help me out."

"Give me time to think."

"Don't take too long, Jake."

"Okay." He stood. "I'll be back soon."

Blades of grass shone from the recent rain, brilliant points sparkling on their tips. He walked along the railroad tracks, heading for his usual thinking spot in the cemetery. He stopped a few blocks past the depot. *What am I doing? I was just there. So where am I going?*

Longacre Brothers was to his left, a big "Closed" sign out front. To his right, a crew was working on the remaining buildings in the rail yard, pulling them apart plank by plank. The building where he'd hid while spying on Red and Marcus was nothing but a concrete pad. *Good thing we got the Goddess out.* Across the tracks was the dilapidated shed he'd seen Marcus kicking, yelling, "Fucker! Fucker! Fucker!" *He had plenty people to be mad at. His dad for dying. His uncle for taking over. His cousin for whatever made him hate his guts.* He sighed. He'd never know.

Beyond the Conoco, a figure in a linen suit paced off an

empty lot and made notes on a pad. Drawing closer, Jake called out, "Mr. Sohi, what are you up to?"

"Jake." Sunny smiled and put away the pencil. "Your friend Randy has got us all signed up for this project of his. Jed is looking through Mr. Alquist's papers at the library, Joanie is writing some philanthropic organization out east, and I," he gestured grandly, "am measuring this lot."

"What for?"

"We're going to build it. We're going to build Ada's Memorial, right here. Randy's negotiating with the city to buy the panels as we speak."

"Wow, he did all that since this morning?"

"That boy's a jinn of energy when he puts his heart in it."

"I'd like to help. How long will it take?"

"Until late July or mid-August I think, depending on how much grief we get from the planning commission. They haven't been completely taken over by idiots, so there's hope."

"So, you'll be around all summer."

"Yes, God help me. But it's worth it. I owe a debt."

"To who? Virginia? Randy?"

In answer, Sunny took out his pencil and drew on the pad without looking, then handed it to Jake.

It was a portrait. "Is this supposed to be me?"

"That's Andy."

Jake looked at it, puzzled. "It doesn't look like the figure on the panel."

"Of course it does."

"Have you seen them? The panels? They're in the Historical Museum, in the old depot. It's just down the tracks a bit. C'mon, I'll show you."

"I don't think—" Sunny started, but Jake waved him along.

"C'mon, Mr. Sohi. They're really cool."

"Of course they're 'cool,'" he muttered. "I made them 'cool.'"

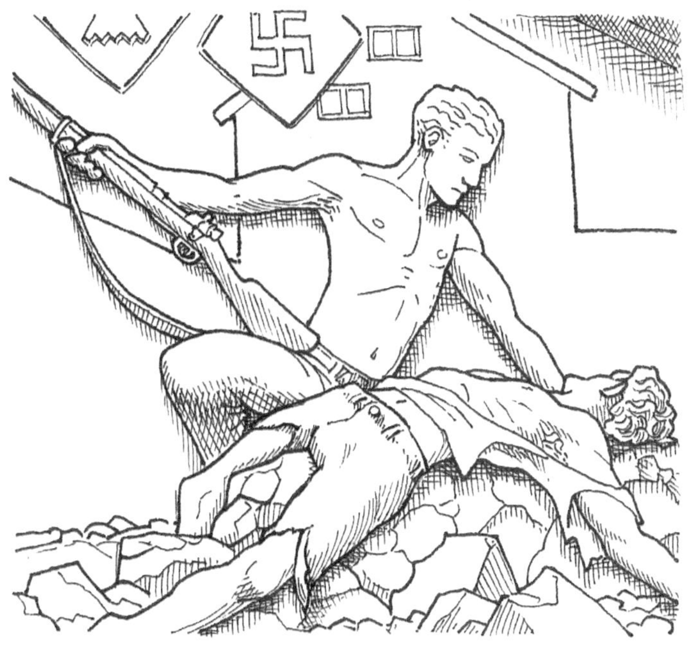

The museum was temporarily closed to the public, but a volunteer working inside let them in. The large center panel, civic pride, was in the waiting room. The soldiers and the tornado were in the cloak room and the baggage room, respectively. The tarps had been removed and the framing crates stabilized. Jake took him to the tornado panel first.

Sunny smiled. "Reverend Jameson still looks heroic."

"He passed about two years ago, same year as my grandfather. And this is Mrs. Oldfield, isn't it?"

"And her husband, Gerald, though he wasn't her husband then."

"She looks so young."

"Yes, hard to believe, isn't it?"

Jake smiled and led him to the civic pride panel.

Sunny laughed out loud. "Did I really make JayRob Pautler that fat? He was mayor back then. No wonder he wanted the thing destroyed."

The soldiers' panel was last. Sensing Sunny's reluctance, Jake took him by the hand and led him to the cloak room. Sunny stopped and stared at the terra cotta figures.

"That's you, isn't it?" Jake said. "The dead soldier."

"Yes, though you aren't supposed to see my face. The panels were meant to be seen from below."

"And that's my father, Andy, beside you."

Sunny shook his head in wonder. "Well, I'll be damned. You were right. It's not at all like I remember him." He reached up and touched the panel, then backed away. He pointed to the background, where a soldier raised a pistol and an outstretched hand as if stopping traffic. "Uncle Crazy Head."

"He still lives out at Pesogi."

"I should probably visit him. He saved my life you know, when this happened." He knocked his leg with his cane. "Him and Jed."

"Jedediah Tucker. You and Coach Tucker were . . . close?"

"What makes you ask?"

"Something Miss Lancaster said. And the way he looked at you at the hospital. I've seen that look before. Someone who wants someone but knows it's never going to happen."

"No, it never happened. Things might have worked out better if they had."

"I wish I'd known. All this time, I thought I had to figure out everything by myself. Instead, there's this hidden history all around me. It'd be easier if people'd just stop hiding things, or erasing them, or pretending they never happened."

"You think life would be better with everything and everyone out in the open?"

"Much better."

"Maybe. That's what I wanted for Andy. Fatal mistake." Jake shook his head. "You too, huh?"

"Me too what?"

"Everyone says they're responsible for Andy's death. It's like some weird badge of honor. But none of you are. He killed himself."

Sunny walked out to the waiting room and sat on a bench, stretching his weak leg in front of him. "It's not that simple, Jake. Uncle Crazy Head used to say it's not the holes that make the net, it's the knots. We pull on each other, even when we think we don't. Andy's death pulled on a lot of strings."

Jake sat across from him. "I feel like that sometimes. A bunch of knots being pulled this way and that."

"You don't always know who you're connected to." He reached into the breast pocket of his suit and produced a sheaf of papers and handed it over.

Jake unfolded it, growing more surprised as he turned its pages. It was a full-color program from last year's Holiday Basketball Tournament, the one that proved to be a dress rehearsal for the state championships. There were color photos of each player, including him. "How did you get this?"

"When I saw Susan's show on TV, I started asking around. I heard she had a boy. He was about the right age, but I wanted to be sure. I thought I'd ask my friends at the network, but it turns out Vince had already met you. He brought this back to New York with him last year. When I saw it, I knew I was right. You're Andy's son."

Jake handed it back. "That's kinda creepy, Mr. Sohi."

"Now that I've actually met you, yes, it is creepy. Are you going to tell your mother?"

"Oh, no way."

"Good. She hates me enough already." He sighed and

put the program back in his pocket. "You aren't Andy. I don't think even Andy is Andy anymore. He's just my memory of him. Like this memorial. We carry these images in our imperfect minds, forward through time. But it's not the real victims or the real heroes we carry. It's not what they were or are, it's what we've made of them, what we make of each other."

"I said that to someone once. I don't think he believed me." He got up. "Thanks, Mr. Sohi. You've cleared up a lot of things."

"I have? I think you've helped me more than I've helped you. I'll have to make that up to you some day."

"You will. But excuse me, I have to settle something."

Jake gathered his mother, Mrs. Oldfield, and his aunt in Mrs. Oldfield's living room. He took a deep breath and announced his decision. "Randy."

"Absolutely not," Aunt Margaret said immediately. "He's just a boy himself."

"Hear me out. He's nineteen-and-a-half, so he's old enough, legally."

"Rubbish."

"He's old enough to go to war," Mrs. Oldfield observed. "And eighteen-year-olds will have the right to vote soon enough."

"Just because the Congress of the United States has fallen down a rabbit hole of idiocy doesn't mean we have to follow."

Mrs. Oldfield was about to reply when Susan intervened. "I think we should skip the politics and hear what Jake has to say."

"Thanks." *She's not objecting outright. That's good.* "He'll be here all summer, working on the memorial, and I want to work on it with him. He's known me for nearly three years.

He lives right next door. And he's Catholic, Aunt Margaret. We go to Mass together. We're practically brothers."

"Exactly my point," Margaret said. "It's children raising children, Susan. You can't consent to this."

Susan turned to Mrs. Oldfield. "Clara, you've known Randy the longest. What do you think?"

She took a moment. "A year ago, I would have agreed with Margaret. I saw warning signs, and I feared he was going down the same path as some of the wilder Edom brothers."

"His father's in jail right now, isn't he?" Margaret said. "Blood will tell. Malachi needs a firm hand, not an accomplice. He should return to Oklahoma City and finish out the year at Saint Albert's. Or a military academy."

Jake looked at Susan. "Is she serious? Does she even know me?"

Margaret continued. "Young hearts and minds are impressionable. You of all people should know that, Susan. Andy was alone in this house for less than a year, and look what free rein did to him."

Clara stiffened. "It was not free rein. He was watched over and counseled. Perhaps too tightly."

Jake put his hands to his head. "If you three want to rehash Andy's life one more time, be my guest. I'll wait outside."

Margaret pounced. "You see? Impertinent!"

"I'm sorry if I offended you, Aunt Margaret, but I am really completely over this multigenerational blood-is-fate tragic drama. Look at *me, now*, not what you were afraid of back then. Sure, I'm impressionable. I'm not—I don't know, *complete*. But I'm getting there. I'm not the same kid you sent down here three years ago, scared of his own shadow."

"No, you're not. Now you're willful and disrespectful, insisting on your own way."

"Reminds me of myself," Susan said.

"Well, there you go," Margaret said, as if that settled the matter.

Jake thought he saw an opening. "Mom, you still haven't said what you think."

"Frankly, I'm concerned. Wasn't Randy the one who took you out to The Corners in the first place?"

"He didn't *take* me. I was in the car. He gave me rides all the time back then, to school, to practice, but he never took me drinking. That first year, he protected me from the jerks at school. He gave me driving lessons, he turned me on to basketball. All of last year wouldn't have happened without him. The team might've still gone to state, but not with me."

"He's been a good friend," she agreed, "but what we're asking him to do takes more than friendship."

Jake hung his head. "I know that. I know I might be asking him to stop being my friend and start being my, I don't know, my adult. But I think we'll be okay even when I don't like what he's telling me to do."

"And when you don't, you'll still do it?"

"Yep. That's the deal."

"What about his wildness?" Margaret said. "His drinking?"

"He hasn't touched a drop since he came back to take care of his mom. In fact, since last spring, when he came back from Lubbock. Am I right, Mrs. Oldfield?"

"Jake is right. I'd know the signs." She took a breath. "I didn't get to finish earlier. I was worried the year before, but Randy has changed. He completely redid that house so Virginia could come home. It meant the world to her, even if it was only for a few weeks. He made it a haven, an easement for her, hard as it was on him. I don't mean the physical burden, though there was plenty of that. But watching the person you love dwindle day by day—it takes fortitude and constancy not to crumble. And when Virginia had to be readmitted, he did it without fuss or self-pity. I think Randy is a young man who has come into his own. He can be your anchor, Jake, and looking out for you can be his. I think it's a good choice."

His mother got up. "Thank you, Clara. Thank you, Aunt Margaret. Jake, tell Randy I want to talk to him before I leave."

Aunt Margaret shook her head. "This is the height of folly. I will not sit here and watch it happen."

Mrs. Oldfield stood. "Let me help you pack, then."

The tribunal was over. Jake had to restrain himself from shouting with glee. *It worked! I convinced them!* As soon as they left, however, a new dread came over him. *How am I ever going to convince Randy?*

True Costs

Late in spring, an out-of-town wrecking crew showed up and took down the iconic neon space ball next to Herman's. Herman's went next, bulldozed in less than an hour. New calls for preserving Croy's history filled the Letters section of *The Croy Evening Call*. They were followed by other letters extolling the construction of a new Sonic Drive-In and how it would bring jobs for locals and draw tourists into town. If *The Call* received any letters about the construction of a wide plinth on the empty lot across from the Armory, they didn't publish them.

They did publish Joan Tibbits's controversial valedictory address delivered at the high school commencement. In it she called for freedom of speech and freedom of the press for high school students. She got as far as describing her encounter with the library board before her mike was cut. After the ceremony, Superintendent Boyd pressed the school board to withdraw her valedictory honors, but they declined.

The Call published her speech in full the next day. It was her last byline. VanDoozer's Clothing, Swofford's Lumber Seed and Supply, and the IGA pulled their ads from the paper for the rest of the month. The following month, the ads were back.

❖

Bobbie Littledeer and Al Mattingly sat in Pastor Mathers's office for their third session of Christian premarital counseling. Bobbie was relieved the sessions were coming to an end. The pastor's non-stop smile wore on her nerves. Although he said the sessions were "to ready you for a marriage you'll love," she felt any answer she or Al gave to even a casual question might postpone or cancel the wedding.

Mathers wrapped up the day's session with, "We should discuss the matter of your vows."

Bobbie tensed. *This is another test.*

"There is, of course, the standard form," he continued, "but some couples like to give the exchange of vows a personal touch."

"I know what I want to say." Al took her hand. "*Whither thou goest, I shall go. Whither thou lodgest, I shall lodge. Thy people shall be my people, and thy God my God.*"

Bobbie adjusted her glasses. "That's what Ruth says to Naomi."

"I know."

"Two women."

Mathers tilted his head. "Perhaps you'd like some other text, Bobbie? A contemporary poem, perhaps?"

"I'd like the traditional exchange, please," she said. "It's what my parents used. I would find that very reassuring."

"Then that's what we'll have," Al said.

Mathers smiled warmly. His phone rang and a button flashed on the front. "Just a moment, friends. I've been expecting this call."

Al took the opportunity to whisper to her, "My parents are coming after all. Reverend Crawford gave the okay."

"Of course he did," she said, ticking one more worry off her list.

"Don't discomfort yourself, Brother Eugene," Pastor Mathers said into the phone. "It will all redound to the glory of God."

He listened further. "Yes, of course. You have a right to

have a say in who goes to school with your children. But have faith, brother. New Life Christian Academy will flourish. That is God's own promise to his people. Life, and that in abundance. God bless you."

He hung up. "I apologize for the interruption. It seems the highest court in the land has just ruled in favor of school busing for desegregation. Some of the saints are concerned, but there is no need." He rubbed his palms together. "There are higher courts."

The knot in Bobbie's stomach tightened.

"Wow," Jake said as Beau lifted the tone arm from the stereo and slid The Kinks' 45 back into its sleeve. *"I'm glad I'm a man, And so's Lola.* Never thought I'd hear that in a rock lyric."

"It's ambiguous, but it's a gimmick. Even Keith Moon in drag is just a gimmick. A pose, not a posture. Once they catch your eye, they go back to being themselves." He lowered himself to the floor in Jake's living room and folded his ankles over his shins.

"I still don't know how you do that," Jake marveled.

"Practice. Do it often enough, you get flexible."

Jake felt the urge to join him. It looked simple enough. He squatted down and grunted and wriggled, but only managed to get one ankle up. "Ow."

"Don't try it all at once. You weren't sinking swishers the first time you played basketball."

"Actually, I pretty much was. Ow."

Beau laughed. "Okay, enough of that. What's this new song you wrote?"

"I wrote it sometime back, but just figured out the title a couple of days ago. Do you still have the Gibson?"

"Yeah, but I didn't bring it with."

"That's okay. It's in my head. I can figure out the chords

later. At first I called it, 'Three Hags and the Moon.' Now it's 'Lullaby for B.'"

"B?"

"That's what Belle calls you, isn't it? It's for the next time you need a lullaby, so you don't have to drag the slaughter of the innocents into it." He sang it through, closely watching Beau's reaction.

Beau furrowed his brow. "Kinda mournful."

"Well it's a lullaby. It's supposed to be sad."

"Huh. I can guess who the three hags are, but who's the moon? Is that you?"

Jake couldn't believe he didn't get it. "No, it's you. You brought us together, you held us together. You're the reason we're all connected."

"Entangled, more like." He ceased his brow. "So, the moon pulls you up, makes you whole. And that's me?"

Jake took a deep breath. *He's not making this easy. I guess that's fair.* "You're more than that. I didn't see it at first. Joanie tried to tell me. Belle tried to tell me. But I was too busy."

"With Frank."

"Well, yeah."

"I can see how that would take up your time."

Jake flushed. "I guess I've been a complete idiot."

Beau cocked his head. "Not a *complete* idiot. But you do have most of the parts."

Jake opened his mouth, but the phone rang. "Hold on," he said. "There's more." His unwound his legs, but the left one had gone to sleep. He nearly toppled reaching for the phone. "Hello? Well, speak of." He covered the mouthpiece. "It's Belle."

"Hey, B2."

"What? No, he's here, at my place. You don't— Well, should I—? All right. Okay." He hung up. "Boy, she's jazzed about something. She was going to pick you up and bring you here, and she's calling Frank in, too."

"Think he'll come?"

He gave a half-smile. "Naw."

"What's up? Did she say?"

"No, but she said to turn on the radio." He reached for it and really did topple.

"Lie down," Beau said. "I'll get the radio."

Jake spread himself on the sofa. Beau tuned the radio to KOMA, then slid into place, propping Jake's legs on his lap.

"Look, what I'm trying to say—"

"Can wait," Beau said. "Let's hear what Belle's all riled up about."

He gently massaged Jake's calves. The tingling faded and a warm feeling flowed out from his center. They stayed on the couch, saying nothing, Jake watching Beau methodically massage all the tension from him.

Belle arrived a few minutes later. "Frank can't make it," she said as soon as she got in the door, "but he's listening."

"To what?"

"Turn the radio up. I heard it last night and didn't believe it, so I phoned it in on the request line. Turn it up!"

They listened to the next song. Jake frowned. "You requested 'Joy to the World'?"

"Shh! No! Listen."

She sat on the recliner while they stayed on the sofa. They strained toward the radio as if waiting for life-saving instructions. The pop tune bubbled to an end, McDonald's assured them they deserved a break today, then the DJ returned. "This goes out to all the quirks in Croy. Yep, that's what it says, folks. The latest hit from Hal Orison."

Jake rolled his eyes and groaned.

"Shh!" Belle commanded.

Slide guitar began a slow intro, then the words floated out:

I need to sleep near a railroad line
Where in midnight dreams I can feel . . .

Jake leaped up. "Holy crap! That's our song!"

"That's *your* song," Beau said, grinning.

"Who's that singing?"

"Hal Orison, like he said," Belle said. "Now shut up. It gets better."

Orison's mellow baritone wove through the opening verses, then the chorus began:

I am the night
I am the rails . . .

It was a woman's voice.

"No way." Jake bounced up and down. "*No way! That's my mom!*"

"Listen to how they end it."

Jake listened, but he didn't really hear it. *My song! On the radio!*

Belle turned the radio off as soon as the DJ came back on. "They're playing it in regular rotation. I heard it last night and again this morning."

"It fits," Jake said, bright-eyed. "It fits her perfectly. The Witch Evangeline. 'I am the soul of your pain.' But how did she get it?"

Beau smiled. "I gave her my copy."

"I could kiss you!"

Beau leaned back. "Okay."

Jake hesitated. He was surprised by how much he really did want to kiss him. He glanced nervously at Belle.

"Oh no," she said. "I've sat through this movie for months now. If you think I'm leaving before the end, you're nuts."

Jake leaned forward, his heart pounding. His lips touched Beau's lightly, delicately. He stood up. He felt uncertain, tongue-tied. "How— How was that?"

"It was nice."

Jake paled. "Nice?"

"I think you got more."

He grinned. "I surely do."

He climbed onto the sofa and pulled Beau into a full embrace. Their lips locked and Beau's arms extended over his head, knocking into the pole lamp.

"Whoa, guys!" Belle said.

The phone rang.

Beau brought his hands to the small of Jake's back and pressed. The phone rang again.

"Are you going to get that?" Belle asked. Their arms snaked to new positions. "Guess not."

She picked up the receiver. "Hey Frank. So, you heard it too? Yeah, I'm over here at Jake's with him and Beau. They're celebrating." She grinned and nodded. "Yeah, they're doing that, too." She listened more and shook her head. "No, I will not give them a big wet one from you. You boys can sort that out yourselves." She hung up.

The boys had flipped positions. Beau was slowly lowering himself on top of Jake. She cleared her throat. "I'm feelin' kinda superfluous here, so I think I'll just go home and, uh, wax my truck or something."

Outside, she hugged herself and squealed. Then she checked to make sure no one had seen her. She got into her pickup and rolled down the alley, singing at the top of her lungs, "*You know you've got it, child, if it makes you feel good!*"

❖

Randy watched Harry go over the plans on the other side of the table. *He's wearing reading glasses. That's new.* His father shifted in his chair as he turned over a sheet and his shackles clanked.

"This here's the problem," Harry said, tapping the sheet. "I never thought these fastenings were strong enough, not for the weight of Sunny's panels. You'll have to get an architect or structural engineer to redo this." He shuffled through them once more. "Where'd you get these, anyway? Lerner's papers?"

"No. Jed and Sunny scoured the library together but couldn't find them."

"Jed and Sunny together? It's The End Times for sure."

"Maybe the plans got disappeared, like some other stuff. But Joanie struck gold with a long shot. She wrote those folks out East, and they still had Lerner's original application. This is a copy."

"Bet that cost a pretty penny."

"We got it covered. There's plenty of money." *Hope he doesn't know I'm bluffing.*

"For the memorial *and* VoTech? You're still going through with that, right?"

"Yeah. Building trades and general contracting. Seems I like it."

Harry smiled. "It's nice to know one of my traits rubbed off on you. Probably the only good one."

He passed the plans across the table. Randy saw the guard go on alert. They would both be searched later.

"You stick with that Joanie," Harry said. "Maybe her good traits will rub off."

Randy hid his smile with his hand. "I think it's actually going the other way." He told Harry about Joanie's valedictory address and the stir it caused.

"Atta girl!" Harry said. "Stick it to the man."

"They wanted to yank back her honors."

"Bastards. They can't do that, can they?"

"Boyd wanted to, but the school board said no. They said it would just cause more divisiveness."

"Well, we wouldn't want any of that in Croy."

They were running out of time. Randy still had things he wanted to talk about. He didn't know where to start.

Harry cleared his throat. "So, how's it going with Jake?"

That's where to start. "It's weird. We've been buddies all this time, but now I'm responsible and suddenly we're not buddies anymore. I feel, I don't know, left out."

"That's the deal when you're an adult."

"And Beau's always hanging around, and that's a whole different kind of weird."

"You don't like him?"

"No, it's not that. It's just— It's like he and Jake have this secret door they go through, and I'm left on the other side. I can't even see the door."

Harry nodded. "You're jealous."

"Yes! Is that weird?"

"Son, you dig deep enough, everybody's weird."

Randy smiled. "Now you sound like Mom."

They were quiet a while.

Randy shook his head. "It's just there's no handbook or rules about how a guy can be friends with a guy who's into other guys."

"No, there is not." Harry regarded him. "How about folks in town? They giving you any trouble over me?"

"Sorry, Pop. You're old news. Mathers has his flock all stirred up over the school board elections. He calls it a referendum on the soul of the city. Everyone's in a tizzy."

"That could cause trouble for Jake and Beau. Maybe they should cool it a while till they leave for college."

Randy snorted. "You think I could tell them that? Jake would pummel me and Beau would, I don't know, chant or something and I'd be levitated off into the yonder. Not to mention Joanie would scratch my eyes out."

Harry smiled. "Best avoid that." He leaned across the

table. "Nothing could keep your mom and me apart. Not Lerner, not the town, not my tribe. When someone finds that secret door in you, it just flies right open. Doesn't matter who's on the other side."

"Yeah. I figured you'd understand. Mom said you handled it pretty well in your day."

Harry creased his brow. "Handled what?"

Randy had gotten right up to the question he wanted to ask and now found he didn't care. "Never mind."

Harry shrugged. "Don't know what she coulda meant."

Randy smiled. *Said one bluffer to another.* "Sure."

Harry pulled back. "This is probably the last time we can meet. They'll transfer me next week."

"It's not forever. And I'll always know where you are."

Harry took off his reading glasses and put them away. Randy saw him wipe his cheek in passing. Looking off, Harry said, "And you know where you'll always be." He looked back and tapped his chest.

He did the same. "Always, Pop."

Joanie thought she'd find the guys at the construction site. She had exciting news, but when she arrived, she saw only Beau and Mr. Tucker and Mr. Sohi. Tucker and Sohi were rigging chains on one of the panels to hoist it into place in the lot across from the Armory. People were already beginning to call the formerly abandoned block "Memorial Park."

Joanie watched Tucker climb into the cab of a crane and bring it roaring to life. She brought her camera up.

"Are you sure you still know how to work this thing?" Sohi called up to him.

"Sure. It's like falling off a bicycle."

"Not helpful, Jed, not helpful."

"Miss Tibbits, if you could stand a little ways off? I'm going to lift the Soldiers Panel."

She backed away, camera in hand.

"Over here," Beau called, ten yards away. "You can get a good angle from here."

The panel rose slowly and swung into position in front of the façade that replicated the front of the library.

She took a few shots then looked around. "Where's Jake? Where's Randy? I didn't think they'd miss this."

Beau shrugged. "Randy's visiting his dad before they ship him off. Jake is at Ace Hardware getting spackle or grout or some such."

He seemed nervous. He kept looking over his shoulder at two guys sitting at a picnic table where Louis Street ended in a cul-de-sac. That would be the parking lot for the park once construction was finished. She shielded her eyes against the mid-day June glare and could make out Marcus Longacre stretched out along the table. She didn't peg the other kid until he threw a knife into the sod next to his shoe. *Billy Swofford. Trying to get as close as he can without hewing off a toe.* "What are they doing out here?"

"Good question. This is the third day they've shown up."

She looked across the tracks. "They'd get nearly as good a view from Longacre's back porch."

"No, no, no!" Sohi yelled. "Bring it down, bring it down!"

Tucker gently lowered the soldiers to the ground.

"I hope they don't mean to start trouble," Joanie said.

"I think I'll find out." Beau started walking toward them.

She ran to catch up. "Is that smart? Billy's got a knife."

Beau scoffed. "Billy's always got a knife." He continued walking.

Not knowing what to do, she turned to the two adults. "Mr. Tucker!" she called out. They looked at her. She gestured at Beau, not knowing what to say.

The two men exchanged a look. "Leave him be," Tucker said, unfastening the chains. "I've got my eye on him."

Just an eye? He needs a steel helmet and a leather shield! But she said nothing. She watched as Beau approached the two boys. A loose strand of hair found its way to her mouth and she clamped down on it.

"Well, lookie here," Billy Swofford said as Beau approached. "It's the chief fairy in charge of building fairyland." He flung his knife into the earth again.

Beau nodded at them. "Marcus. Billy." He looked down at the knife. "I see you're still auditioning for *Hee Haw*."

Billy stretched for his blade and pointed it at the construction. "That thing will be rubble in a month. Folks won't stand for it."

"Well, you're doing your part, that's for sure. You're out here days at a time, staring it to pieces."

Billy leaned forward. "That thing is an insult to every patriot that ever wore a uniform. And they have to come out of the Armory every day and see that pile of shit? It's disgusting."

"Billy?" Marcus said softly.

"What?"

"Fuck the shut up."

Billy grinned. "You mean, 'Shut the fuck . . .'" His smile froze on his face. He folded his knife into his pocket and hopped down from the table. "Screw you, you pussy-eating cocksucker." He spat and strode off toward the tracks.

Marcus grinned up one side of his face. "Ole Billy seems kinda confused what to make of me."

Beau put his hands on his hips. "Why are you here, Marcus? It's not for the view and it ain't for the company."

Marcus stared at him a while, then reached into his back

pocket. "Got something for you." He pulled out a tri-fold wallet. There were enameled crescents in one corner.

Beau couldn't help but reach for it, but as soon as he touched it, he knew it wasn't his. "This is new."

"Got it at the TG&Y."

He turned it over in his hand, then held it out. "It's not mine. Mine had photos of my Poppa and Memaw in it." Marcus didn't move to take it back. Beau placed it on the picnic table. "I don't need this. Maybe you can get your money back."

"What do you want from me, man?" Marcus asked in a low voice.

"What do *I* want? What do *you* want? Why are you out here mooning around all the time? Haven't you got any-place better to be?"

Marcus wiped his hand over his mouth. "I need a job," he said quietly.

Beau pulled back. "You need a what? What's that got to do with me? Randy runs the site."

Marcus looked down and shook his head. "He won't talk to me."

"Well, that's between you and him. Keep me out of it."

"But you're in tight with Jake, right? And Jake's in tight with Randy."

Beau stepped back. *Has he any idea how insulting that sounds?* All he could do is shake his head.

Marcus stood. "I need the money. *We* need the money. It's been hard since Uncle Rusty pissed it all away."

Beau looked down the street to the closed Conoco station with the For Sale sign out front. He shook his head. "No. I'm not your friend. You want to talk to Randy, you do it."

"Look." Marcus held out his hands. "I get it. I was a shit. But you can't take that out on my family. My mom and my sister."

Beau took off his glasses and held them out. "See these? My dad worked double shifts for these. Double shifts for two months. And we ate nothing but Spanish rice the whole time. *Two months!*"

Marcus looked at the lenses darkening in the full sun. He nodded and looked up. "With beans?"

Beau's heart stopped. He heard Sophie crying as their mother dished out Spanish rice for the umpteenth time. With beans. He thrust the glasses forward. "Here. Take them. You can hock them and get something."

Marcus shook his head. "It don't work that way, man. I have to earn it."

"Jesus Christ!" Beau put the glasses back on and started walking away.

"Is that it?" Marcus called after him. He didn't stop. "Beau!"

He spun around.

"I'm sorry, man."

"For what you did then or how you feel now?"

Marcus shook his head. "I don't know. Does it matter?"

It did to him. But whatever being sorry meant to Marcus was something he'd never know. He only knew how he felt about this moment, and how he'd want to feel about it in the future. "I'll tell Randy you want to talk to him. That's it. Nothing more."

Marcus nodded. "Thanks, man."

"Fuck you," Beau said and walked away.

Fare Forward, Voyagers

O n July third, two days before Jake's eighteenth birthday, Jim Morrison was found dead in the bathtub of
his apartment in Paris. He was the third rock star to die at
twenty-seven in less than a year. Belle passed the news to
Beau, who passed it to Jake. Jake left a message for Frank
with his half-sister, Angela, but he doubted she bothered to
tell him. Morrison's grave in Père Lachaise Cemetery became a site of pilgrimage for his fans and others who
wondered what they had lost.

The second body found in the wreckage of The Corners
Bar and Grill was never identified and never claimed. Because of where it was discovered, it fell to Conlan County
to dispose of the remains. The date and expense are noted
on the county books. There are no other records.

Jake and Randy celebrated Jake's birthday at Randy's
house with coffee and a mess of eggs, which was pretty
much the extent of their culinary skills. They were finishing
up when Joanie knocked on the back door.

"Is *The Odd Couple* in?" she asked as she entered.

"Decoupled as of today," Randy said cheerfully.

She joined them at the table. "It's a wonder you didn't
kill each other."

"It's the separate bathrooms that made it work," Randy
said.

"Yeah," Jake said. "His is over here, mine's on the other
side of the alley. Congrats on the scholarship," he added.

She smiled. "Thanks. It made the difference."

"I think your speech made the difference."

"Well, they already had all the application materials. But the scholarship is a relief. We couldn't have afforded Northwestern otherwise."

Randy crossed his arms. "How's your dad holding up? Is the boycott cutting into business much?"

She shook her head. "People we've known for years, whole families, won't enter the store anymore. I suspect it will all die down once I leave for Evanston."

"It's not right," Jake said.

"But there are other folks who make up for it. The other day, Mr. Frye came in just to shake my father's hand."

"He's a real solid guy," Randy said. "The memorial wouldn't be anywhere near done without his help."

"I've got news about that," Joanie said.

"I do too," Jake said. "You first."

"No, it's— I got something in the mail from— No, you first."

Jake grinned. "It's another scoop, isn't it?"

Randy rocked back in his chair. "Oh, brother."

"It could be nothing, really. You first, Jake."

Jake smiled and sat up straight. "Okay. You know that song my mom recorded?"

"Your song?" Randy asked.

"Yeah. Well, it's started paying royalties. Kinda big royalties. And she wanted to know what I wanted to do with them. So as of today, I'm signing them all over to the Memorial Building Fund."

Randy's chair rocked forward with a thud. "Seriously?"

"It's my way of having some skin in the game."

"That's great, Jake." Randy ran his hand through his hair. "And just in time, too. Crane rental is killing us."

"There might be more coming. Mom says the network's so thrilled with the publicity they're going to build several episodes around it—maybe even a movie—about two star-crossed lovers who only connect through the lonely whistle of a train." He beamed.

"Wow," Joanie said, "a movie about two guys?"

Jake squirmed, doubt tinging his pride. "I don't know about that. What's your news?"

"Oh." Joanie reached for her purse. "I got this from the foundation. Remember when we bought copies of the elevations from them?"

"The building fund sure does," Randy said.

"It turns out something was on the back of one of them. They didn't notice until they were refiling the stuff, and they came across this." She unfolded a sheet the size of one of the plans. It was blank except for a note written slantwise across one corner, as if in haste. "The foundation thought, since we paid for a complete set, we should have this, too." She smoothed out the paper. The note read,

> *Dear Philip—*
> *As close as leading can allow*
> *The golden mean we follow*
> *To build today an ark we know*
> *Will hold our hearts tomorrow*

"Who's Philip?" Jake asked.

"I don't know, but I have a hunch."

"And who wrote it?" Randy asked.

"I don't know that either, but I have—"

"A hunch, right. So, are you going to unhunch us, or do we have to guess?"

Her eyes glittered.

"She's enjoying this," Jake said.

"You bet she is," Randy said.

"Do you have the plans here?" she asked.

"Sure." Randy brought them out. They were too large

for the kitchen table, so they moved to the living room and unrolled them on the floor. Joanie flipped through them rapidly until coming across one with a detail of the west elevation. "This one. The windows. Look."

"I know those windows," Jake said. "I always thought the leading looked organic, yet balanced, like poetry."

"Oh," Randy said, nodding. "*Lead*ing, not leading. As in the lead between the panes."

"Right!" Joanie exclaimed. "And the 'golden mean' is the golden ratio Mr. Sohi says it is used throughout the building. Here it's in the height and width of the trim, and sides of the inner pane."

"So, this is a note from the architect about the window design," Jake said. "But why write it in verse, and who is Philip?"

Joanie clasped her hands, barely able to contain herself. "Randy, what's your grandfather's name?"

"Lerner. That's what Virginia always called him. I hear some folks called him New York, but I think that was a put-down."

"No, I mean his full name."

Randy shrugged. "Heck, I don't know. I—" He stopped mid-sentence, suddenly picturing his grandfather's tombstone. His eyes widened. "Lerner *Philip* Alquist!"

Joanie grinned. "Exactly! This is a note from your grandmother to your grandfather. From Ada to Philip. But there's more." She spread out the plans and moved the sheet with the poem across each one. "You see it, don't you?"

"Holy Hannah," Jake whispered. "It's the same handwriting."

"You know what this means? These are *her* plans. She was the architect."

Randy sat back. "Good God. Mom was right. It really *is* Ada's Memorial. It has been all along."

◈

Anti-war demonstrations filled the streets in Washington and San Francisco, but not Croy. Australia and New Zealand withdrew their troops from Vietnam, but the town continued to send its sons. The upheavals of the spring played out in school board elections and local boycotts. The library and the historical museum kept their hours staffed by people who never mentioned the terra cotta panels whose custody they briefly shared.

Susan's television network built several episodes around Jake's song. They brought the show its highest ratings that summer, and one was nominated for an Emmy. The tormented lovers were played by a man and a woman.

Sunday August fifteenth was announced as the date for the second unveiling of the memorial panels, newly mounted on a replica of the library façade. The center panel still showed a chip at its base, representing, so Sunny Sohi declared, the fractured history of the piece. About a hundred townspeople attended. However, no one from New Life Christian Church, as Mt. Hermon was now called, went. Instead, they held an afternoon service to pray for the soul of their city and celebrate their recent victory in the school board elections. The church was packed.

Bobbie Mattingly caught Al's arm before he took his place up front along with the rest of The Father's Five. "Did you speak to him?"

"Bobbie, there's nothing I can do. He's made his decision. He's our pastor and he's head of the Selection Committee. If he says no, then it's no."

"But can't you see what he's doing? What the whole committee is doing? It isn't right."

"It's just a coincidence."

She shook her head. "He said the Lord works in mysterious ways. Now I know what he meant. He meant they could pack the school board with his 'concerned citizens' and at the same time keep any colored kids from enrolling in our school."

He frowned. "There's nothing we can do now. This is a Tremblin' Hour broadcast. It's live. I've got to get to the stage."

"To the sanctuary, you mean."

He didn't look at her as he hurried away. She took her seat with her family, feeling not much like a Mattingly and even less like a Littledeer. Her mother squeezed her hand and beamed.

Mathers based his sermon on the Gospel according to John, Chapter 6, the living parable of the loaves and fishes. His words passed over her like a dream, but one verse kept running through her head:

Jesus, knowing they intended to come and make him king by force, withdrew to a mountain by himself.

She woke as if for the first time that day when Mathers asked for witnesses to the Kingdom. "Holy Spirit, have you sent us a witness? Is there one who can stand up for the Kingdom?"

This was usually where her mother would rise and speak in that strange and thrilling tongue. She rustled beside her, but instead Bobbie found herself floating up, standing amid the congregation.

"The Kingdom of God is with us now, but for us to see it, this world must fall away."

Someone shouted, "Amen!" Pastor Mathers smiled his holy smile. It had no effect on her. *I should be terrified. I'm not. How is this possible?*

"People want a worldly kingdom, a comfortable kingdom. But when the people tried to make Jesus their king, he withdrew. He wanted nothing to do with it. He didn't want power. He didn't want the world's kingdom. He wanted God's."

There were murmurs of assent.

"The Kingdom is not a walled city. It is not a church or a school. It's people. When God answers prayer, He doesn't send a car, or a telegram, or an envelope full of money. He sends a person. We don't know who He sends. The people in Jesus' time didn't know it was Him. We in our time don't know who He sends for us, who His answer is to our prayers. Yet they are among us, if we look. So when we turn away from each other, we turn away from the Kingdom. When we shun, when we condemn, when we seek to separate, we make the Kingdom smaller."

There was no movement, no sound from the congregation.

"Still your tongue, child," her mother hissed.

But she didn't. She couldn't.

"And people—people can also be a prayer, a question God has sent for us to answer. I fear we have not answered as we should. I fear we have not heard the call of God spoken right here in our town.

"When Mrs. Oldfield sought to shelter a troubled boy, she was told to turn him away. He had already lost his father. Then he lost his grandfather and his stepfather. *He* was lost. He was a prayer to be answered. Instead, the church showed up to mock and humiliate him.

"When Miss Lancaster was driven from town, people spat at her. Is that our vision of the new Jerusalem? Is the peaceable kingdom populated with spitting Christians?

"Now the church rejoices in a political win instead of welcoming the poor and oppressed. Kingdoms of *this* world are built with walls. If we strengthen those walls and build them higher, we build the City of Man, not the City of God.

"If faith does not step in where lives are broken and despised, then— Then it is a waste of time."

She stopped and listened. The church was silent. "I hear no amens."

"We don't often hear from you, sister," Mathers said gently.

"I have not been moved before. I doubt I'll be moved again."

"Then perhaps you'd like to take your seat?"

"I don't think that will be necessary." She picked up her purse and Bible. Mrs. Littledeer grabbed her arm.

"If you walk out of here, you are not my daughter."

She detached herself. "That isn't up to you, Momma."

As she walked up the aisle to the doors, she noticed Mrs. Oldfield and Mrs. Armbruster standing silently in their pews. As she passed, they joined her. She hoped Al was behind her too, but she didn't look back to check. *Whither thou goest, I shall go.* She pushed her glasses up the bridge of her nose. *Well, here's hoping.*

The Quirks made their final appearance at the dedication ceremony. At the opening, they performed a completely straight version of "The Star-Spangled Banner," and at the close, they did their signature piece, "The Midnight Train." Jake introduced it by telling the crowd how it helped fund the memorial's restoration. The band wore their Talent Show outfits: chaps, James Dean T-shirt, a man's ruffled shirt, and a dashiki. They each wore a little something extra underneath.

As the crowd thinned, Jake walked over to Frank. Jim was nearby, but as soon as Jake approached he got busy packing up Frank's gear.

"Frank."

He looked up. "College boy."

"Yeah, soon. Look, I just wanted to say, you know, thanks for coming."

Frank shrugged. "It warn't nothin'. I mean, yeah, it was somethin', but . . ." He shrugged again, then abruptly stuck out his hand. "The Quirks."

Jake laughed and shook it. "The Quirks. Speaking of." He pulled down the neck of his T-shirt. Leather straps and a chrome ring gleamed. "What's yours? Your something extra."

Frank looked away. "Somethin' Jim gave me."

"What?"

"I'm wearin' it now. Underneath." He leaned in, his lips brushing Jake's ear. "Under. Neath."

Jake reddened. "Oh. Gotcha."

"See ya, college boy."

Jake caught up with Beau and Belle at her truck. She was saying, "I am not. It's this damned ragweed."

"Belle?" Jake hoped the look on his face asked the right question.

She frowned, then said, "Oh, what the hell," and opened her arms. They hugged until she broke it off. "Okay, that's enough." She turned to Beau and declared, "Onward!"

He saluted. "Onward and Awkward!"

As she got in her truck, Jake asked, "So, what's yours? Your little something extra?"

She gave him a crooked smile. "I go caparisoned in gems unseen," she said and drove off.

Jake was flabbergasted. He turned to Beau. "That was from *Cyrano de Bergerac.*"

"Yep. We read it in Mr. DeWitt's Theater Arts class last year."

"I never pegged Belle for a romantic."

Beau smiled. "Belle is the most romantic person I know." He looked around. "There's Randy and Joanie over by the steps. Don't spend too much time with them out there, okay? We leave in a few hours."

"I won't be late. Have you got everything in the minivan?"

"Everything?" Beau sighed and put his hands on his hips. "If only it were that simple."

Jake walked to the foot of the monument. Randy was standing there, staring up. "You guys got a minute?"

Randy grunted.

"That means yes," Joanie interpreted. "What's up?"

"I want to take you somewhere."

"You guys go ahead," Randy said. "I'm just going to . . ."

"Nope, it's both of you or nothing."

Joanie looked at him sideways. "Where?"

"You'll see."

They got in Jake's VW minivan packed with boxes and large bags stuffed with clothes.

"You're taking all this?"

"My stuff is that box behind your seat. The rest is Beau's." He started the engine. After several complaints, it caught.

"Are you sure this thing will make it to Boulder?" Joanie asked as they headed west down Louis Street.

"It'll be fine," Jake said. "It's mostly flat between here and there."

Randy frowned. "We're not going all the way to Boulder, are we?"

Jake just smiled. He turned off Louis at the paper products plant and headed out the asphalt road to Pesogi.

"Oh," Joanie said, realizing where they were headed.

He turned off the hard road onto a rutted trail that followed Little Bushy Creek. He turned again at a fence with a missing gate and cut a path through the grass. He stopped at the foot of the hill. "All out. Randy, can you bring the picnic basket? It's under that first bag." Jake pulled a large sarape from under the seats and draped it over his arm. Joanie took the other. They trudged through the buffalo grass to the small, abandoned farmhouse at the top of the hill.

"I should apologize to Sunny for what I did to this place," Randy said, looking at the sagging porch and the boarded up windows.

They spread the sarape and sat down. Joanie opened the basket and passed out Sonic burgers and cokes in aluminum cans. They gazed out at the town. It was silent save the rustle of prairie grass and the whir of insects.

Randy pointed. "You can see it from here."

"Where?" Joanie shaded her eyes.

From the hillside, the trees on either side of Louis Street converged on the red brick and sandstone memorial at the far end.

"Look at it," Jake said. "We did that."

"It's so small," Joanie said.

"Hey," Randy objected.

"I meant the town. I mean, I thought so then, when we first came out here, but it seems even smaller now."

"It's changing," Randy said. "It's not the same town I grew up in."

"We're all changing." She put her unfinished burger in the basket and wiped her hands. "This thing has no flavor. Do you know what Mary Kay Halliday had the nerve to write in my yearbook? 'Love ya forever! Don't ever change!'"

"Bless her heart," Randy said.

"I've never been so insulted in my life."

"What'd you write in hers?" Jake asked.

She shrugged. "Same thing. Well, what else could I say? 'Hope you're better soon'?"

Jake shook his head. "I remember when I first got here, afraid to put one foot in front of the other. You know, I nearly turned back that first day? But that's the day I met you and Randy. Now, I can't wait to go on. Onward and awkward, as Beau says. 'Don't ever change'? I hope I never *stop* changing."

Randy gazed at him then turned to Joanie, laying on a thick drawl. "Well goll-darn-it, Big Mama. Our boy Buford done growed up on us." He winced. "Damn. That doesn't work anymore, does it?"

"It does not," Jake said.

"Besides," Joanie said, "Buford wasn't our boy. He was the dog, remember?"

"Oh yeah." He sighed. "We can't play at being people anymore. We really *are* people. It kinda sucks."

Joanie nodded. "Big wet weenies." The boys turned and looked at her. "What? You never heard that before?"

They packed up the remains of the picnic. Standing, Jake smiled at them. "I'll miss you guys."

"Yeah, right," Randy said. "You'll be in Boulder. Beau will be up the pike at Colorado State. You won't have time to miss us."

"And you shouldn't," Joanie said. "I mean, that's the point, isn't it? Valedictory means 'goodbye speech.' Commencement means 'beginning.' It's about moving on, not looking back." She glanced at the town. "We shouldn't miss anything."

"I know what you *will* miss," Randy said.

"Okay Big Man," Jake said. "Lay it on us."

He spread out his arms. "Nothing. But you'll miss it, just the same. Just wait. You'll be in the middle of a crowded street in Chicago, or at a Buffs game with thousands of cheering fans, or buried under a pile of books, and you'll look up and say, 'Boy, I could really use me some nothing!' And it'll be right here, waiting for you. Miles and miles of it." He picked up the picnic basket. "Trust me. You're gonna need it someday."

They headed down the hill back to Croy, the green town already fading in their eyes.

Dear Jake

Queens, New York
October 13, 1980

Thank you for writing. To answer your question, yes, I did attend the rededication of Ada's Memorial. That is what Virginia always called it, you know. The plot of land by the Armory is now the smallest state park in Oklahoma. Randy signed the transfer papers today in a ceremony that reminded me of the one where you and your band performed nine years ago, and of another one further back, a lifetime ago.

The panels have weathered well over the years, so maybe Lerner's insistence on using local clay was the right decision after all. The panel with your father's figure was vandalized a few times when it first went up. Nothing permanent, eggs and such. Red and Marsha Conner put an end to that, he through the VFW post, she through the Ladies Auxiliary. They persuaded them to install a flagpole and "eternal flame" (a spotlight, really) just to the side of the soldiers, lighting them through the night. Now that the grounds are a state park, they may get the respectful attention they deserve. Or not. This is Croy, after all.

I hope you and Beau are doing well in Colorado. Boulder is a beautiful city in a spectacular setting. You were wise to quit Greeley, which is just Croy writ large. The

UCB Theater Department is lucky to have you; I will keep my fingers crossed for tenure.

Mr. Conner and I have struck up a friendship initiated by comparing our respective canes at the ceremony. His is carved from native bodark by none other than Uncle Crazy Head himself. That's him in the background on the soldiers panel, raising his pistol in his left hand to stop the Dachau massacre. He's also the trooper with the machine gun pointed at the German POWs. That story has yet to be told, but as long as there are people willing to seek the truth and tell it, then someday, someone . . .

But you won't find his name on the dedication plaque. He wouldn't want that. He refused to sit for me, citing an ancient belief, so I made the faces deliberately vague. And now he's gone. The old fakir was gathered into the bosom of one of the many gods he worshiped— or, more likely, all of them.

They insisted on putting my name up there, so I made them list everyone else as well. Your dear father Andy, of course, but also Clara and Gerald Oldfield, Reverend Cecil Jameson, John Tibbits, Sr., Lila Armbruster, JayRob Pautler (the old Philistine), and above them all, seated on her throne of light, Ada Alquist, at last credited as the genius behind the library.

They face East, looking across the parade grounds and the old rail yard to the river. The yard is completely cleared now; even the rails are gone. You see glints of the White Horse here and there through the houses and cottonwoods.

I like to think my figures have turned their backs on the town, but that's just my ego talking. The truth is, this is simply a better setting for them than the one I had so meticulously designed for all those years ago. The sun bathes them in gold as it rises over the river. They appear ready to march down the sunlit steps and face the future, unflinching.

I face it with less enthusiasm. The upcoming election is not promising. Overheard at the ceremony were such comments as, "Carter was a mistake. He was neither a true Christian nor a true Southerner." And, "He'll be forgotten come November. Who remembers a one-term president? America will stand proud again!"

I fear they are right.

Fondly,

—Sunny

THE CROY CYCLE - PRINCIPAL CHARACTERS

The Families

The Edom Family

Lerner Philip Alquist – Real estate baron and oil investor, father of Virginia, grandfather of Randy. Went bankrupt trying to construct a memorial library for his wife, Ada, who died in the TriCounty Twister of 1935.

Harry Edom – Contractor, roughneck, and recently escaped felon convicted of stealing supplies from the Oklahoma State Highway Department. Estranged from his wife, Virginia, and sometimes from his son, Randy.

Virginia (Alquist) Edom – Daughter of the once prominent Lerner Alquist, she gave up her prospects to marry Harry. Now a single mother to Randy and *in loco parentis* to Jake while her friend Susan works in New York and abroad.

Randy Edom – Recent graduate of Croy Consolidated High School and recipient of an unexpected legacy. Adrift, he struggles to find a meaningful role for himself that is not entangled with his parents' past.

The Jacobs Family

Reverend Matthew Jacobs – Dismissed as pastor of Mt. Hermon Bible Church in 1952 after Andy Simms's death and his daughter's pregnancy. Father of Susan and grandfather of Malachi.

Susan Jacobs – Daughter of Matthew. Daytime soap opera star as the witch Evangeline DuPere. She escaped Croy to pursue a career in theater but keeps being pulled back to the town by her connections there.

Malachi "Jake" Jacobs – Son of Susan Jacobs and Andy Simms. Changes his nickname from "Mally" to "Jake" and leads the CCHS Rangers to the 1970 State AAA Boys Basketball Championships. Rhythm guitarist for The Quirks. Interests include e. e. cummings, rock lyrics, and figuring out his interest in guys.

The Tibbits Family

John Tibbits, Jr. – Pharmacist and owner of Tibbits Rexall, which he bought from Avril Rosen in the 1950s. Husband of Ruth and father to Joanie, Kyle, and Julia Mae. His father, John Sr., represents ranching on Sunny Sohi's memorial sculpture.

Ruth (Snepp) Tibbits – Wife of John and mother to Joanie, Kyle, and Julia Mae. When Reverend Jacobs is replaced at Mt. Hermon by Reverend Mathers, she and her family leave and join Antioch Baptist. Both Ruth and John remember Andy Simms fondly, if unclearly.

Joan "Joanie" Tibbits – Daughter of John and Ruth. The first person to befriend Jake when he starts high school at CCHS. Senior editor of *The Clarion*, the school newspaper, and sometime contributor to *The Croy Evening Call*. Budding historian and investigative journalist.

Kyle "The Bean" Tibbits – Joanie's younger brother, budding adventurer and talented troublemaker.

Julia Mae Tibbits – Infant daughter of John and Ruth.

The Jameson Family

Reverend Cecil Jameson – Originally a stable hand and groundskeeper for the Alquist family, Cecil answers the call to become pastor at Mt. Zion A.M.E. Church. Eventually founds and heads Marcus Garvey High School, an all African-American school that gets absorbed into the Croy Consolidated School District in the late 1960s. Featured on the memorial sculpture rescuing young Clara Whitlock and Gerald Oldfield.

Reverend Ethan Jameson – Cecil's son who succeeds him at both Mt. Zion and Marcus Garvey High.

Zachaeus "Zach" Jameson – Ethan's oldest son and the power forward on the CCHS championship basketball team. Original lead guitarist for The Quirks. Does an impressive rendition of Jimi Hendrix's "The Star-Spangled Banner."

Adam Jameson – Zach's younger brother. Inspired by Martin Luther King, Jr. and Marcus Garvey, and a student of Latin even after his school drops the subject.

The Craddock/Pellegrini Family

Virgil Craddock – Aging but shrewd farmer whose daughter is unlucky in her choice of husbands.

Arlene (Craddock) Fenton Pellegrini – Virgil's daughter, who runs the farmhouse. Her first husband, Jack Fenton, dies trucking tomatoes in California. Her second husband, Lorenzo Pellegrini, runs off under a cloud of acrimony.

Frank Pellegrini – Arlene's son by her first husband. Takes over as center on the CCHS basketball team when Al Mattingly is unable to play. Originally rhythm guitarist for

The Quirks, becomes lead guitarist when Zach Jameson gets drafted.

Lorenzo Pellegrini – Arlene's second husband. Considers himself a natural-born farmer and a strict but caring father.

Angela Pellegrini – Frank's younger half-sister, daughter of Arlene and Lorenzo.

The Hamilton Family

Scott (Pritchard) Hamilton – Insurance salesman. Disowned by his father for marrying Rachel, he takes his mother's maiden name. Went to high school with Susan Jacobs and sang with her in the Mt. Hermon choir.

Rachel (Rosen) Hamilton – Avril Rosen's daughter. She and Scott met secretly during high school and married despite both families' objections to a mixed Christian/Jewish marriage. They have three children: Beau, Raphael, and Sophia.

Beau Hamilton – Scott and Rachel's son. He conceives of The Quirks, a garage rock band which Jake, Belle, Zach, and eventually Frank join. He is their bassist. They become known for their range of musical styles and quirky outfits.

Raphael and **Sophia Hamilton** – Fraternal twins and younger siblings of Beau. "Rafe" is Kyle Tibbits's best friend and co-conspirator.

Recurring Characters

Al Mattingly – High school buddy of Randy and Red, interested mostly in cars and basketball. Develops bone cancer which nearly kills him. Accepts Jesus as his personal Lord and Savior at Mt. Hermon Bible Church under Reverend Joshua Mathers.

Andy Simms – Music minister at Mt. Hermon Bible Church under Reverend Matthew Jacobs in the 1950s. Friend and contemporary of Harry Edom, Virginia Alquist, and Susan Jacobs. Jake's father. Dies when a train hits his car.

Aunt Margaret – Susan Jacobs's aunt on her mother's side. A conservative Catholic influence on Malachi when he lived with her in Oklahoma City. Sends Malachi to Croy to avoid what she considers the unhealthy influence of Sammy Anderson.

Belle Craddock – Friend of Beau Hamilton and cousin to Frank Pellegrini. An emancipated minor. Fan of Janis Joplin and Ric Lee. Drummer for The Quirks.

Clara (Whitlock) Oldfield – Widow of Gerald Oldfield, who drank away most of his inherited wealth. Landlady to Andy Simms, then Matthew Jacobs, and eventually Jake. She and her husband-to-be appear in Sunny Sohi's memorial sculpture.

Henry "Hank" Ardmore – Head of the P.E. department at CCHS. Football and basketball coach. Recent father of twin girls.

Ida Lane Lancaster – Head librarian at Croy Memorial Library for thirty years and former secretary for the Croy city council. Keeper of records, curator and guardian of books, periodicals, and other library materials.

Jedediah Tucker – Friend of Harry Edom, rejected suitor of Sunny Sohi, construction boss and college football star. Following his college career, becomes assistant football and basketball coach at Croy Consolidated High School. Nephew to "Uncle Crazy Head."

Marcus Longacre – High school buddy to Red Conner, Randy Edom, and Jake. Goes to work for his uncle at Longacre Brothers after his father dies in a car accident during an ice storm.

Marsha "Candy" Sullivan – First runner-up in the Oklahoma State High School Baton Twirling Tournament two years in a row. Her father owns Sullivan's Auto Deals and sits on the city council.

Percy Owen – Former constable under Chief Clay Buchholtz, now Croy's Chief of Police.

Richard "Red" Conner – High school buddy of Marcus Longacre and Randy Edom, taunted Mally when he first arrived at CCHS. Enlists in the Army and goes to Vietnam. Returns with secrets he intends to keep.

Roberta "Bobbie" Littledeer – High school friend of Joanie Tibbits until her fundamentalist parents enroll her in New Life Christian Academy. As a Candy Striper at St. Joseph's Hospital, she develops feelings for Al Mattingly.

Samuel "Sammy" Anderson – Friend and neighbor of Susan and Jake when they lived in Oklahoma City with Aunt Margaret. Also known on certain Friday nights as Sister Many Agonies.

Sundar "Sunny" Sohi – Byronic self-taught sculptor, student of Bruce Goff, and creator of the sculpture destined for the Croy Memorial Library. Andy Simms's lover.

AUTHOR'S NOTES

The incident at The Corners Bar and Grill is based on the December 27, 1987 fire at The Peoples' Bar in Fort Collins, Colorado. Two people died that night: Donald Kirk, 51, of Cody, Nebraska, and Alden Klein, 32, of Loveland, Colorado. A friend of Klein's I spoke to after the fire believed he was trying to help Kirk escape through a window in the men's room when they were overcome by smoke. The fire started when a patron touched a lit cigarette to a Christmas tree to prove it was fireproofed. It was not. The bet was for five dollars.

Two chapters pay homage to *The Dismissal of Miss Ruth Brown* by Louise S. Robbins (Norman: University of Oklahoma Press, 2000). My account of Miss Lancaster's trouble with the town is fictional, but Miss Brown's story anchors it in Oklahoma history. I am grateful to Geri Ceci Cupery for calling my attention to it. One chapter title directly paraphrases the title of Robbins's book, and the following chapter, "The Storm," is a nod to *Storm Center*, the Bette Davis film based loosely on Brown's ordeal.

The 45th "Thunderbird" Infantry Division was one of three divisions that liberated the Dachau concentration camp on April 29th, 1945. Outside the camp, they encountered boxcars loaded with rotting corpses; inside, bodies were "stacked like cordwood" and inmates milled around "like walking skeletons." At some point after the camp's surrender, several camp guards and SS officers were lined up against a wall and machine gunned. Lt. Col. Joseph Whitaker investigated the incident and concluded that the number killed "most certainly did not exceed fifty." Other witnesses put the number at over three hundred. Whitacker's report, *Investigation of Alleged Mistreatment of German Guards at Dachau*, was classified "Secret" until 1991.

Ada Alquist's role as the genius and architect behind Croy's Memorial Library parallels the role Adah Robinson played in the design and construction of the Boston Avenue Methodist Church in Tulsa, Oklahoma. Robinson's contributions were central but often overlooked because she was a woman and never held a degree in architecture. She went on to chair the Art Department at the University of Tulsa.

Robinson was assisted in the Boston Avenue project by her pupil, Bruce Goff. Goff also had no formal training in architecture and, like Robinson, went on to head an academic department, the School of Architecture at the University of Oklahoma. He resigned that position in 1955 when reports of an affair with a male student surfaced. The Bruce Goff Chair of Creative Architecture at O.U. is named in his honor.

The chapter titled "Passenger of Infinity" is named for Kristin Nordeval's setting of three Emily Dickinson poems for piano and mixed chorus. The text of the third poem, "Into the staunch Dust," is sung by Belle in the novel. Nordeval's setting was commissioned by the Lesbian/Gay Chorus of San Francisco. You can find their recording of it on their 1994 CD, *Together In Harmony*.

ACKNOWLEDGMENTS

It takes a village to raise a village, and in the twenty-odd years it has taken me to write The Croy Cycle, my little town has been built up by early readers, authors, editors, librarians, native Oklahomans, correspondents, and book clubs.

This final book in the series owes much to its first readers, some of whom have been with me from the start: Surajit Bose (who published the first excerpt from the cycle in *Trikone Magazine*), Rémy Ceci, Jim Richards, Steven Brook, Rick LaReau, Patrick Ennis (my guru for all things rock'n'roll), and Judith Lancaster. Anthony Gonzales of Nevada City Gas advised me on automotive repair. These readers and reviewers checked everything from historical accuracy to punctuation and continuity. Special thanks go to fellow authors Bill Konigsberg for support and encouragement, J. Marshall Freeman for recommendations on the Principal Characters section, and Jerry L. Wheeler for clear and precise editing. If any quirks of fact, grammar, or reference remain, they are entirely my own.

Jennifer Rain Crosby brought the citizens of Croy to life with her evocative line drawings. Many are based on photos of neighbors, friends' pictures in old yearbooks, or models photographed by Dot. They include:

Brent Waxdeck and Billy Jim Crawford (Mally Jacobs/Jake Jacobs)
Jamaal Bradshaw (Zack Jameson and young Cecil Jameson)
Kel Hamilton and Brian Bauer (Beau Hamilton)
Brendan Forrest (Frank Pellegrini)
Kelley Ann Stewart (Belle Craddock)
Ulikens Polin (Sammy Anderson)
Jean Reynolds (Agriculture/Lila Armbruster)

Jeff Reynolds (Government/JayRob Pautler)
Major Mugrage (Ranching/John Tibbits, Sr.)
James Harker (Slain soldier/Sunny Sohi)

Many talented people helped me turn "The Midnight Train" from audio dream into fully realized recording. Richard Thomas put me in touch with Stepside, a local Nevada City band; performing with them helped me hone the lyrics and melody. Their keyboardist, Stephen Miller, wrote and played the piano accompaniment. Jonathan Hansard added his rich baritone, sounding just like Hal Orison did in my head and bringing all the layers and mood swings to life. Paul Emory Studios provided the recording studio, and Mr. Emory himself mixed the master. The recording is available on the Les Croyens Press web site (www.beautifuldreamerpress.com/les-croyens-press).

The first prospect of Croy appeared in a screenplay I wrote for a Radio, Television and Film scripting class at Northwestern University. The instructor was so enthusiastic about it he showed it to some friends in the film industry. Although they liked the characters and dialog, they didn't think they could sell a major motion picture whose central character was a gay teenager. That was in 1979. When I found myself out of work in 2002, I pulled the screenplay from a trunk and reread the instructor's comments. I decided to take his advice and expand the story. In a final scene in the novel, Joanie, Randy, and Jake sit on a hill outside of Croy, looking down at the town. A street draws a line from the farmhouse behind them to the memorial they built. That street is named Louis after my Northwestern mentor, the first believer in Croy.

ABOUT THE AUTHOR

Louis Flint Ceci was a high school teacher of English and speech in Benton, Illinois; an assistant professor and chair of the Department of Journalism and Mass Communications at the University of Northern Colorado, Greeley; a commercial actor and freelance science journalist in the Denver-Boulder area; and a software engineer for several companies, including Skype, where he helped design and implement a user interface for the blind and visually impaired.

His poetry is published in *The Colorado-North Review* and *Impossible Archetype*. His scholarly articles on linguistics and poetics have appeared in *College English*, *Language and Style*, and *Literature in Performance*.

His short stories have appeared in *Diseased Pariah*

News, Jonathan, and *Trikone Magazine,* and in the anthologies *Queer and Catholic, Best Gay Erotica,* and *Gay City Volume 4: At Second Glance.* He has twice been a finalist in the *Saints+Sinners: New Stories from the Festival* short fiction contest, and was inducted into the Saints+Sinners Hall of Fame in 2017.

He is an avid U.S. Masters swimmer and won two gold and three silver medals at the 2020 International Gay and Lesbian Aquatics World Championships in Melbourne, Australia. He won the Gold Medal in the Poetic Justice Poetry Slam at the 2002 Gay Games in Sydney, Australia.

He lives in Nevada City, California.